Rayder's Appeal The Brantons Book 4

The Brantons, Volume 4

Bonnie Edwards

Published by Bonnie Edwards, 2020.

RAYDER'S APPEAL THE BRANTONS BOOK 4

First edition. July 31, 2020.

Copyright © 2020 Bonnie Edwards.

ISBN: 978-1989226254

Written by Bonnie Edwards.

This book is dedicated to scorned women everywhere.

May revenge be sweet and the grovelling sweeter.

And for Ted, always.

5 Stars – Entertaining— Great story

"The characters are rich and full and flawed and I couldn't help but fall in love with them!" C Cae – Amazon

"4.5 stars! Enjoyable romantic suspense

I was not expecting to enjoy this as much as I did." Badass Lioness – Book Reviewer

5 Stars -Delightful Romantic Mystery

"Rayder has a lot of amends to make...You'll have to read this book, but trust me. You'll love it."

- Joan Reeves, NY Times and USA Today Bestselling Author

5stars – BookBub Review

"Not only is there a "man from the past" romance in this book, there is intrigue! Bonnie Edwards' excellent writing will keep you glued to the page until you reach the end." H Rowan

CHAPTER ONE

ELEANOR MACKLIN'S FOOTSTEPS echoed in the cavern-like stillness of her underground parking garage. She wanted to ignore the flickering shadows and crackling buzz of dying fluorescent lights overhead, but she couldn't. She clutched her keys in tight fingers and picked up her pace. Finally reaching her car, she unlocked the door and slid behind the wheel. She released a soft exhale of relief.

She needed coffee and longed for her first cup of the day. Hoping her make-up hid her exhaustion she checked her reflection in the rear-view mirror.

That's when she saw him.

A man watched from the long-fingered shadows of the pillar directly across from her.

She told herself she was imagining the man. She was tired from stress and lack of sleep. That's all it was, she thought as she studied the still darkness by the pillar. Nothing stirred in the shadows, just in her mind. This was a secure building with twenty-four-hour security. No one could get in who didn't belong. There couldn't be a man watching her. Not at this time of the morning. Not on a day like any other. *Not today.*

But, still, she locked her door, the click loud and reassuring in the emptiness.

She checked her mirror again. And shivered when she saw movement. There was a man.

He stepped out into the weak light and strode quickly toward her car. His full-length leather coat swayed as he moved with sure strides. She gasped in fright. The edges of the open coat lifted and reminded her of raven's wings. He was over six feet, and the thunder in his expression made her think of righteousness personified. Hardly the attitude of a street mugger, but more dangerous.

She kept her eyes trained on him in the mirror, prepared for anything. She fumbled with her keys, trying to insert the correct one into the ignition without looking for the keyhole.

There was something familiar about his walk, the cut of his jaw, and his hair.

Long hair with a blackbird sheen. *Oh, God, not him.*

Black, so black. All but his eyes. *Please, God, not him.*

Eyes so crystalline blue they could laser through a woman at thirty yards. Except the distance between them was only ten feet.

And ten long years.

Rayder Cole.

She inserted the key and turned it, gunning the engine and wished for the nerve to run him down. He slowed but continued toward her. Fear battered her ribs and threatened to beat its way out.

Panic rose. *Breathe! Breathe!* She'd wondered how she'd react if faced with him again. Pride came to her rescue. She forced the panic down and replaced it with full seething anger.

She opened her window. "What the hell are *you* doing here?" she demanded.

Surely, she was wrong. Her exhausted brain had tricked her into thinking an innocent man was Rayder Cole. But everything about the man was right: his eyes, nose, high cheekbones, even the small puckered scar on his upper lip. Every detail of his face was indelibly etched in her memory and stood in full living color before her eyes. She blinked but he was still there, only a foot away from her car window.

"You ripped me off and you're surprised to see me?" His voice was hot and dark with anger.

"Answer my question. What are you doing here? You've already stolen what you could from me." *Her money. Her trust. Her heart.*

His jaw twitched. "Don't play stupid, Ellie, it's not your style," he said. "I know about the forgery. I know you ripped me off." He leaned closer. "I *know*.

"I don't have a clue what you're talking about," she said. "You're the one who ripped *me* off, remember?" She heaved in a breath, startled by the release of pent up anger and humiliation. "Ten years ago? Five grand in cash?" She refused to admit the deeper hurt, how he'd taken her virginity while his belongings were in the trunk of his getaway car. How'd she'd woken to find him gone.

"Oh, I remember," he said, soft as lake mist. "And that's why you've taken your revenge," he said, his tone sharper.

His hands gripped her car door, tempting her to close the window on his fingers. She ignored the temptation and focused on what, exactly, he'd said.

"Revenge?" She furrowed her brow and tapped her chin with the tip of her middle finger. "I don't think so, no, I can't recall cooking up a revenge plot." She kept up the pretense of intent consideration. "In fact, I don't remember as much as thinking about you in the last decade," she lied.

His eyes narrowed.

She liked that. It felt good to pull off a quick, nasty jab to his ego.

His intent gaze roved across her features and settled on her hair. His intensity brought up a blend of memories and emotions. She was glad she'd braided her hair, so it was tight and safe.

He'd never again comb his fingers through it, lift it to his face and pretend to love the feel of it.

Rayder gave her an insolent smile and stretched the moment for maximum effect, infuriating her. When he leaned down to the car window, an incredible vibrancy enveloped her. His. Again.

Eleanor wasn't up to this sparring today: she wasn't awake, she wasn't sharp, and she wasn't prepared. And, he knew it, which is why he'd chosen this moment to approach her. He'd always sought the advantage.

He leaned even farther into the open window, bringing in cold air, exhaust fumes and menace.

"Ellie," he said, his eyes warming as he used the name from long ago, when she believed he loved her. His face came close enough to kiss her, to slip his hand behind her head and tug her to his mouth. The flare in his eyes told her he knew it, too, but she didn't retreat; didn't flinch.

"I must be crazy," he murmured. "You look good, Ellie," he continued with a mature male's husky appreciation. "Really fine."

She felt his breath, warm and scented by coffee. His eyes, so startlingly blue they glowed, watched her with too much interest.

"Why flatter me?" she responded dryly. "It won't get you anywhere. I learned my lesson." He was a thief and a liar ten years ago and she'd bet her life that he still was.

"And I learned about you. What you like, where you like it and how you like it done. We're older now. We'd be even better than before." His gaze followed the lines of her body from her knees to her mouth. "Slower. Hotter."

"As thrilling as the sex talk is, I have work to do." She sat up straight, forcing him to back his head out of the window, but not far enough to satisfy her. She wanted to start the car and leave him there, but he'd piqued her curiosity. She opened her door with a hefty shove and knocked him back a step. Pleased, she climbed out of the car to face him square on.

She set her hand on the car door to keep grounded so she wouldn't slap his smug, handsome face. "Get to the point. Then get out of my way."

His mouth quirked with that damned pucker in his upper lip, but he said nothing. He'd told her his cousin had split that lip with brass knuckles the year before she'd met him. That was probably a lie too, like everything else he'd said.

When he didn't speak, she went on, "I don't know what plot you imagine I've dreamed up, but I've accepted the loss of my money and moved on. Obviously, you have a problem, but it has nothing to do with me."

At her denial Rayder's eyes burned. His lips thinned into a grimace and he leaned over her. Eleanor stood her ground, no more the easily intimidated college girl he remembered.

The harsh light in his eyes cranked up to a glare. "Look, I want to give you a break. Let me have the original, and we'll call ourselves even."

"What original?" Her confusion must have made an impression because he turned his glare down to a simmer.

"The Lady Emma Hamilton miniature," he said as if talking to a child. "I retrieved what I thought was the stolen original but now I find I returned a forgery and the original is your vault."

She remembered the tiny portrait. The Lady Emma was one in a collection of thirty miniatures owned by a woman recently widowed. Why a con artist would be interested in one specific art piece was beyond her. Rayder hadn't even liked art when she knew him. He'd been studying law, or at least he attended some classes. A con artist studying law was so ludicrous she laughed.

Her neighbor who parked three spots up stepped off the elevator and walked toward his car. He gave her a look that asked if she needed assistance. She smiled and waved. Nice guy. She let him think this was a perfectly normal conversation.

The break seemed to ease Rayder's tension. He swept his fingers through his hair and leaned against her car as if he had all day to chat. Which she didn't.

"The contents of the Macklin Gallery vault are no concern of yours." She'd check into his claim one of the pieces was stolen as soon as possible.

"You're wrong. When I first learned about the forgery, I assumed the owner had it copied and passed the copy off as the original. Not very sophisticated, but, sometimes the most effective cons are the simplest." He crossed his arms and looked as if he was enjoying the tale. "Then I found out you had access to the original and I believe you're behind the forgery. Considering your grudge against me, your connections, and your easy access to the pieces, naturally I'd assume you're involved. You've got motive and opportunity."

Stunned, Eleanor blinked and thought fast. "For revenge? I hate to break it to you, but I don't want revenge. I want to forget that we ever met." She frowned as one question rose to the top of her mind. "Why dismiss the owner from your short list of suspects?"

"Celia Brand has recently inherited the collection and has no expertise. From all accounts she's a society-obsessed woman. She'd have no way to pull this off. Also, she's loaded, so there's no motive. But your motive is personal."

Except Eleanor didn't care about him or about what he'd done to her. Not anymore, and certainly not enough to exact revenge. "You're romancing Celia Brand and want me to keep quiet about what I know about you."

Celia Brand was the only client willing to trust the gallery with a substantial collection. Eleanor and her brother Nick had worked hard to gain her trust and losing her support now would be a catastrophe.

"I've spent the last two days with her," Rayder admitted.

"And nights?"

He set his lips firmly, blurring the puckered scar into a thin line.

"Suppose I tell her about how you stole from me," she probed. "You wouldn't be in her good graces for long."

"Don't threaten me, Ellie. We both know the art world runs on trust or the lack of it, depending on which side of the law you're on. Honest collectors are cautious. And semi-honest collectors are downright paranoid." His calm, light tone, frightened her more than his dark anger and phony outrage.

"If you expose our past, I'll drag the Macklin Gallery down with me," he added. "Considering the conspiracy to commit fraud charge you barely avoided three years ago . . ." his voice faded away because he didn't need to continue.

The gallery's position had been precarious ever since the police had bungled their previous investigation into a fraud that appeared to be connected to the Macklin Gallery.

"We were never charged because we didn't do anything wrong." Her stomach clenched. "The rumors and innuendo nearly killed us." Her voice broke over the last word. How many times must she explain before the stain went away?

Threatening to expose him had only made him angrier. She looked at Rayder, wanting a sign that he was joking, that he wouldn't hurt her again, but there was no softening in his hard gaze. All he wanted was to win, at any cost.

"Do you have any idea how much I hate you?" she whispered, unable to hide the hurt in her voice.

He blinked and the light in his eyes dimmed. "Yes, I do."

"What do you propose?" she asked, sickened she had to listen. The Macklin Gallery was her responsibility. It was also her greatest joy. She'd never made a secret of her ambitions, especially with him. She would stop at nothing to protect the generations-old family business, and he knew it.

"This is a draw. We're even, Ellie. You've had your revenge. All five-grand worth."

She opened her mouth to deny it, but he raised a palm to put her off.

"And for the record," Rayder went on, "I am not conning Celia Brand. All I want is to buy the original and get out of Toronto. I'll be gone in a matter of hours. We'll be there at nine."

Eleanor had learned the hard way no one waited for the truth to come out before branding an art dealer fraudulent. Even a whisper of impropriety with a piece of art could ruin a legitimate business. It was to the credit of the Gallery's decades-long stellar reputation that she'd been able to hold the business together over the last three years.

"All you want is to buy that one piece of Celia's collection?"

He nodded. "Right."

"And what do I get?" she asked.

He cocked an eyebrow. "Rid of me."

She wanted nothing more. Except time to think. And to talk to Nick. She'd have to tell her brother about Rayder. She'd have to explain why she'd abandoned university and come home so suddenly. Nick would support her through the sale of the painting and never mention Rayder again. But first she'd have to make her brother promise not to tear Rayder's head off.

"My schedule's too full to see you at nine," she said smartly. "Make it eleven."

CHAPTER TWO

ELEANOR CLIMBED INTO her car, buckled up and pulled away. In her rear-view mirror, Rayder faded back into the shadows of the underground parking garage. It wasn't until crisp November air blew the smell of fear out of her car, that she wondered how he'd gained entry into the garage in the first place. She must tell Bruno, the doorman, about the lack of security. He'd figure it out and report back.

Twenty minutes later, she walked into the Macklin Gallery, her pride and joy.

Ignoring her own office, she went straight into Nick's at the back. They shared a connecting door, but her office was much smaller, having been carved out of the larger one that her father had preferred. He'd been unhappy but Nick had agreed Eleanor needed her own space. The new configuration worked for both siblings.

Inside the office, three portraits hung on the walnut-paneled walls. The Macklin men, from her great-grandfather down to her father stared at her, in silent chastisement her for allowing a new threat to the gallery they'd loved above all else.

"Three years since the last time, Eleanor? How could you?" echoed down from the stern faces. She shook off the guilt and crossed to Great-grandfather's huge walnut desk, now Nick's. Papers cluttered the expansive top.

It was too early to expect Nick, so she searched for a clue to help her learn what Rayder was up to. Using the desk phone, she dialed her brother's home number and glanced through the mess on his desk, as she waited for him to answer. Again, she replayed what Rayder had told her.

He'd retrieved the original Lady Emma Hamilton miniature. *From where?* He hadn't said. He'd since learned it was a forgery. *From whom?* He hadn't said.

Rayder, a victim. The thought amused her, and she sat in Nick's chair and laughed out loud until tears sprang to her eyes.

Her call still hadn't been answered. She disconnected before his voicemail kicked in. Nick was likely in the shower. Or still asleep. If so, she hoped the call had woken him.

But what, exactly, had Rayder meant by 'retrieved'? Was he working as an insurance investigator? Impossible. That job was too legitimate for a man like Rayder. He was the lowest of the low: a smooth con artist who preyed on vulnerable women for money.

Humiliation nipped at her insides as she acknowledged, for the first time in years, how much his love con had cost her. She'd changed so much after being victimized. She'd once been warm, loving, and ingenuous; willing to think the best of people. Today, people referred to her as an ice queen. She wore the nickname like a shield.

At twenty-eight, she was fiercely dedicated to running an international art gallery. She'd pushed and cajoled her brother into helping her pull it out of a disastrous scandal and worked long, hard hours to bring it back into the black. She would not let Rayder Cole blow into town and ruin everything she'd worked for.

She had to bury whatever scandal he was trying to brew. To do that, she needed Nick. She tried his cell phone. An automated voice said the phone was out of range. Weird.

Nick was her ace in the hole with their clients. Art collectors could be secretive, flamboyant, paranoid, or obsessed. Artists were often downright strange. Nick handled them all with flair and a sense of amusement she'd never been able to muster.

But lately, Nick had been distracted or dissatisfied, she wasn't sure which. Frowning at the thought, she tried him again. Still out of range. But as far as she knew there were no dead zones in the city.

Eleanor set to work on the papers on Nick's desk, looking for any reference to Celia Brand or her collection. An orange notice regarding an auction fluttered onto the floor, reminding her of leaves in autumn.

She reached for the paper, but an errant puff of air made it skitter away. She stretched farther and came smack dab upon a memory of Rayder, picking a big yellow leaf out of her hair. She trembled with the memory, tried to deny it, and failed.

The sun had been warm that day, the air filled with the strong tangy scent of fallen leaves. Rayder had tugged her down into a pile beneath a sugar maple and kissed her senseless. He stretched his long body along the length of hers. She allowed him to wedge his leg between her thighs as desire rose thick and heady between them. He kissed her.

His lips were chilled at first but heated quickly. He looked down into her eyes and flattened the tip of her nose with his palm. "It's cold."

Ellie laughed; her heart filled with love. She let it fill a lot of other places, too and shifted beneath his legs in invitation. "You know what they say, cold nose, warm heart."

"That's not what they say." He grinned and covered her face with a crinkly golden leaf. She blew it off and found him looking at her, his eyes alight with joy. His thigh moved against her urgently and made her tremble with need.

Eleanor balled up the orange paper and tossed it in the trash can along with the memory.

Nonsense. It wasn't young Rayder that made her shake, it was the dark, dangerous man he'd become. Not for the first time, she realized his name was tellingly appropriate. He was a raider. A raider of hearts.

She heard the rustle of paper and the low humming sound of a photocopier warming up. Anne, the assistant she shared with Nick, was settling in to work. If Anne was here already, there was no time to waste. She called her in.

"Good morning, how was your trip to New Mexico?" Anne Hetherington, tall, slim, and brunette sauntered in, empty coffeepot in hand. "Find any interesting potters?"

Eleanor must have looked as frazzled as she felt because Anne stopped suddenly and gaped at the mess of papers on the floor and all over the desktop. Her expression made Eleanor stop and take stock of her actions. The office was in a worse state than when she'd come in.

"What's going on?" Anne asked. "Where's Nick?"

"He's not in yet and I've got a couple of questions for him. I hoped I'd find the answers in this mess." She held up her palms.

"Maybe I can help," Anne suggested. "You must be exhausted. You didn't get into the airport until three a.m. Heaven knows when you went to sleep."

Eleanor sighed. She'd been too excited by the artists she'd discovered in the southwest to sleep much.

"I'm okay." She pushed away the fatigue and smiled. "Is Celia Brand still happy with our service? Did anything unusual happen while I was gone?"

"No, nothing. And if Celia Brand had a complaint, believe me, she'd have told everyone."

Eleanor nodded, relieved.

"I'd be happy to call my mother, to be certain." Anne's mother was a maven of society with a penchant for gossip. With the Gallery's interests in mind, Anne regularly pumped her mother for any information on divorce settlements, pre-nuptial agreements, and inheritances. Idle gossip was often important to a business that survived on shifts in wealth. Information Anne gleaned from her mother had proved useful in the past.

"Yes, please. Call to see if Celia's mentioned the gallery in a negative way." She smiled, relieved that not all in her world had gone awry. Anne was still the best assistant ever and the world still turned.

"Consider it done," her assistant said.

The phone rang. "I'll get this," Eleanor offered. It's probably Nick, anyway." She hesitated with her hand on the receiver.

"Coffee's a priority this morning," Eleanor explained. "I haven't had any yet. Would you mind making the first pot?" As much as she trusted Anne, she still didn't want her assistant to overhear her conversation with Nick.

With a smile and nod, Anne stepped out of the office, closing the door behind her.

"Good morning, the Macklin Gallery," Eleanor said clearly.

"Eleanor?"

"Hi, Dad," she said, sorry she'd answered. He thought it unprofessional for the gallery owner to answer the phone. She'd given up arguing that it made her seem accessible. Besides, she didn't do it often.

"Where's Anne?"

"She's busy making coffee, Dad. What's up? How's Mom?" When her parents had retired to Florida, she'd hoped these calls would stop. She should have known better.

"Fine, fine. We're golfing with the neighbors at three."

"Wonderful." She waited, expecting him to do it again.

"Is Nick around?" he asked.

There it was. She should quit hoping her father would ask her about the business. She'd always be his little girl and Nick would always be the man in charge. She sighed.

"No, Dad, he's not. What can I do for you?"

"How is he handling the sale of Celia Brand's collection? Do you know?"

"I don't know what Nick plans to do with it, but *I* want to offer it at auction in the spring. London hasn't seen a collection like this in years. Response would be good." She kept her voice even. The dutiful daughter. She frowned.

"Well, that's a wonderful idea, Eleanor," he said, as if she'd just learned to tie her own shoelace.

She waited for him to ask about her buying trip.

"Mom says hello and wants you both to come down for Christmas," he said with an air of finality.

"Sure, Dad, we will," she responded. "I've a question before you go. What can you tell me about Celia Brand?"

She imagined her father's brow furrowing. "Not much," he said, "except she's more interested in collecting husbands than art. Axel was besotted with her and left her everything, even though she knew nothing about his art collections and cared even less." He paused. "Why?"

"I'm curious. That's all." The comment by Rayder about semi-honest collectors rang through her head. "We'll be seeing more of Celia and, as you've said, it's useful to understand who you're dealing with."

"You'll pass this on to Nick?"

"Sure, thanks Dad." She hung up, less concerned with Celia being vulnerable to Rayder's charm than she had been.

She tried Nick again and got the same odd message. Aggravated with the technical glitch, she supposed he'd left home without checking his voice mail, in which case he'd be here any minute.

Anne brought in a cup of coffee and left it on the desk for her. Grateful, she drank it quickly and checked the time. Feeling pressured by the minutes ticking by she continued her search. She found delivery slips, work orders for repairs, and even old invitations to events, but she discovered nothing about Celia's collection.

It had been a relief for Eleanor and a coup for Nick when Celia had placed her collection in the gallery's care. If anything were to shake Celia's confidence now, the gallery was as good as dead. She glanced at the portraits again and cast about for an idea to help her.

She called an art dealer in New York. One short conversation would confirm Rayder had lied through his teeth about 'retrieving' stolen goods. Did he think she had no resources to check out his story? Or perhaps he underestimated her, and assumed she was still the gullible girl he'd abandoned in a rumpled bed.

RAYDER WATCHED CELIA Brand breeze through the door of the Macklin Gallery offices ahead of him, with the air of a woman too busy to be polite and too rich to care.

"Where's Nick?" she demanded of a woman caught in the act of settling a morning cup of coffee onto her tidy desk.

The woman didn't miss a beat. "Good morning, Mrs. Brand. It's nice to see you again. Mr. Macklin's not available, but "

"Don't be ridiculous," Celia cut the woman off. "I can hear him in there."

Rayder watched as Celia cocked her ear to listen at an office door. The brass plaque announced the space belonged to Nicholas Macklin.

The widow's hair was black as coal and sparkled too brightly to be natural. Her choice in clothes seemed a size too small, except for the low cut of her tops. Her avaricious nature made her ripe for a shake down. Too bad he was no longer in the shake down business.

"That's a fine-smelling cup of coffee," he said with a smile directed at the pretty receptionist.

She looked up at him. Her slate gray eyes widened, and she smiled back. A faint hint of color rose in her cheeks.

"Sorry we're here so early, but...." He turned the smile up a notch. Everything was coming together perfectly. He wanted to buy, Celia wanted to sell, and Ellie wanted him gone.

"Nick!" Celia called through the office door. "I must see you." She opened the office door and walked through uninvited. "Oh," she said, pointedly, "it's you."

Rayder followed her into the office. Ellie was leaning over a large desk, making a phone call. She looked startled, then angry when she saw him. He didn't think she'd care that an eleven o'clock appointment had been too late for him to make his twelve-thirty flight.

Resigned to the interruption, she set the receiver back into its cradle. Apparently, she didn't appreciate this morning's warning of his arrival. No matter, she would after she had time to process.

Against the impressively paneled walls, her dress was two shades deeper than her sea-green hazel eyes. She looked lush and inviting, the braid that kept her thick honey hair tightly in check made him remember the lushness of her waves. The promise of beauty he remembered in the girl was more than fulfilled in the woman. She took his breath away and he wondered which of them was in control of this interview.

"Yes," she said smoothly to Celia, keeping her gaze locked with Rayder's, "it's me. I'm sorry Nick's not here to meet with you, Mrs. Brand." She waved them into chairs in front of the ornate desk.

Celia's surprised huff echoed his own disappointment. It would have been simpler to deal with Nick Macklin directly. Rayder's reaction to Ellie was stronger than he'd anticipated. Even after all this time, Ellie tugged at him; made him want.

Celia looked ready to explode in a tirade. He considered allowing it, but he needed to catch his flight. He didn't want Celia sidetracked.

"I'm certain Ms. Macklin is perfectly capable of helping us with our request," he cut in, with a smile for Celia. She visibly controlled herself and smiled back, her ice-blue eyes glittering.

"Ray and I," Celia explained, "are here to see my collection." Rayder already knew Celia preferred to deal with men. He suspected she thought it gave her an advantage.

"Ray?" Ellie asked with a cool smile. "Short for Raymond?"

"No, Rayder," he said evenly, holding back a grin. "Rayder Cole." At one time, he'd considered an alias, but his family's reputation and connections had been too useful to throw away. While the other Coles broke the law, Rayder used his name as a key to 'informed sources' all over the world.

"You haven't met?" Celia chimed in. "Of course not, how silly of me. Ray only arrived on Saturday." She looked up at him with a predatory smile that hadn't irked him until now. "It's been a very instructive two days."

She looked sharply back at Ellie. "But, Eleanor, you seem disconcerted. Surely Nick told you my collection's in your vault for safekeeping?"

"Of course, he did mention how happy he was to have been of service. But I've been out of town, Mrs. Brand, and Nick didn't tell me you planned to show the collection to anyone," Ellie explained.

"I've decided to sell it," Celia announced. "The miniatures were Axel's favorites. I never cared much for them."

"Oh, I see," Ellie said thoughtfully. "And Mr. Cole says he wants to buy them?" She slid a glance in Rayder's direction. "Perhaps you've forgotten our suggestion to sell the collection at auction. It would be more profitable than selling privately. Sotheby's–"

"Mrs. Brand is in a hurry, Ms. Macklin," Rayder cut in. "She can't wait for the spring auctions and she's too late for this fall." He aimed his next words at Celia. "You selling privately wouldn't do much for the gallery's profits this quarter," he said, appealing to Celia's greedy core. He let a lazy grin steal across his face, as he pointed out Ellie's fiscal responsibility as if profit were a dirty word.

Ellie's only response was a tightening around her eyes.

"I suppose I could be greedy and take Eleanor's suggestion," she said, with a sly glance at him. "But then why should I wait for spring?"

She smiled happily. "Ray is eager to purchase and I'm eager to sell. A match made in heaven."

"You want the whole collection, Mr. Cole?" Eleanor probed.

"I won't know until I see it, will I?"

"Of course." She stood and Rayder got caught by the long curve of her waist and hip, emphasized by the draping silk of her dress. "If you'll wait right here, I'll bring it to you."

"I'd much rather see the vault. I'm fascinated by security systems," he said with a wink meant only for her. The look she flashed back was lethal.

SEE THE VAULT. Rayder would see the vault over her dead body. She closed the door to Nick's office gently and leaned over Anne's desk.

"Keep them busy," she whispered urgently. "Take them coffee, make small talk, but keep that man in my office."

"Shucks," Anne whispered back. "I want to keep him in *my* office. He's gorgeous." She picked up a loaded silver coffee service from the credenza behind her and smiled sheepishly. "What can I say? He noticed how good it smelled."

"I know, I know," Eleanor said. "He's a charmer." She picked up the linen napkins Anne had forgotten and slipped them onto the tray.

Anne smiled her thanks and Eleanor headed down the short back hall, not in the least surprised at Anne's response to Rayder. He had a dangerous knack for making women want to please him. Getting Anne to make coffee and serve it in the good silver was typical of a man who wanted to show his skill in manipulation.

If she were forced to consider her impressions of this grown-up Rayder, she'd say he was more devastatingly attractive than the boy she recalled. And he'd been difficult enough to resist. Who was she kidding? She'd melted like toffee in the sun as soon as he'd looked at her.

The vault sat behind a clever screen of potted palms and Schefflera, devised sometime in the nineteen twenties. Her father had updated the security system before he'd retired. She punched in the numbers of the security code with more force than necessary and wrenched at the heavy door with impatience born of fear. Once inside, she leaned against the vault wall and took several deep breaths.

At least Rayder had the good sense to have warned her this morning. Even if the warning had contained an element of blackmail, she was grateful he'd prepared her for this meeting. Oh, hell, she thought, now he had her feeling grateful.

She checked her watch. It was five after nine and already she'd been through more than a weeks' worth of disasters. She'd expected to be overrun with work today, but she thrived on hard work.

Rayder's return had her in an emotional maelstrom she didn't need. She couldn't focus. First, she'd dealt with Rayder's reappearance, then her father's lack of confidence in her and now Nick was late. *Very late.* She couldn't worry about that, there wasn't time.

She would not let her emotions boil over and she mustn't let her memories ambush her again. Spying the box that contained the miniatures, Eleanor took it off the shelf. Each miniature was kept in a velvet lined individual drawer inside a sturdy handmade oak box. The box had a handle for easy transport.

She cursed Rayder for not waiting until eleven o'clock. But she should have known he'd arrive at whatever time suited him. Celia and Rayder's arrival had prevented Eleanor from placing her call to the New York art dealer. Without talking to her contact, she couldn't accuse Rayder of trying to con Celia.

All she could do was turn her back to the door to shield the box from view. She carefully slid out each drawer. One at a time, she compared the names of the subjects painted and their corresponding inventory numbers with a list on the inside top of the box.

Only five more to go, she saw, wishing this nightmare would end. Any moment Nick could sail in, his usual happy smile in place, and save her from spending one more second with Rayder and Celia. She wished hard but Nick didn't come.

The next drawer was stiff, and she gave it a stronger pull. It opened, but it was empty.

The miniature of Lady Emma Hamilton, mistress of Lord Horatio Nelson, was gone.

CHAPTER THREE

GALLERY POLICY PROHIBITED any piece from being removed from the vault without a note being left in its place explaining where the piece had been taken and why. There was nothing on the shelf. Anne didn't have the combination of the vault.

Her brother had left Eleanor no choice. She'd have to cover for him. Quickly Eleanor grabbed a piece of notepaper and wrote the note.

Sweat broke out on her body. She'd never been a good liar, but to do it on paper. She shuddered. She had no other option.

Eleanor secured the vault and quickly carried the oak box back to Nick's office, dread making her hands cold and her heart thump.

She got to the office door and looked inside. Her assistant flashed brilliant smiles in Rayder's direction. Pretty, cheerful Anne never let an opportunity to flirt pass her by. Eleanor couldn't blame her.

Rayder looked incredibly virile in casual navy slacks with a Christmas red vee neck sweater over a snowy shirt. The white collar at his neck brought out the brilliance of his eyes. No, she couldn't blame Anne, but she'd warn her off. It was the decent thing to do.

"Excuse me," Anne said, when Eleanor entered. "I have email to tend to." She left quickly, slanting Eleanor a quizzical look as she brushed past.

Celia's lips lifted into a cool smile. "There you are," she said to Eleanor. "We were wondering if you'd absconded."

"Nick rearranged while I was out of town, and it took me awhile to find the right box." Eleanor shook off the guilt of another lie and set the box on the desk. "Let's take a look, shall we?"

She pulled out each drawer and set them side by side on the coffee table. When she came to the empty drawer, she guiltily mimicked everyone else's disappointment. "Oh, that's odd, I wonder—"

Rayder looked at the label on the bottom. "Lady Emma Hamilton, George Romney, 1800," he said with a grating edge in his voice.

"What? My Lady Emma?" Celia interjected. "Where is it? What have you done with it?" Her agitation grew with each question. Frantic suspicion froze her usually mobile face. She glared at Eleanor.

Eleanor shifted uneasily. Her guilt for lying might color her perception, but Celia's overreaction seemed forced. She looked jumpy as a hare in hunting season, as her gaze shifted from Eleanor to Rayder and back, as if she suspected them of trying to pull something over on her.

Being in accord with Rayder brought on a nervous giggle. Eleanor coughed to cover it.

"I'll check with Nick about where he sent the piece," Eleanor replied as soon as she could.

Rayder watched Celia closely, his expression unreadable. He picked up the folded square of notepaper that sat in the tiny drawer.

"It says here that it's been sent out for cleaning and frame repair," he read aloud. He turned his lethal gaze on Eleanor. "Unless you use a lot of different restorers, you know where the miniature is, right?"

When Eleanor hesitated, Rayder went on. "The initials are N.M. For Nick Macklin, I assume."

"Of course," she said brazening it out. "Who else?" The heat must be turned up high. The room was too warm. Eleanor flushed from chest to forehead. She shifted uncomfortably.

Rayder gave her a 'gotcha' grin as Ellie fought a wave of nausea. How could he read her so easily? Flustered all over again, she took the note out of his hand. She folded it and placed it on the desk behind her. "It'll take a couple of hours to reach Nick and ask him how long it's been gone and when it'll be ready."

"Why call Nick? Call the restorer, he'll tell you what's happening," Rayder goaded.

"I can't," she blurted, damning herself.

"Why not?" Rayder asked. His eyebrows rose.

"Before I left for my buying trip, Nick may have found someone new." It was a bluff. Jack Burke was the best art restorer in the city, a master craftsman. The Macklins only used the best.

"That's great," Celia whined on a gusty sigh. "It's gone and you don't know where." Celia's strident voice scraped Eleanor's spine.

"It won't take long to find out." She could think fast, but these lies had stacked up. She'd need to make notes to keep all of them straight. She'd be damned if she let Rayder catch her in a lie. She avoided looking at him.

"Why didn't Nick tell me he'd sent it out?" Celia's expression looked calmer, but her lips tensed as she rolled her shoulders.

"If he'd known you were planning to show the piece, Nick never would have removed it from the vault." Eleanor reached back to the desk, picked up Nick's appointment calendar, open to today's date. She circled the blank morning. "You didn't have an appointment," she pointed out in a gentle tone.

Eleanor needed to tread carefully or lose Celia Brand's business. She smiled at the other woman.

"When a piece is left with us," she explained, "we do all we can to present it to prospective purchasers in the best condition. Clearly, the Lady Emma wasn't as pristine as the rest of this magnificent collection."

Eleanor held her breath until Rayder snagged her glance. He smiled in an amused, proprietary way that sent shivers down her back. He admired her performance. It aggravated her that she hadn't fooled him. A new question arose in her fright-filled mind. What was his next move? Would Rayder have Celia call the police?

She had to find Nick. She checked the time. Nine-twenty. Where was he? But if her brother did show up, he'd be at a loss as to what was

going on and she'd be caught in her web of lies. She had to get these two
out of here.

Rayder had a mischievous twinkle in his eyes. He was enjoying
himself, the sick bastard.

"Emma Hamilton?" he said in a voice laced with curiosity. "I just
told Celia about a legend that surrounds her."

"I'm sure it's very interesting, but . . ." Eleanor trailed off and stood,
expecting them to stand with her, but neither of them moved. *Get out!*
But of course, *this* thought Rayder refused to read.

Celia's expression eased into one of amused interest as she
continued telling the legend as if Eleanor hadn't given them a clear
sign of dismissal. "Apparently, if it comes into a widow's possession, she
dies penniless." She nodded, enthralled with the telling. "After Lord
Horatio Nelson, the great British admiral, was killed at sea, Emma
ended up in Calais, went to debtor's prison and died in poverty. The
last thing of value she owned was this miniature that had been in Lord
Nelson's hand when he died," she said, with a dramatic sigh. "She had
to sell it to pay for her own funeral. Can you imagine?" Celia asked
Eleanor.

"No, I can't," Eleanor murmured, as she shifted from foot to foot.
There'd been a subtle change in Rayder's attitude when Celia had
responded so wildly to the miniature's absence. The change was in
Eleanor's favor. She wasn't sure how she knew this. Perhaps it was a
shadow of their past connection, but she read Rayder in ways that
surprised her. He didn't like Celia and didn't like seeing Eleanor squirm
as much as he pretended to.

"I'll study the rest of the collection," Rayder said, as if the missing
piece was inconsequential.

Now he wanted to waste time looking at the rest of the collection.
She groaned silently and her stomach clenched as she glanced at the
time again. Her only way out of this was to leave and tell Anne to warn
Nick away when he arrived.

"We can catch up with the Lady Emma as soon as she's returned," Rayder continued in a reasonable tone. "I'd arranged a flight for later this morning, but I'll rearrange my reservation."

If Eleanor had needed any more proof Rayder was up to something, she didn't now. He was far too agreeable. It wasn't Rayder's way to accept no for an answer.

"Excuse me, I'll be right back," she murmured, and hustled out of the room before they could stop her.

Anne agreed with one nod to shoo Nick away when he arrived. Eleanor's stomach unclenched and she returned to her visitors.

Rayder admired all the other pieces, explaining brief histories of most of them. His broad knowledge impressed her, and Celia hung on every word.

Eventually, Celia's gaze came to rest on the empty shelf and Eleanor thought fast to prevent the conversation turning to the Lady Emma's current location again. "George Romney was a portrait artist, not a miniaturist."

"He was, and miniatures were different from full size portraits. There were much better artists in miniatures available at the time. I've seen pictures of the Lady Emma, and it isn't particularly good," Rayder explained.

"Then why would he attempt a miniature?" Eleanor asked, intrigued.

"His fascination with Emma was well documented. Hers was the only miniature he did. And he had to do it from memory. Emma never sat for him."

"Romney was beguiled by her, as was Emma's husband, and Lord Nelson, and probably a host of other men." Celia laughed. "They all crashed and burned at Emma's feet. What a life she led." She clicked her tongue. "And to end it all in poverty."

Celia shook her head with a sickening smile for Rayder. "Like the legend says, a widow who owns the miniature...." Her smile turned speculative as she trailed off. "But a widow who sells it is another matter entirely."

Rayder smiled smoothly and stood, hooking Eleanor's glance. She kept still, refusing to let him see her inner unrest. Her nerves stretched taut. She wanted Celia and Rayder out of this office, out of her gallery, out of her life.

She put the miniatures' case back together, closed it and ushered Celia and Rayder out of the office. She'd talk to Nick, get the Emma Hamilton back, and save the gallery from another scandal.

WITH THE COLLECTION locked away, and another phone call to Nick unanswered, Eleanor called Anne into the office.

"Interesting pair, aren't they?" She asked, hoping the question encouraged Anne to share her perceptive opinions.

Anne nodded, smiling. "I'll say. Wasn't her last husband old and rich?"

Startled by the idea of Rayder as Celia's new or next husband, Eleanor nodded. "Yes, but Rayder and Celia aren't married."

"Not yet. But believe me, Celia Brand's already on the lookout for wealthy number three. I've heard she's been cornering any male who's not standing beside his wife."

"You got this news from your mother?" Eleanor was constantly amazed by how much information Anne had.

"Just because Daddy lost nearly everything in the last recession doesn't mean Mrs. James Hetherington is without contacts." She gave her chin a haughty tilt, mimicking her society-conscious parent.

Eleanor smiled, thinking of her own father. "Doesn't it seem that the older our parents get, the quirkier they become?"

"Yeah, I've often wished my mother would get a job. Then she wouldn't have time for all this gossip."

"The love of which her daughter has inherited," Eleanor teased, thankful at times like this that Anne was quick to share any tidbit.

Anne laughed. "Okay, you got me. But seriously, I got the impression Celia was edgy or nervous. Especially when she looked at Rayder. There was a distinct scent of desperation about her."

"I noticed that, too." Eleanor tapped a pencil on the desktop. "But I didn't get a feeling he reciprocated the interest."

"No way. But he was definitely on red alert. Especially around you. He was charming and relaxed when you were in the vault but when you came back, he changed. I think you scare him," Anne said quizzically. "How could you scare anyone?"

Eleanor mused aloud. "I don't know, but you may be right." She hoped so. She wanted to scare Rayder. Scare him right out of town.

With Nick not answering his phone she had to ask Anne painful but necessary questions.

"This may be touchy, Anne, and I don't mean to bring up the past, but have you seen Jack Burke lately?" Perhaps Nick really had sent the miniature out for repair. Jack did all the work for the gallery. Nick may have become lax about tracking which pieces were there at any one time.

"That skunk? Not likely." Anne made a face.

"Not even here?"

"He was in a couple of weeks ago when you were gone to lunch. He spent a few minutes with Nick and left." She pursed her lips. "He had the nerve to speak to me as if nothing had ever happened." Anne squared her shoulders and tilted her chin. "Only a man could propose marriage and then forget he'd said the words." With that, she stalked out of the room.

Eleanor heard drawers slam but controlled the impulse to ask Anne to take it easier on the furniture. She was sorry for asking about Jack, but she'd had no choice.

Jack Burke was an excellent art restorer, known for his attention to detail and fine craftsmanship. He worked at home, refused to hire staff and rarely answered his phone. He said his work was too sensitive to have other people, even an office assistant, around, but Eleanor thought he was a loner. His unexpected romance with Anne had caused months of speculation that he'd been shaken out of his self-imposed social exile.

But, in the end, his desire to be alone had won out and Anne had been hurt. In the last months, she had put the pieces of her heart together again.

Eleanor sighed, knowing too well how it felt to be betrayed. Shaking off the melancholy thoughts, she hoped Jack would answer the phone, tell her he had the miniature and it was ready for pick up. She doubted her luck would have changed that much but she had to try.

When Jack didn't answer, she kicked off her shoes, slipped on her boots and collected her coat. She couldn't sit around any longer. She felt too impatient to wait for Nick, too agitated to stay and do nothing. She'd go to Jack's house and get the Lady Emma back, ready or not.

She slipped on her coat and bent to pick up her purse. The office door opened.

Rayder lounged in her doorway, tall, smooth and intimidatingly alone. "Anne's in the showroom," he said, arching one eyebrow expectantly. "I have you all to myself."

"What are you doing here?" Eleanor demanded, pointedly looking at her watch.

"Is that any way to greet the man who just saved your gallery?" Rayder's smile was dangerous and slyly intent.

"You save my gallery? That'll be the day." She stepped back, then realized retreat made her appear frightened. She straightened and glared at him. "Get out."

Of course, he didn't move.

"That scene with Celia. Really, Ellie, I thought you'd be more skilled at subterfuge by now."

"Don't be ridiculous," she said fiercely, to drown out the sound of intimacy in the silent office. "I'm not the liar." If only she'd left one minute earlier, she'd be on her way to Jack's.

Rayder stepped to the center of the room, crowding her, making her feel invaded despite the four feet between them. In no mood to dally, Eleanor stepped right up to his face and got in it, enjoying a glow of satisfaction when she read surprise in his eyes.

Her palm itched, tingling deliciously in anticipation. She swung it up and across his handsome cheek. The sound of the slap was sudden and sharp in the quiet.

He stepped back. "I'm glad to see you haven't lost all your spunk."

"I've wanted to do that ever since I went to your landlady's door and found out you'd left," she said. She couldn't trust herself to say, "left me." She rubbed her palm on her thigh, relishing the sting, suspiciously aware that he'd goaded her deliberately.

His cheek was red where she'd slapped and she knew, *she knew*, it must burn. But, damn him, he didn't make a move to touch it. "I'll allow you that slight revenge," he said softly, "and now that it's done, we can get down to business."

"Please do," she drawled.

He glanced at her abandoned high heels, one straight up, the other on its side on the deep plush rug. He let his gaze run from her toes to her eyes, taking in every inch of her with audacious calculation. "Uncle Shamus told me a woman never forgets her first time or her first man. I can see it in your eyes." He watched her speculatively. "Shamus is right."

"And what makes you think you were my first?" She tossed out the comment as if nothing could be more amusing. He was toying with her, taking her mind back to a time when they could read each other's thoughts.

The low flame in his eyes flared dangerously. "I was there, remember?"

Unfortunately, she did. "It's ungentlemanly to gloat. But then, being a gentleman was never on your agenda."

He blinked. She'd stung him. *The first one who blinks loses.*

"Even so, our previous relationship allows me certain insights into your behavior. Body language, for instance."

"That particular advantage goes both ways. I remember more about you than you realize." She hoped that was true because Rayder was tough and resilient.

"You knew before Celia and I saw the collection that the Lady Emma was gone," he said smoothly, with no touch of rancor. "Your lies may have worked with Celia, but you couldn't fool me."

"That's not true." She shifted uncomfortably. How could she convince him of that one particle of truth amid all the other lies she *had* told?

"You're lying again, Ellie. I see your tells. You shift your shoulders. You shrugged a lot this morning." Was that enjoyment she heard in his voice? Or anticipation?

She gauged the distance to the door. It wasn't far, but Rayder stood solidly in the way.

She looked into his eyes.

Big mistake.

CHAPTER FOUR

RAYDER BORE DOWN ON Eleanor like a warrior, making full use of the four extra inches he had on her. Inexplicably, she recalled something about ancient Picts painting their faces blue to frighten their enemies. Rayder didn't need paint, the blue brilliance of his eyes was pure threat.

"Exactly where is your brother? You smoothly avoided answering earlier. If he took the miniature, where did he take it? Don't hand me that garbage about him sending it out for repairs. I recognized your handwriting on that note."

She shook her head, denying the written lie, but he kept coming. She took a deep breath, fighting the urge to scream. Frozen to the spot, she waited, caught by old memories and long-buried responses.

A memory of Rayder borrowing her notes for an art history class they'd shared unnerved her. Of course, he knew her handwriting; he'd spent hours poring over it.

He stepped closer but she refused to give an inch. The leather scent of his coat and the deep musk of his aftershave played across her nose. Rayder smelled too damn good, like usual.

"You won't intimidate me," she said clearly, holding her ground, not sure where the strength to resist had come from.

Rayder stopped and eased back a step. He grinned a little-boy-caught kind of grin. "It was worth a try."

The tension popped like a balloon and, ignoring her better judgment, Eleanor grinned back.

"You're incorrigible," she said, even as she wondered what tack he would take next. "Why is that particular piece of so much interest? Even Celia–"

"Overreacted?" he interrupted smoothly.

She bit her lip. Obviously, Rayder had noticed the same thing she and Anne had seen. "She did, didn't she?"

"For a woman who said that her husband's collection means nothing to her, Celia was very aware of one piece." Rayder cocked an eyebrow and waited.

He wanted to pump her for information, use the old "we're in this together" routine.

"No matter how charming and sexy your eyebrows are, you will not get me to trade on the confidence of my clients." In one fell swoop she'd told him she knew he was using his wiles on her and that she took her clients' privacy seriously.

She kept her shoulders level and dropped her arms to her sides. The stakes were too high to make a mistake with this man. Everything was muddied by emotion.

"I'll make you an offer, Ellie," he said softly. He brushed his knuckles across her cheek, sending deadly little blitzes of electricity down her spine. "I'll trade what I know for what you know. We'll both win."

She blinked and regained her equilibrium. "What do you take me for, a fool? Celia won't wait–"

"I'll handle her, too," he interrupted quietly, making her wonder how he'd "handle" a woman like Celia. His gaze held Eleanor locked. Fine lines had formed at his eyes, his jaw had sharpened; the man chiseled from the boy. "As long as she believes I want the whole collection, she'll give you time to get the Lady Emma back."

There was something in his speech that confused her, but she was too rattled to sort it out. His fingers danced along her cheek and jaw line, so tenderly she felt an ache deep inside.

"It's been so long since..." Rayder said in a seductive timbre that pulled at her vitals. He traced her tight French braid, trailing his fingers down the loops, looking for a way to loosen it. She looked up, startled at how near he was and how suddenly open his desire. Open and compelling.

"This feels good. To touch you. To see your smile," he said roughly, his fingers tugging on her hair. His eyes gleamed with feral intent in the fluorescent lighting. "But there's fear and distrust in your eyes. I want to make love to you until your eyes are filled with nothing but me."

Her throat betrayed her, and she squeaked an inconsequential sound that told him how terrified she was that he'd make good on his threat.

"Why?" she whispered. "Didn't you hurt me enough ten years ago? You want to gut me this time?" She wanted to avoid talk of the past, but she was confused, her thoughts swirling with emotion, not clearheaded logic. Lord help her if he sucked her into the maelstrom of his lovemaking. She'd drown in him again, exactly the way she had before, and it would kill her afterward. That thought brought her back to solid ground and she tried to pull away.

Rayder tugged her closer. "Call it curiosity." His gaze roved her features in a silent inventory. "Call it renewed interest but don't deny it. Don't deny you wonder what it would be like, too. I can see it. I can read it in every glance." His voice went lower, hollow with leashed desire. "You remember how it was. How good."

She nodded in silence. He placed her hands on his chest and pushed them up to cup his shoulders. He was strong, toned, broader than he'd been. Heaven help her she loved the feel of him.

"My chest has more hair and my shoulders are filled out. I'm a *man* now, Ellie. And I can take you places you never dreamed of."

"Bastard," she whispered hoarsely, so caught up in his images she wasn't sure what was real anymore. His flesh beneath his sweater seemed super-heated, as if burning with his vital life-force. She held on, needing to feel more.

"My Ellie," he whispered. "Now we're getting somewhere." His voice became an intimate massage for her grated nerves. "Let it out," he crooned, "let it all out."

She squeezed her eyes shut to hold herself in, battling a deep chord of response. Eleanor willed him to go away, to disappear into the mists of memory, taking her pain with him.

"Don't call me Ellie, you don't have the right." It was a weak retort, but the best her befuddled mind could come up with.

"You said you loved hearing your name on my lips," he said smoothly, cocking an eyebrow. "I was the only one you permitted to call you Ellie."

"Anything I said to you ten years ago means nothing now. I don't understand why you keep talking about it." Her voice went edgy. "Why are you making this so hard?"

His lips were inches from hers. His eyes were diamond bright and intent. Rayder in full seduction mode. She gasped as she got her answer.

He needed to talk about the past. *He* needed to come to terms with what he'd done. And *he* was the one who hadn't been able to move on with his life. She filed away her conclusions to sort through later.

"Correction. You're the one making me hard." He tugged her hand to his chest again and held it there. His hand over hers felt warm and strong and oddly comforting. Slowly, inexorably, he slid her palm downward and she marveled again at the firm, smooth muscles under his clothes. He'd kept himself in devastatingly toned condition. He closed his eyes as she allowed him to move her hand lower still.

This was dangerous. It was wrong. But she was caught in a seductive web of sensual curiosity, the scent of him, and the sight of him, eyes closed, nostrils flaring. The flat of his belly heated her and then the clasp of his belt buckle felt cool.

He didn't need to push any lower because he'd risen to meet her. Her fingertips danced lightly across the tip of his arousal that strained at his belt.

He sighed raggedly with her touch. He opened his eyes again and shocked her by pushing into her hand. He slid her palm along the full rigid length of him. "I meant to buy the miniature this morning and leave." He looked fierce and wild. "But now you've got it stashed somewhere," he said, freeing her hand from his grip. "And I mean to get it."

"With sex as a weapon?" Eleanor yanked her hand away from him, furious with herself for allowing him to gain control so easily. "Get out!"

"You've got two hours to consider my offer to trade information," he said, checking his watch. "When I come back, I'd like you to answer a question for me."

"That is?"

"Axel Brand was a well-known collector, with the accompanying fear of theft. Why would his widow, with a security system like Fort Knox, need to put anything in your vault for safekeeping?"

CHAPTER FIVE

RAYDER'S QUESTION RICOCHETED in Eleanor's mind after he left. Why would Celia need to use the gallery's vault? Was she involved in forging a piece of her own collection? Maybe Rayder wasn't involved in the forgery. She shook her head to clear it. Of course, he was involved in whatever was going down.

He was probably lurking outside right now so he could follow her if she left the office. She slammed down the phone on her latest attempt to reach her brother.

She removed her coat and slipped back into her shoes. How could she leave and check with Jack Burke with Rayder watching her?

The intercom buzzed and she picked up the phone. "It's Farley and Associates on line two. It's their V.P. of Finance," Anne said. "Shall I take a message?"

"No, I'll take it Anne, thanks." She needed to keep up the appearance of business as usual. As much as possible, she should keep the same hours, see the same people, and do the same things. Nothing should look different, out of place, or suspicious.

Once Nick showed up and was able to look after the gallery, she'd be free to pursue her investigation. Because, sooner or later, the gallery would come under police scrutiny. With any luck at all, she'd hand over damning evidence and prove she and Nick had nothing to do with forgeries. Now or ever.

But knowing what she should do, knowing Rayder was probably watching her, knowing the police would eventually be called in, only frustrated her more. To change gears, she shook her head and answered the waiting call.

Farley and Associates was an investment firm that had decided to sell three watercolors they had purchased for their office reception area several years ago.

Eleanor confirmed what Nick had already told them; the Macklin Gallery would rent them several replacement paintings. With rental artwork being changed regularly, the company image would be one of fresh thinking. The Vice-President agreed, while focusing more on the profitability of selling the artwork they now owned.

She arranged an immediate meeting and hung up. For the first time today, something had gone right. Lack of sleep, traveling, three separate confrontations with Rayder in one morning and worry combined to make her lightheaded.

"Anne?" she called. When her assistant popped her head around the open door, Eleanor explained. "I have several errands to run, starting with an appointment at Farley. I'll be back after lunch. If Mr. Cole returns, please tell him I'm too busy to see him today."

Anne pursed her lips. "Too busy? But he's a buying agent. Can we afford to ignore him?"

"I'm not ignoring him, but I must see the V.P. at Farley right away." It was the coward's way out, but she was in no shape to have another meeting with Rayder. Like a wound-up toy that had been running too long, she was out of spring. "I'm not sure how long I'll be. I need to court Farley to keep them rotating their rental art. But don't worry, I have a feeling Rayder Cole will be more difficult to get rid of than either of us realizes."

The strange look Anne gave her made Eleanor grimace. "If my brother deigns to show himself or call, please tell him I need to speak with him immediately."

She'd deal with Farley's VP and then run personal errands with a visit to Jack Burke's sandwiched between. That way, if Rayder followed her, he wouldn't understand the significance of her stop at Jack's. With

Jack's loner attitude, he didn't even advertise his business by putting out a sign. Rayder would never know she was picking up the miniature.

With the Lady Emma safely in the vault, Eleanor would feel confident dealing with Celia and Rayder. It was possible Rayder would purchase the collection and the forgery would never be discovered. *If there even was a forgery.*

She shouldn't believe a word that came out of his mouth.

Eleanor left the gallery at ten-thirty, checking the street with furtive, sidelong glances for Rayder. He was nowhere in sight, so she hunched her shoulders against the biting wind and booted it the half block to the parking garage. The snow swirled around her. Once inside the relative protection of the garage, she hurried to her car, relieved to see no men in the shadows. Her relief would be temporary. She'd have to face Rayder again eventually.

But for now, she had a brief respite to steady herself. Obviously Rayder's suspicions of Celia were growing. Why else would he question the woman's actions?

She reviewed what he'd told her in the parking garage of her building this morning. He'd 'retrieved' a stolen miniature and then been told it was a fake. When he'd discovered the original was stored in the Macklin vault, he'd jumped to the conclusion that he was a victim of a plot to discredit him. A plot masterminded by Eleanor, or her brother, Nick. He'd dismissed Celia as a culprit because he'd decided she wouldn't have the expertise to pull off a fraud as beautifully orchestrated as this one appeared to be. What would he do with Celia's Lady Emma if he got it?

She shivered and started the engine, needing to drive and clear her head. Rayder couldn't be involved in a forgery plot. It was too much like real work. He had an insolent charm that nullified effort and made everything look easy. Even charming a money-motivated woman like Celia Brand.

If he was involved in a forgery plot, he'd have no reason to alert Eleanor to his presence. In fact, he'd probably go to great lengths to avoid bumping into her. Perhaps he'd thought to move in on Celia's distress at her recent widowhood and get his hands on a valuable art collection. But again, Rayder would avoid Eleanor.

Why would he return to her office and try to foster memories of their time together? Sickened by his feigning interest in her again, she clenched her teeth. How transparent. Did he think she was that gullible?

Rayder Cole had sunk low. It was a shame, really. He'd once had so much promise. As a student, a man, a lover; even a husband. Eleanor sighed. All that potential lost. Such a waste.

Agitated for no reason she wanted to understand, she turned on her car stereo. Her agitation turned to aggravation. Of course, she thought, it would have to be this song. It had been theirs. Hers and Rayder's.

She turned off the radio.

Maybe if she worked hard at it, she could forget she'd ever been eighteen and in love with Rayder Cole. Maybe she could forget how he'd made her feel today; breathless and warm and tingly.

She turned off the heat, found the parking garage under the office tower that housed Farley and Associates and parked. Shoving away all thoughts of Rayder, forgeries and seduction she concentrated on what to say during her hour-long appointment. The reassuring feel of the leather of her portfolio handle calmed her. She took comfort in the routine of presenting her gallery as the best in the business.

Sixty-five minutes later, pleased with the success of her meeting, Eleanor drove north again, nervously dividing her attention from the road ahead to her rear-view mirror. If she caught sight of anyone remotely resembling Rayder driving behind her, she'd abandon her plan to go to Jack's.

But first she needed to add a couple of personal errands to her afternoon. With that in mind, she picked up her dry cleaning and dropped off a donation bag of gently used clothes.

Forty-five minutes later she turned onto Gloucester Avenue. She parked half a block from Jack's house. With no sign of Rayder, she felt less jumpy. She imagined the thwarted frustration she'd see on his face when she told him to go to hell and that she didn't need to trade information.

She locked her car and walked the half block. Most of the houses on Gloucester had offices or other small businesses operating out of them. A photographer's studio shared a common wall with Jack's house.

Within an hour she'd have Celia's collection intact. She was only a phone call away from ending Rayder's game. Celia would know Rayder had lied about wanting the whole collection. Eleanor smiled with a delicious sense of justice. How right it was that it should be Eleanor to thwart Rayder's plans.

She knocked on Jack's front door several times before giving up and peering in the front window. Gauzy curtains did nothing to block the view. A love seat, two tub chairs, a coffee table and one floor lamp filled the front room. There were no pictures, no vases, and no magazines. Funny how she'd never noticed the sterile atmosphere before. On her previous visits to the place, of course, she'd had appointments and Jack had led the way to his third-floor studio immediately. The live-in areas of the house had been private.

She stalked the three steps back to the front door and looked through the window into a vestibule. An umbrella sat propped in a corner. A blue recycling box filled with newspapers took up the other wall. She cupped her hands around her eyes to see better, but it was no use. She couldn't read the date on the top paper. "Damn."

She banged on the door in frustration. Things seemed to be careening out of control again. The hair on the back of her neck prickled in alarm. *Rayder.* Was he watching her bang on the door after peeking in a window? This must look like a desperate errand rather than a casual one.

She straightened her shoulders, preparing to turn and face the street calmly when the next-door neighbor opened his door.

"Looking for Jack?" The man asked, peering over the top of the wall that divided the verandas. He had short cropped blond hair and friendly blue eyes, ringed with long black lashes. Gold hoops glittered in both earlobes.

"Yes, I am." She smiled widely. "Any idea where he is or when he'll be back?"

"With Jack, you never know. But lately, he's been gone more than usual." His blue eyes widened with curiosity. He walked past the divider to the front steps where he could get a better look at her.

"Could you please give him my card and tell him I was here? It's rather urgent." She held out her business card.

He took it and read it over. Then he smiled. "I've been to some shows at your gallery. Nice place. I'm a sculptor. Maybe you've seen my work?"

"Maybe I have. What's your name?" A lead on an up and coming sculptor could be great for business.

"Brian."

She waited for three breaths. "Just Brian?"

"I think it's a statement, don't you?"

"Yes." She smiled. Now was not the time to suggest a more memorable name. "You will tell Jack I was here? I really need him today."

"Oh, I doubt he'll be back anytime soon. He left with suitcases. Lots of them. Looked to me as if he'd be gone for some time."

Reeling with shock, Eleanor stepped back, her hand at her throat. She couldn't breathe. "Jack's gone? Where?"

"No idea. But he left about four a.m. Are you okay?" He looked concerned.

She nodded. "It's just so important I talk with him."

"Sorry I don't know anymore, but I'll keep your card. And I'd love to set up an appointment for you to check out my work."

Her mind a terrified blank, she managed to murmur a response and made her way to her car. When she drove away, she only ground the gears once.

She clenched her teeth as she drove by the gallery on her way to the dry cleaners. After that, she'd go to the bank, wasting more precious time because, if Rayder was watching her, she didn't want him to know the importance of her visit to Gloucester Avenue.

Damn Rayder for turning up in her life at a time like this. When she needed all her energy focused on clear-headed thought, he'd come back and scattered her concentration like chaff in the wind.

After wasting a full hour on errands that could have been done at any time, she returned to the gallery.

Anne was on the phone when Eleanor walked to the back of the gallery. "Hold on, Nick," Anne said, "Eleanor's here now." She held out the receiver. "He's in Tokyo."

"What?" She took the phone. "Nick, what the hell are you doing there?" She turned away from Anne's startled expression and pressed the phone more tightly to her ear.

"Go to your office, sis. We need to talk."

"What's wrong?" She said as soon as she settled behind her own desk. The door was closed for privacy and she spoke quietly, tense with fear. She massaged her forehead.

"I'm at the Tokyo airport," Nick said quickly. He sounded excited. "My flight's being called."

"Hurry up and tell me." She demanded again, fully frightened now.

"There's a duplicate miniature of the Lady Emma Hamilton."

"So I've heard."

"How did you find out?"

"I had a visit from an old frenemy. He told me this morning. He said something about having retrieved what he thought was the original."

"Oh, yeah? Well, I was told there was one for sale in a small gallery in Kyoto, so I guess that makes three."

"You're right. Three. One he retrieved, the one you're after and Celia's. You'll buy the one in Kyoto?"

"That's my plan."

"I'm glad you moved quickly on it. But it would've been good to be informed."

"You were flying home, and I didn't want to text you. Too cryptic."

She nodded. "Okay." She was so tired. "You took Celia's Lady Hamilton out of the vault. Tell me you didn't give it to Jack."

"Yeah, I did, late last night. I dropped it off with Jack. He'll authenticate it. We need to know which one is the original, especially now that we're dealing with three."

"Did he say anything about going out of town?"

"What did you say? You're breaking up."

She couldn't explain without a clear connection "Nothing. Get home as soon as you can."

"Sure. They're calling my flight. I'll call you later."

She had no proof Jack had taken off because he was afraid of being caught. Maybe he really was on vacation as his neighbor said. There was nothing Nick could do from Japan.

For a moment, her mind teetered on the edge of despair. She was so tired. Weary to the point of surrender.

Weary of the financial juggle, weary of fighting innuendo and rumor, weary of letting everyone, including her own parents, think Nick was the Macklin that ran the gallery.

With Nick in Japan, she felt alone. She had no one, not one person she could go to for help. Her father was out of the question, her brother was out of the country, and Rayder Cole was back in her life. *Oh, God.*

CHAPTER SIX

ELLIE HAD ROCKED RAYDER to the core. He paced his hotel room. He should have hung around and followed her, but after he'd felt her hands on him, he'd needed time to reassess the situation.

He was sorely tempted to forget the whole thing and go to New York. He could walk away. A museum there needed him to track down a tapestry they'd paid for and promptly lost on a train from Istanbul. It sounded like one of Ian Thompson's tricks. And old Ian would claim he'd found the parcel under a seat and planned to turn it in.

Yeah, he'd go to New York. Get back to simple fraud, old con men and mysterious packages delivered under cover of night. That was what he knew, what he wanted to do, what he was comfortable with.

He was not comfortable with Ellie's accusing eyes boring into him, her fleeting smile making him feel guilty, and her hands making him all kinds of horny. He jabbed his fingers into his hair and scrubbed at his scalp. That's it. He was out of here.

His reputation could survive a smear. Hell, no one could work at what he did for as long as he had without picking up muck along the way. The Calais museum would believe he did his best and had come up empty. *Yeah, sure.*

The phone beside the bed rang as he reached for his suitcase. "Yes?" he answered, expecting the front desk.

"Did you get it?" The old man's voice was gravelly but strong in spite of the stroke he'd suffered a few years back.

"No. Eleanor said it was out for cleaning. Why?" He dropped the suitcase on the bed. Opened it.

"We've got trouble."

"What trouble?" He asked his Uncle Shamus automatically, already thinking of the possibilities. The phone cord stretched enough to reach the dresser. He opened the drawer.

"The curator in France wants the museum's reward money back or she'll go to the cops." Anger hummed through each of the old man's words. "I told her we don't give refunds. I told her you'd get the original and deliver it pronto."

Rayder gave up packing and focused on the conversation. "I've decided to go to New York and move on. We'll return the reward, no problem."

Shamus snorted. "All this time we've been straight as arrows and one mistake shoots us down. This honest living is a crock." His uncle's voice turned dismissive, as if the threat was minimal, but Rayder knew better. Shamus had spent too long behind bars not to have a healthy fear of justice. And the fact they'd done nothing illegal wouldn't mean much. Prison was still prison whether you were guilty or not.

"She hasn't called the cops yet," Rayder decided, "so she's in no hurry to let the world know she accepted this fake." He reconsidered New York. "To show our good faith, we'll put the money in escrow until we find the original."

"Got a time frame for that?"

"Tell her two weeks." He looked around the hotel room.

"I'll see what I can do."

Rayder sighed, forcefully, into the phone.

"You okay, son? That Ellie gettin' to you?" He chuckled. "As I recall, she was a sweet little thing."

"Not anymore, Uncle, not anymore." He thought of the bruises he'd put in her eyes, the mistrust he'd put in her soul and wanted to go back ten years and see that sweet Ellie again.

"Take it easy on yourself. You were a kid trying to prove yourself."

"Sure, I was." He'd never been just a kid. Childhood in a clan like his lasted until you found your first mark. Most times, that was in the schoolyard.

Childhood might be easily discarded, but family loyalty never was. Shamus was afraid of the museum curator's threat to go to the cops. Prison would kill the old man and it was up to Rayder to set things right.

He'd have to stay, would have to deal with Ellie. Even harder, he'd have to face himself.

"Find me a place to stay here, will you? I'm sick of hotel rooms. Oh, and Nick Macklin wasn't in the gallery this morning. Makes me wonder if he's in the city. If he's not, find him."

"One more thing. Your cousin Teri Branton's getting married."

"Again? Not to the same guy, right?"

Shamus chuckled. "She met this new one while she was on her honeymoon alone. It's quite a story, but romance always is. I hope this guy deserves her."

Teri had been left at the altar. The last Rayder had seen of her had been at the church steps as she refused anyone's help and hailed a cab. She jumped in with a gaggle of women surrounding her, all yelling at once. A grand escape. She must have taken off and found the right guy.

Oddly, it gave him hope. "When's the wedding?"

"Six weeks. It's at a resort in the Caribbean."

"We're going," he said. He'd have to find a plus one and Teri needed as much family there as she could get.

CHAPTER SEVEN

THREE POSSIBLE MINIATURES. What Nick had told Eleanor rattled around inside her mind like metal marbles. How could she prevent this mess from becoming public? And if a scandal erupted, could she keep the Gallery's name out of it?

She heard a quick knock on her office door and looked up, dreading the interruption.

"Come in," she called. The door opened and Anne stepped in and held the door closed at her back.

"Rayder Cole's back," she announced with a saucy grin. "I told him at noon you'd be too busy to see him. But he won't take no for an answer."

Eleanor heard a bell ring. Not a tinkling bell, but a ringing sound like the bell that rings between bouts in a boxing match. She put her head down on her crossed arms and sighed. If only she had time for a power nap. But, no, Rayder had returned, as if he knew when she was at her weakest.

"Eleanor, are you all right?" Anne asked.

She raised her face. "Yes, I'm fine. Please show Mr. Cole into Nick's office in five minutes. I just need five minutes to think."

Anne looked concerned and opened her mouth to speak. But she closed it again with a nod. As she quietly left the room Eleanor sighed. Anne would be better off if she knew nothing of the events unfolding.

At this very moment, Nick was running for a plane to Kyoto, determined to find and buy the duplicate miniature. He still didn't know Jack Burke had left in the middle of the night, probably with the piece Nick had trustingly handed over. Her thoughts whirled. Her stomach churned. All this had gone wrong in the space of four or five hours.

She sighed again, wondering if it might help to throw herself on the floor, kick her legs and hold her breath until she turned blue. Not likely, but if things didn't improve soon, she may have to try it.

Her stomach growled as she crossed her office to the connecting door into Nick's space. She grasped the handle, took a deep breath to fortify herself, and stepped into the other office.

"At least you'll be happy to see these, even if the sight of me turns your stomach," Rayder said, holding up a bag from her favorite delicatessen. "Pastrami on rye."

"You remembered," she said, surprised. Her stomach growled again, and she couldn't stop the smile that broke over her face. "They smell delicious." She'd introduced Rayder to her favorite sandwich so the odds were good he had two in the bag.

Rayder saw her reaction and smiled back, deeply and directly into her eyes. She blinked to lessen the powerful effect.

"Mm, yes, well," she smoothed her skirt and headed toward the safety of Nick's desk.

Rayder went for the sofa and sat down, patting the cushion beside him. "If you want to eat, you have to come here."

"Brute," she muttered loud enough for him to hear. But she took the place beside him and reached for the bag he offered. The smells were mouth-watering. "Thank you. But how did you know I wouldn't have time for lunch?"

"Anne said you were too busy to go out with me. Besides, you forget to eat when you're upset."

She unwrapped the sandwich, keeping her face down.

RAYDER STUDIED HER as she bent over her sandwich. Her nose was too long to be pert; her eyebrows were beautiful wings that framed her large, wide eyes and her mouth was what it had always been: tempting.

"How did you manage to get all your hair under control?" He ran his fingers lightly along the knotted lengths. Earlier it had been tighter, impossible to get his fingertips into, but now, if he wanted, he could press into the twining mass, loosen it, and hold her hair in handfuls. He wanted to its warmth, silken and alive.

She froze at his touch and he considered releasing her, but something dangerous grabbed at him and he couldn't. The remembered warmth of her rose in his mind. The sighs, the heat, the wanting, the scrambling to get out of his clothes before sense and honor won out over hormones.

He couldn't let her go. He remembered all the details all at once. He trailed the braid down her back until he found the clasp. One flick and all that glorious hair would be released.

She looked at him then, all wide-eyed fear, the sandwich forgotten in her hand. He didn't mean to frighten her, but her lips were glossy and full, half-parted and begging for his mouth. He should stop.

But this was Ellie. His Ellie.

The realization slammed into him, hot as a comet and twice as fast. He'd used that name earlier, of course, but only to rattle her. He'd learned early to use whatever advantage he found, but now it hurt to see her fear.

"I let you blackmail me into keeping quiet this morning with Celia," she said firmly, "but that does not mean I will allow you to swindle anyone." The fear was gone from her eyes, replaced by the fire of vengeance. Her lips went tight and prim, her posture stiff and her gaze unrelentingly hard. His fiery Ellie.

He laughed at her fierceness and dropped her braid. *Back to business, Cole.* "I don't swindle people anymore. Not since"–no, she'd never believe that–"not for a long time."

"Yeah, right," she said derisively.

He unwrapped his sandwich, unwilling to explain, and refusing to acknowledge that it mattered to him what she thought. Because it shouldn't matter. He was here to do a job and get back to his own life, such as it was.

They ate in silence for a few moments. "You mentioned Shamus earlier. Is he well?" she asked when most of her sandwich was gone.

"He had a stroke."

"Oh," she said quietly. Her gaze softened sympathetically. "I'm sorry. I know you were close."

"I didn't say he was dead, I said he had a stroke. He works for me now." He popped open the can of cola from his bag and took a long drink.

"Oh! I'm glad he's all right," she said, with genuine relief in her eyes. The relief clouded. "And what would that nice old man be doing for you?"

The implication was clear. She couldn't see Shamus going along with a con man. Ellie wasn't ready to believe the truth about what Rayder did for a living. She preferred to believe he was still the bastard he'd been at eighteen. Sometimes he wondered the same thing himself. "Shamus gathers information for me. He's a whiz on the internet."

He took a sip of his drink. The cola sparkled against his throat as he swallowed. When he looked at her, he was surprised to see her watching him. Her gaze seemed riveted on the muscles of his neck as they worked. Her lips parted even as he watched.

"I forgot you and Shamus hit it off." He was sorry he spoke even before the words were out of his mouth. Seeing the awareness in her eyes had reminded him, vividly, of the passion she'd once felt for him.

"Yes." She blinked and the moment passed. "I liked him very much." She narrowed her eyes suspiciously. "Although after you left, I wondered if he'd been sizing me up for something." She cocked an eyebrow at him.

"Maybe he was." He shrugged. "Shamus had an eye for the ladies. He says that's why he never married. Too many women, not enough time."

His comment made her grin even wider. The idea of cigar-smoking, bandy-legged Shamus charming the ladies was so funny he laughed. This was one of the things he'd loved most about her, sharing their humor.

"I get the impression he's had an interesting life." She slanted him an amused glance. "A very interesting life."

"You're right." He leaned toward her and played with the end of her braid, his fingertips brushing her spine. It had been so stupid to think he could come in, get the miniature and leave without being affected by this woman. He left her braid and smoothed a palm down her back. His response to that affect that worried him. "Someday I'll tell you about it."

"That won't be necessary." The chill she put into the words went Arctic cold. "Besides, we won't have a 'someday.'"

Words that echoed his own thoughts. Regret was a new concept; one he didn't want to explore.

She bent to pick up the empty bags and napkins and he curled his fingers around her upper arm. He tugged to get her attention. "Are you certain of that?" he said.

She looked steadily at him over her shoulder. "I'm dead certain."

He let her go. She finished gathering the remains of lunch and stood. As soon as she straightened behind the desk, she became Eleanor again, cool and efficient and determined to block him at every turn. But something about her had gone askew, some inner confidence or knowledge had been shaken. She was finding it difficult to meet his eyes.

"Have you given any more thought to my offer?" he asked quietly, studying the flickering emotion in her green-eyed gaze.

"Of course not. Sharing information with you would be a mistake." She sat down and primly laced her fingers together on top of the desk. She stared straight at him now, as if to prove she wasn't afraid. "Frankly, I'm surprised you brought it up."

"Really? You've figured out what Celia's up to? Because I don't have a clue."

When she didn't reply, he pressed his advantage. "What happened to shake your confidence?" He waited but she said nothing, only set her chin. "I believe you don't know where the miniature is now. I'm sure you thought you knew earlier, regardless of your performance for Celia's benefit." He paused for effect. "Maybe I know something that can help you. I certainly have more investigative experience than you do."

When she still said nothing, he snapped his fingers. "Unless you're counting on your brother Nick to save the day."

The flash in her eyes confirmed what he'd wondered about earlier. Eleanor was the real brains behind the Macklin Gallery. He wasn't surprised, this was the fulfilment of her greatest dream.

"Shamus has contacts all over the world," he added, offering more information than he'd intended; a measure of how much he wanted to have an excuse to be with her. "They've been useful in the past. You'd have access to a whole network." He held out the offer. It appealed to her if he was any judge. She'd soon see it as a possible way out of her predicament, whatever it was. Ellie was a woman who embraced cooperation.

She opened her mouth and closed it again. She frowned, her brows knitting in concentration. Rayder waited, patient. She'd come to the decision he wanted in her own time.

ELEANOR WAS TEMPTED. She could use his uncle's network and Rayder's information without giving him anything useful in return.

"You first," she said by way of acceptance. "And start by saying something you think we both know."

He grinned in a way that irked her because he knew darn well she couldn't resist his offer. "The Lady Hamilton miniature was copied," he said.

"Who did it?"

"Not so fast," he held his hands up, palms out. "Now you give me something."

Eleanor bit her lip. "You were right, I was lying this morning. I did write the note on the shelf where the miniature should have been."

"That's a cheat. I'd already deduced as much."

"That's all you're getting. For now." She tacked on the last two words as insurance. She might find a need for more of his information as this thing unfolded.

"But you do know who has it?" His eyes lit with interest.

She exaggerated a sigh. "I might know who is in possession at this moment, but then again, I could be wrong." For all she knew Jack Burke had passed it off to someone else, someone they'd never find. She went on, "I thought this network of Shamus's would have provided you with more answers."

He grinned. "When it does, I promise I'll share."

"How about you call Shamus right now and see what he's come up with?" She held out the telephone.

"Why don't you save the old man some trouble and tell me where Nick's gone?"

"When pigs fly," she drawled.

"So, he has left town," he said with a nod, his eyes laughing at her.

Infuriated by his arrogant expression, she stood. "Look, I still have a gallery to run and mounds of paperwork to get through. I got next to no sleep last night and I'm exhausted. While I appreciate the food, I need to get back to my regular routine. Check in with me tomorrow. I may have everything together by then," she said, hoping he'd take the hint and leave.

He stood and assessed her in silence for a long moment. "I'm sure I'll have more news by then, too. And you'll see how much easier it would be to work with me."

After he left, she relaxed for the first time that day. Massaging her temples to work off a tension headache, she called Anne on the intercom. "Did Nick leave a number where he could be reached?"

"Yes."

"Thank God."

Anne gave her the number and after a couple of minutes struggling with rudimentary Japanese and English, she managed to convince the hotel clerk to put her call through to Nick's room.

Finally, he answered.

"Nick? It's Eleanor," she said into the phone. "I'm glad you let Anne know where you are."

"Yeah." He sounded sleepy. Very sleepy.

"Are you awake?" She checked her watch. Three p.m.

"I am now. Did you know it's three in the morning here?" He yawned.

"Sorry, but we've got a problem. Jack Burke's gone. I don't know where and I don't know if he's taken the miniature with him." She heard a muffled curse. "Are you there?"

"Yes, um, sure I'm here." She heard a soft rustle of movement and assumed he shifted to a sitting position.

"Jack's neighbor told me Jack left around four a.m. with suitcases. Lots of suitcases. The house looks the same. Nothing's been moved."

Nick grunted. "It's not much to go on. But, Eleanor, remember this is Jack. He's no thief."

"But is he a forger?" She kept telling herself there was no reason to believe the worst of Jack, but all the evidence pointed to it. The question was: how did Rayder fit into Jack's scheme?

"Jack a forger? Of course not. But he takes off a lot. If it isn't a woman, it's camping in Algonquin Park. Give him a couple of days, he'll turn up."

But this is November, she thought. Camping involved sleeping bags and gear and warm weather, not suitcases. And she didn't want to ask Anne if she'd heard about a new woman in Jack's life. It would be too cruel.

"There's something else," she said. "Celia came in with a buyer for the collection. His name is Rayder Cole." She held her breath, wondering if Nick had heard of him. The art world was small considering it spanned the globe. It was possible Nick and Rayder had met without Nick mentioning it to her. "Do you know him?"

"No, but I've heard of him. The gallery's missed a handful of important auctions in the last three years, so we've never crossed paths. But he's a buying agent."

She thought again of her friend in New York. She'd forgotten to phone him in all the commotion. If she hadn't been so tired, she'd have called before this. "I'll check on his story."

"You mean Celia wants to sell privately now?" Nick asked, sounding more awake. "Damn, I had hopes that sale would bring in new business."

"Me, too. But I think she's only listening to Rayder and what she doesn't know is Rayder's only after the Lady Emma. He's leading her on, letting her think he wants the whole collection."

She recounted everything that happened during the initial meeting with Celia and Rayder. It crossed her mind to mention she and Rayder shared a past, but she thought better of it. This wasn't the time to mention to Nick that his big sister had once been conned by this very same Rayder. And that's exactly what he was, she reminded herself, a raider.

"Destroy the note you wrote as soon as you can. You don't need any evidence against you when I'm the one who screwed up by handing the piece over to Jack. If it turns out that Jack's a thief, a forger or both, I want the jail time to be mine."

"Jail time? Why would you think you'd go to jail for trusting a man we've worked with for years? We were the ones who were duped. All we're trying to do is find the truth, expose the forgers and keep our gallery out of the news."

"What police officer in his right mind would ignore that investigation three years ago? They'll assume we were guilty then, so we're guilty now. They'll come after me with a vengeance."

"Don't talk that way. As soon as you get the fake, we'll learn the truth. If we have solid evidence the forgery had nothing to do with the gallery, we'll be exonerated. You'll see."

There was an ominous pause. "There's another problem."

"Of course, there is." She waited.

"The miniature that was here was sold, Eleanor," Nick said quietly. "I couldn't get it."

"What are you saying?" Her voice quivered with her fear. She twisted the telephone cord around her fingers.

"Someone bought it almost a week ago. But I've got a line on a dealer who knows where it went. I'm returning to Tokyo tomorrow to see him."

The third miniature was now in the hands of another party. One step closer to disaster. Her hands shook as she tried to clear her mind and stay focused.

"Keep in touch. I need to know exactly what's going on all the time. And, Nick, be careful."

Her irrepressibly spontaneous younger brother snorted before he hung up. She wondered what jail would do to a man like him.

She had to find out where Jack Burke went. Tracking him down couldn't be all that hard, could it?

CHAPTER EIGHT

RAYDER RELAXED INTO the apartment's sofa and put his feet up on the coffee table. He'd expected having a complete studio apartment to himself would be a change from hotel rooms, but the comfortable ambience only reminded him of the things he didn't have. The things most average men took for granted.

He was grateful to his uncle for arranging the short-term rental, but the place gave him the creeps and he'd only been here a few hours. He'd started picturing Ellie here, doing things like putting groceries away with him, washing dishes with him, dancing slow and close with him, falling into bed with him.

Damn, why had she looked at him the way she had? She couldn't have realized the message she was sending. For a brief moment she'd remembered being with him; the way their bodies had fit, how good it had been. He rubbed his palms across his eyes to banish the images and reached for his phone.

"Shamus," he said when his call was picked up. "Any word on Nick Macklin's whereabouts?"

"Not yet, but I'm working on it."

Shamus would work every angle. He had a brilliant mind for detail and an uncanny knack for discerning artifice. "Have you got any information on the Macklins business network yet?"

"Yeah, they use a guy named Jack Burke for their restoration work," Shamus said. "He's good, but kind of an oddball." He gave Rayder the man's address.

"Why? What kind of oddball?"

"The story is that he started out as an artist but made more money cleaning and restoring. He could be busier than he is, but he's an expert at avoiding real work. He's had some sweet offers, but the money's never good enough for him or he doesn't like the people making the offer. People don't think of him anymore. His prima donna routine wore thin."

"Got any friends I should be aware of? Patrons?"

"No, he's a loner. Except for rich women."

"Gloucester Street's not far from here." And not far from Eleanor's gallery. "What's happening with the museum? Has the curator been hassling you?"

A brief pause. "She mentioned Shaughnessy at Interpol."

"Damn. That SOB would love to see either one of us do time. Did Shaughnessy contact her?"

"She didn't say, but he makes it known he'd like to get you. You never should have messed with him."

"Maybe he shouldn't have done that convent out of their fifteenth century tapestry, either." That was all he needed, Shaughnessy on his tail. The man was dirty, but he and his uncles were the only ones who knew it.

Setting aside the thorny Shaughnessy problem, Rayder thought of one more place to look for Ellie's brother. "Call Jimmy Matsukawa in Tokyo and ask if he's heard about Nick Macklin asking around."

Japan was the first place Rayder looked for any stolen art. Under Japanese law if a hot item is held for two years and the owner provided an affidavit saying he didn't know it was stolen, it was considered free and clear. This law made Japan an international holding ground for stolen art and artifacts. If Nick knew anything at all, he'd go there first.

"What do you want me to do if Jimmy's seen him?"

"Ask Jimmy to put the word out to give Macklin the run around for a few days. I want Ellie off balance. Without her brother here, she'll be more likely to work with me. I've offered to share information. It looks like she's in over her head."

"Is she threatening you?" Shamus asked.

In too many ways. "No worse than I did her," Rayder said.

"Good." Shamus snorted dismissively. "Then she won't cause any trouble."

Rayder laughed. Ellie had already caused more than her share. "That depends on what you consider trouble."

"She gettin' to you?" His uncle's voice lowered confidentially.

"It's old stuff, Shamus. Nothing I can't handle." Ticked off with himself for no reason he cared to name, his temper snapped. "Can we get off the subject of Ellie Macklin? Our butts are on the line, here."

"Nothing you can't handle," Shamus grumbled. "That's what you said ten years ago," Shamus pointed out grouchily. "And look at you, traipsing around the world, no wife, no kids. No prospects either."

"Did you have any of that?" He sounded ragged and felt bad for snapping, but it was an old song and he was tired of hearing it. The way his uncle acted sometimes you'd think Rayder had never gotten over Ellie.

"No, but I had you to raise." The old man snorted. "And you were more than enough to handle." Shamus coughed, long and hard.

"Have you been smoking?" Rayder asked resignedly.

"Just one cigar. Can't a man enjoy anything anymore?" His voice came back gravelly but firm again.

Rayder didn't answer. The cigar smoking was a symptom of Shamus's stress. The threat from the museum was enough to push the old man back to old, unhealthy habits.

"You think the girl's innocent?" his uncle asked. "You're sure she and her brother didn't arrange for you to buy the fake?"

"Ellie's no girl." He thought of her flaring anger and composure under pressure. "She's all grown up, but she's not vengeful. She's focused on the gallery. Getting back at me isn't high on her priority list." The kicker was that he felt he should be important enough for her to want to avenge herself. *Weird.*

"And the brother?"

"Nick's not the driving force behind the gallery. My guess is, he does a decent job, but leaves the decisions to her."

"Maybe he's letting some other woman call the shots. Would he work against his own sister?"

Rayder's hackles rose. He'd never let Nick get away with hurting her. Never. She'd had enough betrayal for one lifetime and Rayder had been the betrayer.

But family was strange sometimes. He just had to look at his own for confirmation of that sad fact. The only blood relatives that gave him any sense of connection was his mother's side, the Brantons. They were good people and he cared deeply for all of them. A ragtag bunch, the Brantons were honest, decent people.

Cousin Tyce had recently married. Another of the Brantons, Teri, had been left at the altar. The last Rayder had seen of her was her climbing into a cab with a stunned, devastated expression on her face. His sweet cousin had left New York and found love on her honeymoon cruise and now, she was taking another chance on love.

The groom who'd hurt her sat on Rayder's list of people to deal with.

"When we're done with Ellie and this situation, I'm heading to the west coast," he declared. "I haven't seen my cousins in too long. From there, we'll fly together to see Teri get married." Destination weddings were fun, and he'd need the distraction after leaving Ellie.

"Yeah, but Washington State's cold and rainy this time of year."

"It feels like home. This time, you should come," he said. "Since you missed the disaster of Teri's first wedding."

"Maybe I will. The place seems to agree with you." Shamus mused aloud. "That Tyce. His mom still single? Maybe I can escort her to Teri's beach wedding. The Caribbean's my kind of place when the nights get cold."

"Yes, she's single," he replied with a chuckle. "And taking her to the wedding would be a nice touch."

Shamus sighed. "Then I'll take a vacation with you and talk to her about it then."

"I'll hold you to it."

"Hey, I went to Tyce's wedding. He married that rich widow."

"Which is the only reason you went. You wanted to see how many other wealthy people were there." *Old habits die hard.* Shamus had been in the grift for most of his life. But not anymore.

"Back to business," Rayder said. "It's possible Nick Macklin's absence has nothing to do with the miniature," Rayder suggested half-heartedly, loathe to consider what would happen to Ellie if she was double-crossed.

"Then why won't the girl co-operate?"

"She's got lots of reasons. Me being the biggest."

"Maybe so," Shamus agreed.

"Check into Nick Macklin's association with Celia. See if they've been involved in any previous deals together. Maybe as far back as three years. Ellie may not be involved in this mess, but Nick could be."

"Sure thing. I'll put the word out. We should hear something soon."

Soon. He'd wanted to be gone today; back to the life he'd made for himself when falling for Ellie Macklin had changed the life he'd planned. But he was in too deep in too many ways to leave yet.

SIX A.M. WAS EARLY to be skulking around Jack Burke's house, but Eleanor needed to find a clue to his whereabouts. She peered into the front window as she had yesterday. The little room was empty. The furniture had been cleared out.

She tore back to the front door and rattled at the doorknob, dismayed to see the front vestibule empty as well. She pressed her forehead to the windowpane on the wooden door and sagged with disappointment. The door swung inward under the weight of her body and she missed a step, catching her heel on the doorstep.

She lost her balance and tilted forward in a free fall.

Suddenly, strong hands gripped her by her forearms and hauled her upright.

"Ellie. Are you all right?"

Rayder. He let go with one hand, reached around her and closed the door. She was trapped in a five-foot square area with Rayder's hands roving all over her, apparently checking for injuries.

"I'm fine. I slipped, that's all. Let me go." She shrugged out of his grasp and stood straight. "What are you doing here?" There was no point demanding to know *how* he found out about Jack.

"Keep your voice down. People are moving around next door. If I can hear them, they can hear us."

"What are you doing here?" She whispered again, shrinking against the wall at her back. He was too close, especially after the incredibly erotic dreams she'd had all night. Not that they'd been about Rayder, of course. Just her usual dark stranger in a long, black coat. She pulled her fingers away from the lapels of his leather coat as if they'd been singed.

"I suspect I'm doing what you're doing. Looking for Jack Burke. And since he's obviously flown the coop, I'm looking for clues as to where he went."

"Well?"

"Well what?"

"Have you found anything?" She demanded in a less-than-patient tone.

Rayder shook his head no. "Just you."

"Still, you won't mind if I look around myself?"

"Fine. Be quiet about it." But he didn't move out of her way. He stood solidly blocking her into the corner.

She didn't want to look up at him, didn't want to see the look in his eyes, or feel what hummed through his body. Because the same awareness filled her every nerve-ending.

Eleanor went to move around him. He gripped her elbows and held her still. Her power to shrug him off deserted her. He nestled his chin into the hair above her ear. They stayed like that a long moment, Rayder holding her lightly, she, succumbing to the desire to lean into him. His strength and scent were a support for her. His vitality and masculinity were her downfall. Finally, fulfilling her instinct for survival, she pushed past him and stepped through the inner door into the hall.

She already knew the front room was empty, so she walked past the staircase into the second room. The plate rails a couple of feet below the ceiling told her this used to be a dining room. Jack had used it as an office. There was still a surge protector plugged into the electrical outlet on the far wall. A few scattered scraps of paper blew around on the hardwood floor from the drafts produced by their footfalls. She bent and picked up two of them.

"There's nothing on them," Rayder said from behind her. "There's nothing, period."

"Not even in the loft?"

"No, nor the bedrooms on the second floor. Have you been here before?"

She nodded. "Jack used the third floor as a studio. When he worked on restoring frames, he was in a basement room."

"Did you hire him?"

"No, my father ran the gallery then, so Jack's been with us for years. Ever since I returned." She nearly said "from university" but didn't want to bring up that subject. He didn't need to know she'd run like a scared rabbit when she'd discovered him, and her money, gone.

Rayder walked past her toward the kitchen at the back of the house. It, too, was empty. Every step she took farther into the house, depressed her more. Jack was gone, so very gone, that she didn't see any way of ever finding him.

Rayder caught her glance and she tried to hide her crushing disappointment. Obviously, she didn't do much of a job because he dragged her into his arms in a comforting, caring hug. She allowed the hug for an all-too-brief moment, tempted beyond reason to rest her head against his shoulder the way she had in the vestibule.

He set her aside, much to her chagrin. She could've stayed there a bit longer. "We need to work together. Please, Ellie. Between us, we can find him, and the Lady Emma."

"Why is she so important to you?"

"She was stolen from a museum years ago and I got the contract to retrieve her. I found what I thought was the original miniature and returned it. I got the reward and within a week, was told it was fake. When I discovered the connection to you, I figured it was your revenge."

"THAT'S WHEN YOU FOUND Celia, ingratiated yourself and stormed back into my life." Her lovely brows knit in a frown as she mulled.

Rayder gave her a moment. "Pretty much. Yes. I told Celia I wanted to buy the whole collection."

"You lied," Ellie deadpanned.

"An expediency."

"Where did you find the one you returned?" She asked and went still. Her question revealed more than she realized. Her brother must have tracked the same piece to Kyoto, and hightailed it there, only to find it gone because Rayder had beat him to it. "If I tell you where I found the forgery do you promise to work with me, to share information? Fully and completely?"

"You're asking me to trust you with my gallery, my life and all I've worked hard to regain."

If he could take away the pain and disappointment he saw in her eyes, he would. But life kicked the crap out of you, and everyone had to learn sometime. Unfortunately, Rayder had been her teacher. He couldn't be sorrier.

She dragged in a breath and let it out in one sorrowful sigh. "You, a con man, a thief. You, above everyone, knows what the gallery means to me. Even my own father doesn't see my commitment. You're the only one who ever did. And you're asking me to leave it in your hands."

He nodded. "Yes. Even back then I knew you'd keep your dreams front and center. That no matter what I did to you, you wouldn't waiver."

She bit her lip and blinked back moisture in her eyes. "Where did you find it?" she repeated.

She hadn't answered him, but he didn't have the heart to press her any more than he already had. "Japan."

"In Kyoto?"

He nodded and she seemed to spring back to life, released from her frozen state of fear.

She spun around, searching. She lifted the receiver from a wall phone covered in dust. "This line's disconnected. How did Jack get moved out in record time?" She opened her arms to encompass the emptiness. "Where did he send everything?"

Rayder hid a grin. "However he did it, I'm sure he ditched his landline years ago."

She glowered at the handset and hung it back up.

"Damn. My cell phone is in the car for charging." She started back toward the front door.

"Wait," Rayder said, following her. "What's going on?"

"Nick went to Japan to track down the fake you had already bought. He's on a wild goose chase." All that money wasted. "Come on, we'll go to the gallery. It's closer than my condo."

They slipped out the front door quietly, aware the city was beginning to stir around them. Joggers in sweat suits ran past the house, apparently oblivious to the two people who didn't belong. Eleanor and Rayder sidestepped piles of yesterday's snow and continued down the street.

She headed for her car, but Rayder tugged at her hand and directed her to his instead. "Here, it's closer." A plain black sedan, Rayder's rental was indistinguishable from a thousand others.

Before he pressed the start button, Eleanor began questioning him. "How did you find Jack's place? Did you follow me yesterday?"

"I didn't need to." The engine purred to life. "I have Shamus. He found out who you use for restoration work and I looked up Jack's address. However, I was as surprised as you when I got there this morning and the place was cleaned out." He pulled into traffic and headed north. "Any idea how we can get a line on where he might have gone?"

"There's only one person I know who would have any interest in Jack's personal life."

"And who would that be?" Rayder glanced at her and waited. She bit her lip and looked oddly guilty about sharing Jack's romantic secrets.

"I'm taking a giant leap here, Rayder. If I confess that you broke my heart years ago, it'll be no surprise. But now, if you betray me, you'll break my spirit. Tell me you understand all that that means."

"I will not betray you." He had no other words to convey everything he wanted to say. Traffic snarled up ahead when someone made a dangerous lane change, preventing him from facing her. "I'm sorry and I hope my word on that means something to you."

"Okay, then I'll commit to this investigation with you." In his peripheral vision he could see she watched him with a calm, level gaze.

The snarl of cars cleared, and he could focus more on her. "Thank you. For helping and for your trust. I won't let you down." At a red light, he turned to face her, but she stared out the side window. Her jaw worked, and she turned away even more so he couldn't see her face.

"I understand this is tough for you," he murmured, wanting to touch her thigh, her chin, anything to make her relax. He clenched the steering wheel instead.

His heartfelt words didn't appear to move Ellie in the least. He waited but when she didn't respond he continued. "Who's your source for information on Burke?"

"It's Anne, my assistant. She and Jack were engaged for a short time last year. When he found out Anne's father was no longer as wealthy as he once was, Jack drifted out of her life." Her confusion and sympathy for her employee were evident in her expression.

"Drifted?"

"Ghosted her. Yes, it was odd, even for Jack, who's a loner. He stopped calling. Became suddenly busy with work. Avoided her. Anne tried to confront him, but he was as difficult to catch as smoke."

"Let's hope we have better luck," Rayder said grimly. "Is she certain it was the lack of money that made him take the coward's way out?"

"There doesn't seem to be any other reason and the whole episode did a number on her." She faced the front window again but flashed a glance at him from the corner of her eye.

He'd take it as progress.

"I don't know her," he said, "but she seems smart and sophisticated. I hope a lovely woman hasn't been ruined by one idiot." Too late, he realized what he'd said.

Ellie snorted. "Good one," she retorted dryly.

CHAPTER NINE

ELEANOR DIRECTED RAYDER to park in her reserved spot in the parking garage halfway up the block from the gallery. She read the time and estimated the time difference in Japan as they tramped toward the gallery.

"Nick planned to return to Tokyo. He said he had a line on a dealer there who knew where the miniature went."

"That must be Jimmy Matsukawa. He's a friend of mine. I'll tell him to let Nick know it was me who bought it. Jimmy's heard from Shamus by now and without a word from me, he won't tell Nick anything."

She slipped her key into the lock of the gallery's back door and disarmed the security system being certain to cover the keypad with her other hand. Beside her, Rayder sighed at her caution. "How big is this network you mentioned?" she wanted to know.

"Global."

"You never did think small."

He grinned.

As they walked to her office in the back, Rayder called and spoke with his friend Jimmy Matsukawa. Rayder spoke clearly, uncaring that she could hear every word. That boded well, she thought.

"Is that right?" he asked. "Yeah, his sister's with me, she can speak with him directly." He passed her the phone and she took it.

"Eleanor?" It was Nick. "Is this true? Rayder Cole's the guy who beat me to the piece in Kyoto?"

"It appears that way. He returned it to a museum in Calais and the curator told him it's a forgery. He tracked the original to Celia who told him we had it in our vault." He didn't need to know about her previous relationship with Rayder. Maybe she'd never have to tell him his sister had been duped by a con man.

"Oh, no. When I panicked and handed Celia's over to Jack, I caused a boatload of trouble." He sighed.

"You could say that. At least we're certain there are two Lady Emmas: the one Rayder bought and the one you gave to Jack." Two was better than three. She glanced at Rayder who looked content with the outcome.

"I'll text Anne my flight information," he said. "Jimmy wants to take me to one of his favorite bars first, though."

She groaned. "Just be back tomorrow," she said before hanging up.

The enormity of the trust she'd put in Rayder hit home. Her heart rate picked up and she sat down heavily in Nick's chair. She silently counted to ten. She needed the time to collect her thoughts.

"You were great," Rayder said reassuringly.

"Pardon me?" she asked. Rayder stood waiting, a bemused, tolerant expression lighting his eyes.

"You made a gut instinct decision to trust me and went with it. And now, here we are, working together, pooling information. What was the word you used? Ah, yes, committed. I like it."

"I don't understand why I decided the way I did." She usually avoided snap decisions. But all that had been since Rayder had conned her and by conning her, changed her fundamentally. Once, she'd been young and trusting and impulsive. Her rash decision to work with him reminded her of the young woman she used to be.

"The why doesn't matter. You've got no reason to believe I'm not the cocky, arrogant kid I was. But I'm not." He reached into his inside jacket pocket and extracted an envelope. "Back then I knew you wouldn't waver from your plan to dedicate yourself to this gallery. You didn't waver. You're running the gallery and running it very well, whatever your father thinks. From what I've seen, the con job I did on you changed your life far less than it did mine."

Her cheeks warmed with his praise.

He slid the envelope onto the desktop then pushed it toward her with one finger. "Go ahead," he said. "Open it."

The envelope was small, white and ordinary-looking until she recognized the handwriting on top. They were doodles. Familiar doodles. "Mr. and Mrs. Rayder Cole", "Dr. Jones, 2:15", "Mrs. Ellie Cole", "quiz - art hist."

It was the envelope containing the money she'd given him in good faith ten years ago. While she recognized it as the cash, he'd supposedly needed for a sister who'd found herself in a jam, she couldn't understand what it was doing here.

"It's yours, Eleanor. I kept it. I expected to need it to win your trust, but you outsmarted me again."

Until this moment, deep inside in a place she'd never looked, was the seed of hope that maybe there had been a sister; that maybe he'd left for a more noble reason than a clean getaway. "You thought you'd need to buy my trust?" Her voice sounded rusted out.

"No, to earn your trust. I thought you'd like to know I've never had the stomach to use this." He tossed the envelope on the desk and several of the bills spilled out.

She couldn't take it, couldn't move, as the shock of what he was giving her subsided.

"It's all there," he said. "Five thousand. Just as you gave it to me."

"I don't want it." Was that her voice? It sounded hollow, as if her soul had shriveled, dried and blown away on the wind. "How dare you try to give it back." She clenched her hands into tight fists, releasing her completely from her frozen shock. "How dare you think it was the money that hurt. The money was nothing!"

"I can't give you back the other stuff. If I could, I would." His eyes went damp and he blinked.

"You still don't get it," she said, bitterness welling and spilling into her voice. "I've earned it all back: my pride, my judgement, my self-respect, all of it." A clean, killing rage boiled through her.

"And you've turned into a bright, savvy businesswoman who's pulled this gallery back from the brink of bankruptcy. And now, you've joined forces with the only man you'd like to see dead, on nothing more than instinct. You're one hell of a woman, Ellie."

The compliment confused her, and she wondered if he'd deliberately thrown her this curve to get under her skin.

"Now, where's the coffee maker?" he asked briskly. "I'll make a pot while we're waiting for Anne." He checked his watch and stood. "We've still got at least two hours before she shows up." He wandered out to the reception area and she heard him run water. Another couple of minutes ticked by and she heard the gurgle of the coffee maker.

ELEANOR SETTLED INTO the cushioned comfort of the sofa and prepared to pump Rayder for information. By unspoken agreement, they'd avoided talking about his apology and her confusion around it.

The coffee was gone, and Anne would arrive in less than an hour. They'd passed the time comparing notes on old classmates, discussing the changes in recent European politics, and had become aware of each other on several different levels. The awareness of Rayder the man confused Eleanor more. She'd subtly edged away from him, to avoid the scent of his aftershave and the heat of his body.

He'd just as subtly moved closer.

The envelope he'd passed to her still lay on the desk. The money represented more than an attempt to gain her trust today. The envelope took her back to a time when she'd trusted completely, a time too long ago for the woman she was today.

She stood, walked to the desk and picked up the envelope. She faced him again, tapping the envelope against her chin. "I meant it when I said I didn't want this back." She walked to him and slid the envelope into his shirt pocket.

She patted it for good measure and took her seat again. "What, exactly do you mean by 'retrieve' when you talk about your work?" she asked.

He played with the end of her braid, his long fingers flicking it around his palm. "I hunt down stolen art. Then I get it back to the people it was stolen from. Sometimes that means it was looted during the war, and sometimes it means a more recent theft."

"When was the Lady Emma stolen?" Her mind raced.

"Three years ago, from a museum near Calais, France."

"But it's been in Axel Brand's collection for years." At least, that's what his widow had said.

"A year. He bought it in Japan when the so-called 'owner' offered it for sale. After the two-year cooling off period, of course."

"Why didn't you get it then?"

"I don't do work on spec. I only retrieve the goods that a museum wants back. They asked me to locate it after all their own efforts failed. Besides, the insurance company had already paid off."

"Museums and collectors come to you? Why would they trust you?"

"Because I've never cheated a client." She gave him a world-class eye roll that he deserved.

"And you don't work for the police?"

"If I did, I'd never have gotten this far. People in this game trust me specifically because I'm not a cop. I've had offers from insurance companies, but that's not my style." He shifted closer. "No, Shamus and I do better operating in the shadows."

She felt the tug of his fingers along her braid, like spritzes of electricity.

"But you're catching criminals, aren't you?"

"No, I don't catch anybody. I can't pass judgement on these people, Ellie. If collectors weren't so eager to collect, the market for stolen goods wouldn't be there and thieves wouldn't steal." He grinned self-consciously. "Surely, you remember what I used to be. I can't throw stones."

She cleared her throat, trying to frame her next question. His electric blue gaze caught on hers and she leaned closer, too. He smiled warmly. The old Rayder peeking out from behind the hard shield of the man.

Abruptly, he pulled out his phone and tapped it. He passed it to her. "See for yourself the people I deal with. The kinds of people."

Rayder had attempted to charm and beguile her with stories from his career in retrieval. He was confident, at ease with the highest levels of society worldwide.

She looked at the phone in her hand. He had billionaire collectors, museum curators, high-end art thieves, and special Interpol agents in his contact list.

Without asking for her discretion, he trusted her to keep his secrets. He probably could trust her, she thought, wryly. Eleanor wasn't one to betray a confidence or a friend.

Her next question would reveal more than it should, but she had to ask. "Have there been other women? I mean . . ." She trailed off suggestively.

"You mean that I stole from? No." He sighed, long and hard. "No, I suppose you could say you ruined me for other women." He waggled his eyebrows.

She straightened away from him. "You're teasing me."

"Am I?" The look he gave her made a thrill of awareness run over her skin from her ears to her toes. He leaned closer and she wondered if she'd let him kiss her. In the end, there was no question and as his lips settled easily on hers, she sighed, knowing it had been inevitable.

The kiss was smooth, familiar, and so right, that it put her on edge immediately. Eleanor placed her palms on Rayder's chest and held him back from drawing her close. Still, she allowed him to deepen the kiss. Rushes of awareness coaxed her to give in completely, to allow him to hold her, but she held back.

Rayder retreated and looked at her, his eyes cheerful. He smiled. "Thanks, I needed that."

Her skeptical expression caused him to laugh.

"Shh!" she whispered. "I hear something."

They listened. "Sounds like Anne's here," he said.

Eleanor went to the door and asked her to come in.

"Hi!" Anne said. She saw Rayder on the sofa and stopped short. She swept a speculative gaze over the two of them. "What's up?"

Eleanor glanced at Rayder and took his cue for her to begin. She walked to Nick's desk, preparing her questions in as friendly a manner as she could. "I'm not sure, Anne. It's serious and we'd appreciate it if this went no further."

"What's wrong? How can I help?"

"It's Jack, Anne. He's moved without telling me where." Quickly, she told her assistant as little as she could without giving her away information that could hurt her should a police investigation begin. She didn't want Anne involved in a conspiracy, even if that conspiracy was only an attempt to clear the gallery's reputation. "Is there anything you know about Jack's recent behavior; what he's been doing or who he's been seeing?"

Anne slanted a look at Rayder and then back to Eleanor, who nodded. "I talked to my mother last night," Anne said. "Celia Brand has been seen with Jack." She frowned. "It looks like Jack Burke's moved on to the lonely, rich widow."

"Oh, Anne. I'm sorry I had to ask."

Anne shook her head, her eyes telegraphing concern. "I'm sorry I didn't know yesterday when you asked me about him, but my mother never mentioned it to me before. You can guess why." Then, Anne smiled a bitter smile. "They deserve each other."

"You're right," Eleanor said hollowly, slipping quickly into the chair, unsure if her legs would hold her. "This explains a lot. Thank you."

"Hey, no problem. I stomped and fumed a bit when my mom told me, but obviously, the guy's a jerk and I'm better off without him."

Rayder stepped smoothly toward Anne and ushered her out the office, murmuring his thanks and a reminder to keep this conversation confidential.

"I'll make coffee," Anne before she stepped out.

"No, thank you, we've just finished a pot," Rayder said before closing the door. He spun toward Eleanor. "Celia had Jack copy the Lady Emma."

Eleanor closed her eyes and covered her face. "And Nick handed the only evidence over to him. We've both trusted Jack for years." *Again, she'd been swindled again.* Her shoulders slumped. "When will I learn that I'm a terrible judge of character?"

RAYDER COULDN'T HELP Ellie understand that she wasn't the one at fault for trusting people. Jack had probably been trustworthy for most of their acquaintance. "Don't blame yourself. Maybe something in Jack's life turned him. It happens. No one can really know what will make a man change. It can be lack of money. Lust. Love. Or even blackmail."

Ellie looked devastated. Her trust had been destroyed, just when Rayder needed it most.

"The copy's in the Calais museum," he said, "so the original is with Jack. If Nick had left things as they were Jack wouldn't be in the wind."

"This is my fault, not my brother's."

"I'll get Shamus to have the museum dust the copy for prints. Although, they'll probably only find mine." Her expression of horror cheered him. Obviously, she didn't want him implicated in this plot.

"Why didn't Celia know Jack had the miniature yesterday morning? You saw her reaction as well as I did. She was furious when the Lady Emma wasn't in the vault. She'd have been more collected if she'd known Jack had it."

"If she'd known, Celia would not have brought me here. Is Jack trying to stiff her?"

"We won't find out sitting here." She checked her watch. "It's nine fifteen."

She stood, cool and in command once more. "I'm confronting her. I've had enough of this nonsense and it's time I put a stop to it. Besides, if I tell her Jack's lit out, maybe she'll admit to something and we can take it to the police."

"Ellie, charging into a situation like this can be dangerous. You've got to learn to control those impulses."

"Mostly, that's what I do." She pulled her lower lip into her mouth in the sexiest way. "Ever since you barged back into my life, I've felt impulsive and off kilter."

More like her old self, he thought. "It's best if I go see her."

Ellie hesitated and Rayder was disappointed to see doubt cross her lovely features. "You can come with me," he offered, trying again to prove she could trust him.

"Great." She looked relieved. "Let's go."

"But you have to stay in the car," he added as he went to help her with her coat. Her braid trailed across his fingertips, alive and silky, and he was tempted to kiss the exposed nape of her neck.

"I'll stay in the car if you stand close to the living room window, where I can see you," she said.

CHAPTER TEN

THE STREETS IN THE Rosedale neighborhood were lined with huge old oaks and sugar maples. At this time of year, the canopy of green leaves had gone, making the mansions appear like society matrons waiting for their cloaks. They were still well-dressed but looked cold. Fancifully, Eleanor imagined them shivering.

Streets curved in wide and narrow avenues and cul-de-sacs spread like fingers. It was a stately old area bordered by busy uptown commercial streets on two sides and the sweeping Don River Valley on the other.

Many of the mansions came complete with carriage houses and servants' quarters that had been turned into separate residences. But not the Brand mansion. It stood alone, well back from the street, its manicured lawn brown in the weak November sunlight.

Rayder parked across the street, to provide Eleanor the camouflage of the shade trees that lined the boulevard. At least this way she wouldn't have to crouch and hide while watching him from the car.

RAYDER RANG THE DOORBELL and waited with the unblinking stare of Ellie at his back. Of course, she stared, he felt the itch between his should blades. He understood her caution with him. Still, it he hated having to earn someone's trust after all the years he'd been straight. He'd taken client's trust for granted. He had a great rep and was well thought of, but it hadn't always been that way. He'd had to live down the Cole family infamy first and that had taken hard work, dependability and determination.

He set aside the useless thoughts and moved on to more pleasant recent events.

He'd kissed her and he was glad. Relieved, too, that she'd kept him at a distance. One inkling that she'd respond as fully as she used to, and he'd have pushed for more. Making love to Ellie would be the biggest mistake of his life. Even bigger than the last time. Because this time, there would be no luggage in his trunk, no clean getaway and no way to ever excuse himself.

When the door still hadn't been answered, Rayder rang again, certain a curtain twitched in the living room window. He had to get his mind back on track and away from Ellie Macklin.

The door opened and Celia smiled at him. "Why, Ray, what a pleasant surprise."

He inclined his head and smiled. "Celia, as lovely as ever. I'm sorry to take you from your busy morning, but I've been thinking about the missing miniature..." He let his voice trail into a question.

"Yes?" she responded. She stood her ground, making it clear she didn't want him to enter.

"Surely, we can't discuss this on the doorstep." he said smoothly. "I've heard disquieting rumors about the Macklins." He leaned close, catching a whiff of her perfume. Too sweet and flowery. "I came by to warn you," he said, lowering his voice to an intimate level, and catching her gaze. He held it.

"Oh? In that case you'd best come in." Her words may have been appropriate but the edge in them was off kilter. The rumors disturbed her in some way, and she was furious.

Rayder grinned, enjoying nothing more than a game of cat and mouse. No matter if he was the hunter or the hunted. His only wish was that Ellie could be here to join in.

He stepped into the entrance hall and made deliberately for the living room, leaving Celia to follow. He passed extravagant compliments while Celia smiled coolly. The living room windows were covered in filmy sheer draperies and Rayder made a show of flicking them open to look out across the front lawn. "Nice view. Nice neighborhood."

"Coffee?"

"Yes." He wanted the time she'd be gone to give the room a quick search.

She left and a moment later, he heard her voice in the distance. She must have help and that meant he wouldn't have as much time as he'd hoped. But the living room held no desk or cabinets with drawers. Just extra-long upholstered sofas facing each other and a couple of wing chairs in front of the fireplace.

He opened the gauzy drapes wide. *Let Ellie sit out there in a cold car watching like a suspicious cop. He'd give her nothing to complain about.*

Celia returned and stood with him near the window. Her glance flicked to the open drapes, but she didn't comment. "The coffee is on the way." She raised her eyebrows in curious interest. "Now, what rumors have you heard, Ray?"

"Only that certain pieces of your husband's collection may have been a little *warm* when Axel bought them. A Picasso? A Manet?"

Her eyes lit with appreciative cunning. "I thought this was about the Macklins?"

"It's about buying some of those pieces, Celia. I have clients who would be most interested in picking up a bargain. It's hard to unload pieces when you can't prove ownership."

"Buying my art. Huh! It's about picking my bones. And my husband barely gone, too." Her eyes snapped with fury, but he'd grabbed her attention. He planned to lead her into a discussion on some of the other artwork Axel had collected, manipulating her into admitting an alliance with Jack Burke. If he handled her correctly, Celia would tell him far more than she realized.

"I should be offended that you accuse my dear Axel of nefarious dealings. I assure you if he bought a piece of stolen art, he was tricked. He was completely trustworthy and always aboveboard."

He nodded gently and smiled. "Of course, he was, and if this had come to light before he passed away, I'm certain he would have returned every piece to the rightful owner."

Mollified, Celia was cool and unflappable and willing to play along. Now to make her expose herself and he'd let the police know. The Macklins would be cleared and he'd tell the museum in Calais that the Lady Emma would be available when the investigation was complete. The miniature wouldn't be where it belonged for some time, their claim of ownership would be rock solid.

If the plan worked, Rayder could go back to his own life. He and Ellie would be free of each other. But did he want to be free of her?

The treacherous thought hit him like a blow and his mind reeled with the implications. He'd missed her. Every single day for ten years.

His life stretched before him, barren and wasted. An image of Shamus flashed up and he swore he wouldn't live the way his uncle had.

ELEANOR SAT IN THE car, denying her chattering teeth. It had been a reasonable compromise between doubt and trust that had prompted her to insist on coming along. She *needed* to watch Rayder through the window of Celia's home. Her trust wasn't fully formed

He'd entered the house, leaning close to that woman's face, probably smiling his megawatt smile, teasing Celia in the offhand way he had to get what he wanted. Was he kissing her right now? Using the same tactics on Celia that he'd attempted with Eleanor?

The front curtain opened wide and revealed Rayder, arms outstretched to give her a good view of the room and Celia in the background. Celia turned and left and Rayder let the curtains fall back into place. She could see well enough to know the black shadow that was Rayder didn't move. A moment later, he opened the curtains a slim crack, reassuring her he would keep his word and let her watch him.

She tried to relax and thought to start the engine for some heat, but Rayder had taken the keys.

Damn.

Snuggling deeper into her coat, Eleanor noticed a movement at the side of the house. A car.

Eleanor hunkered down so the driver wouldn't see her. The car crept toward the street and closer to where she sat, feeling exposed. She ducked her head to hide because Jack Burke was driving.

Jack e was leaving Celia's house and Eleanor was stuck in the car unable to follow him. How infuriating that Jack had been hiding at Celia's. They'd never considered this possibility.

Damn, she went for her purse to get her cell phone and when she pulled it out realized Rayder hadn't given her his number.

There was nothing to do but signal him to come out. *Now.*

She waited until Jack had driven out of sight and got out of the car. Eleanor dashed across the street keeping to the side of the neighbor's large cedar hedge. Celia's back was to the window, with Rayder facing her. Frantic with excitement, Eleanor started to wave, practically doing jumping jacks on the front lawn.

RAYDER WATCHED CELIA pour coffee from a silver coffee service. Distracted by a flash of movement over her left shoulder, he caught sight of Ellie.

Ellie, on the front lawn, gesturing wildly, waving at him when she saw him watching.

Celia chatted about her husband's sterling reputation and how he could never be involved in less-than-honest dealings.

"Of course, I'm not saying Axel *knew* these items were stolen. Honest collectors are tricked all the time," Rayder soothed. He smiled and nodded, and tried to focus on Celia, but Ellie's antics distracted him. She mimicked driving a car and pointed down the street. She was telling him she wanted to leave immediately. The shock of seeing her out there, endangering them both, acting out a bizarre game of charades sent a shiver of alarm along his spine. He raised his hand and smoothed the back of his head, hoping Ellie would take the gesture to mean he understood.

"On second thought, I'll pass on the coffee," he said into Celia's slightly mollified gaze.

On the lawn, Ellie turned and hurried away toward the street. Good. He needed to get out and see what had got into her.

"I'm able to wait a few days to see the Lady Emma. There's no hurry," he assured Celia. "Not when other pieces of Axel's collection may be of interest. I'll be in touch with my clients to tell them you're amenable to offers. We won't need to involve the Macklin Gallery at all."

"You don't mind doing them out of their commission? I thought I detected a whiff of history between you and Eleanor."

"No history. Of course, the art world is small and it's likely she's heard of me." He lifted one shoulder insouciantly. "Even Eleanor Macklin would not deny you the right to make a private sale. I'm sure Axel would be proud of the way you're handling things."

She tilted one side of her lips into a wry smile. "Yes, I think he would."

With the pleasantries out of the way Rayder started toward the door, hoping Celia would follow him without looking out her front window. Thankfully, the last view he had of Ellie was her climbing into the passenger side of the car.

He took his leave of Celia, hastily kissing her extended fingers. "I'll be in touch."

Rayder stepped outside, buttoned his coat against the brisk wind and hurried out to the car. Ellie must have hidden in the front seat.

He climbed into the driver's seat and started the car immediately. Over the throb of the engine, he said, "What the hell was that all about?"

Ellie kept her head down and spoke toward the floor. "Jack Burke just left," Ellie said. "Hurry, we may still be able to catch him." She pointed down the road. "He went that way."

"He's long gone."

"So? That means you won't try?"

He sighed. "What kind of car was he driving?" He pulled out and started down the street.

"A black one."

"Well, that'll be easy to spot."

"It had four doors and was shiny. I'll know it when I see it."

At the corner, she instructed him to turn right. There wasn't a car in sight, black or otherwise.

"Damn." she said. "Turn around. We'll confront Celia right now. I want to—"

"Get a grip. If we do that, we'll blow my cover. I've got her convinced I'm interested in more than the miniature and I don't want to arouse her suspicions."

Ellie's green gaze narrowed. "How much more?"

"What?"

"How much more does she think you're interested in?" The emphasis on the word "more" made Rayder glance sharply at her.

"Well, well, aren't we the jealous one?"

"I'm not jealous," she denied hotly.

"Artwork, Ellie. Celia thinks I'm interested in buying a Picasso and a Manet. If she finds out I'm not just a buying agent she and Jack will disappear, taking everything with them. Turn off that murderous look. It makes me nervous."

"Good. It's about time you looked anything but smug."

CHAPTER ELEVEN

ELEANOR SETTLED INTO the Volvo and headed west on a twelve-lane beauty of a highway that dipped and swelled through the city, effectively slicing the city into north and south. She had to meet Nick at the airport. They needed to talk in private as soon as possible. He'd wanted to take a cab, but that would delay the conversation.

She'd left Rayder parked in front of Celia's house. Alone. It grated to leave him on his own, but she'd done it anyway. She had no choice but to trust him with the surveillance, with Celia, with the knowledge she'd shared with him, and ultimately with her gallery.

She only hoped he lived up to her trust this time.

To be fair, if she'd never known Rayder before, she'd have instinctively trusted him. Without the baggage of their past to weigh her down, he'd have been exactly the kind of man she found attractive. Decisive and in command. And challenging.

Rayder Cole was oh-so-very-challenging. She let a smile lurk in her heart at the thought of him. It wasn't long before it danced on her lips, as well.

It was no surprise she'd enjoyed the kiss they'd shared in the office earlier, she rationalized; she'd loved kissing him at eighteen. What had worked for her then worked for her now. Just the right pressure, taste and even scent. He'd always smelled so good.

She took the exit onto Airport Road and relaxed into her seat. Rush hour was over, and she enjoyed driving the express lanes when traffic flowed as it should.

Maybe she'd been unduly mistrustful when she had insisted on going with Rayder to Celia's home. Worse, she had handicapped

Rayder when he was with Celia. She could only imagine how ridiculous she'd looked prancing around on the lawn like a crazed mime.

She hated the comment he'd made about her being jealous. She was aware of how sexually attractive Rayder was; how charming he could be with that grin he had and the way the scar on his lip thinned. No wonder Celia had met with him when he'd called out of the blue claiming to be an old acquaintance of Axel's. Proof he could charm snakes.

Since Rayder had exploded into her own life she'd been bombarded with memories of their brief time together.

For ten years she'd brutally cut off all thoughts of that last afternoon with him. The rare times the memory invaded she chose rage to color the recollection. But she was no longer angry, not at him and certainly not at herself.

It had been November, just like now. In upper New York State, all but the most stubborn leaves had long gone. It was cold and generally windy, grey and lifeless, except for the world she and Rayder had created. Between them was the wonder of new love, deep, passionate, young, and exciting.

He was due to arrive at any minute. The landlady Ellie suspected of being a spy for her parents had left for a weekly afternoon bridge game.

She and Rayder would be alone. If things went the way Ellie wanted, she and Rayder would be one, forever. She watched out the upstairs bathroom window and waited for him to park and come to her.

She saw his car and excitement thrummed along her nerve endings. His long, determined stride thrilled her. His face was a mask of determination. A strong, virile male come to claim his mate. And she would be claimed.

She ran downstairs and opened the door to tug him inside. Then they were against the wall, kissing. Rayder ran his hands all over her back, waist, behind. Holding her, pressing her back to the wall, his mouth left hot trails of desire as he nibbled her ears, neck, jaw line. Finally, he reclaimed her mouth and groaned into it.

"Rayder," she whispered. "Let's go to my room. Mrs. Decker's gone. We have two hours."

"Are you sure, Ellie?" He kneaded her breasts. Arrows of desire rushed to her center, only to melt and flood into pools of heat.

She nodded. "She's playing bridge."

"No, I mean are you sure you want to?" He stood back, his blue eyes seemingly at war with what his hands were doing. His thumbs flicked her risen nipples and she nodded again, more rapidly this time.

She walked steadily to the stairs and looked over her shoulder at him. He hesitated, watching her, his eyes still a confused blend of emotions. She read desire, reluctance, love, and doubt. He needed some coaxing, she thought, deciding his love for her must be truly deep if he wanted to hold back, even now, after all these weeks.

"I want this, Rayder. I really, really want this. With you." She continued up the stairs without looking back. Before she reached the top, she heard his sure step behind her. Ellie couldn't contain her excitement and grinned all the way to her bedroom.

Eleanor's lips curved into a fond smile as she remembered Rayder's funny, fumbling attempts at gentleness. She suspected now that he'd been covering up his own inexperience, but his earnest declarations of love had been all the reassurance she'd needed. How sad that she'd forgotten the wonder of those moments in his arms. Not simply forgotten, she corrected, but deliberately subjugated under the anger she'd felt at his subsequent betrayal.

Afterward, when she'd been dozing in his arms, Rayder had tried to rouse her, had tried to talk about something, she recalled vaguely. He'd said he wasn't good enough for her, didn't deserve her and that her parents would never let them be together. She'd mumbled something back and kissed his cheek. When she'd woken, he'd been gone.

At first, she'd assumed the time had flown, and Mrs. Decker had returned. But when she'd searched for Rayder, his landlady told her he'd packed and left hours before. Horrified, she realized that he'd planned to leave even before he took her to bed. He'd taken the money she'd handed him for his sister and left town. But she'd given him so much more than money.

She'd given Rayder Cole her heart, trust, and her virginity.

She'd left Mrs. Decker's home within the hour.

Eleanor hadn't examined that afternoon clearly, without anger and humiliation, until now. She'd expected it to still hurt, after seeing Rayder again, she no longer held a grudge. They'd been kids; all hormones and need. And in his own way, Rayder had loved her. She was sure of it. And he'd been right about her parents not allowing their relationship.

The sign for airport parking came into view. She took the exit, aiming for the area closest to the terminal.

Inside, she found her way to Arrivals and waited impatiently. Finally, she saw Nick weaving his way through the throngs of international arrivals. "Nick! Over here!" She waved until he saw her.

Her brother smiled, waved, and approached her. Even red-eyed and haggard-looking, Nick Macklin turned female heads. Dressed in his brown leather jacket and tan slacks, his dark blond hair tousled from the airplane pillow, he looked adorable. Just like a younger brother should. But to women seeing him as a man, Nick looked like the real thing. Brawny shoulders and warm brown eyes could invite and entice women of all ages. She was swept up into his embrace and his excitement. She laughed, unable not to.

The relief of being able to share her burdens made her nearly giddy.

"Hey, what's up?" He passed her his flight bag and she dropped it immediately.

"I don't carry your things for you anymore, remember?"

He laughed. "Not since I was six and you were seven, but it was worth a shot." They strode out to the car together, Nick making a steady stream of comments about Japanese galleries.

When they were buckled into their seats, and could have a private conversation Nick said, "It *is* Jack Burke, El. As hard as it is to believe, he's the forger."

She nodded. "I know. He's working with Celia. I'm sure there are other forgeries from Axel's collection, too. But we can't concern ourselves with that. We have to stay focused on the Lady Emma. That's the only one tied to the Gallery."

Nick whistled low before he went on. "He's the one who consigned the fake in the shop in Japan." His voice was rich with disappointment and self-condemnation. "You were right. I never should have trusted him. I shouldn't have trusted anybody."

Eleanor tapped her credit card to pay for the parking and pulled out of the lot.

"Don't blame yourself. Jack's worked with us for years. I'm sure he wasn't always a forger. Dad would have caught wind of it years ago and stopped dealing with him. I'm sure this is a new development."

"Speaking of the old man, how's he taken all this?"

"I haven't told him."

"What? He'll go into coronary failure when he finds out."

"So, maybe he won't have to." She glanced at Nick as she smoothly changed lanes. "If we play our cards right, we can make this all go away."

"If we did let him know he'd be on the first flight home. I hate to say it, but he'd get in our way. No one can do outrage quite like the old man."

She smiled. "Exactly. He'd call all his contacts and friends and we'd lose whatever chance we have of keeping this quiet."

In the panicked time since yesterday morning when all hell had broken loose, she'd been too upset with her own situation to wonder what her parents would say. She didn't want to think about it.

"How did Celia get involved with Jack?" he asked.

"Any number of ways. They're two snakes who found each other, I guess. Celia had control of Axel's collection after he died, and Jack has the skill. Between them, they found people willing to buy a bargain. Only the bargain would be a fake."

Nick nodded. "Some collectors have too-little knowledge and too much greed. That's a combination that means they can be fooled."

"Apparently even the experienced can be tricked by Jack's work. I think he's found his calling."

"Was this Rayder Cole tricked?"

"Yes, he was." It still surprised her. "He's the one who bought the Kyoto miniature and returned it to the museum for the reward. He assumed it was the original because it was in Japan. The two years were up, the piece appeared on the market, and he jumped on it."

"Where is this Rayder now?"

"Watching Celia's house." She went on to explain everything that had happened since they'd last spoken: finding Jack's house empty, sharing information with Rayder, asking Anne about Jack and going to Celia's place only to see Jack leaving and having no way to follow him.

"What do you know about this Rayder Cole?"

Too much and not enough.

She watched for a break in traffic and merged into the stream heading for a southbound ramp. "He's a freelancer who tracks down stolen pieces for the reward. When he bought the fake and returned it, fooled into thinking it was the real thing, the museum gave him a week to get a line on the original. His uncle, who works for him as a researcher, found out Celia was offering Axel's miniature collection for sale."

"Which is how the gallery came into this."

"Yes. Rayder came to buy the Lady Emma four days ago." She didn't think it necessary to remind Nick that he'd been the one to hand the miniature back to Jack. "All he wants is to protect his reputation. Rayder's not interested in catching crooks."

"So, why's he helping us?" Nick's suspicion rang through his words. "He doesn't strike me as the altruistic type. Sounds like he wanted to be in and out fast,"

"I refused to share information and I left him no choice." She said firmly, wishing it was as simple as that.

Nick watched her shrewdly. "Is that all?"

Her cheeks warmed and she turned her head to glance out the window at the side mirror so he wouldn't see.

"I'll take you home to get some rest. Then I'll check with Rayder, to see if he's still at Celia's house or if he's on the road following her. The Ryan's fund raiser for the Children's Burn Unit is tonight. I'm sure Celia will go, if only to compare tonight's festivities with the ones she's hosted. We're taking turns watching her, but we're glad you're home to help."

Nick sighed and settled against the headrest. "I'm bushed. I need a good couple of hours sleep before I do much of anything. But after that, I'm all yours. I'll meet you at the fundraiser. Between the three of us, we should be able to keep track of one woman."

Nick was right, especially when the woman was Celia Brand. She and Axel had sponsored the first fund raising attempts for the special unit at Sick Children's Hospital years earlier. Eleanor was certain Celia wouldn't let the event occur without her now. Axel's sudden death had been the reason given for Celia's bowing out of hosting the event, but now, Eleanor wondered if there were other reasons as well.

RAYDER SLOUCHED IN the seat of his rental car, keeping one eye on Celia's drive. What he wouldn't give for a wiretap on her phone.

But this wasn't Europe and his reputation probably wouldn't stretch to getting police help. He had to do without.

He considered asking a friend from England, but by the time Gerry Hobbes got here the case could be wide open.

Soon enough Celia and Jack would tip their hand. After Nick had asked Jack to authenticate the miniature, they had to know the jig was up. That kind of pressure made for desperate acts.

Thinking of desperation made him think of Ellie. She was a promise of all the best life had to offer. She was straight and honest, with no grey area between right and wrong. The way she wanted to charge into Celia's house and confront her amazed him, even though that part of her personality was what attracted him most. Even at eighteen, Ellie's enthusiasm for life had captivated him. He could see it, still, in the way she focused so single-mindedly on saving her gallery.

Ellie was different from anyone else he'd ever met; totally forward-thinking and moving, never confused by moral questions. What was right was right and that's what she'd do.

Her unwavering belief in him ten years ago had made it easy to steal from her, while at the same time making it impossible to forget that he had. Ellie had touched him in places and ways he'd never dreamed possible.

Leaving her behind, hurt and humiliated, had been a watershed for him. No matter what became of him, Rayder Cole was a better man than he'd had any right to expect to be because Eleanor Macklin had once loved him.

Suddenly, she opened the passenger door and climbed in beside him. The cold fresh air invigorated him, and he wanted, badly, to take her into his arms.

"How goes it?" she asked briskly.

"'It' goes to the beauty parlor. I had to sit in a coffee shop for over two hours drinking coffee while Celia had some goop applied to her face and had a manicure. Since then I've been on a caffeine high and dying for a washroom."

"Ooh, that is a sticky situation." She chuckled. "We didn't consider those mundane facts of life," Ellie said with a genuinely amused smile. "I'll take over for a while if you want to take a break."

"I'll pick up lunch, too," he said. He reached for the door handle and held out his hand for Ellie's car keys.

She dropped her keys into his palm and snickered at his predicament. He couldn't resist pulling her chin toward his face for a quick kiss.

Her startled eyes made him laugh in turn and he left her with a smile on her lips.

He picked up burgers from a greasy hamburger joint, and returned to her in about half an hour, more refreshed than he'd expected to be. He parked behind her and she waved in welcome.

He had a flash of what it might be like if they continued seeing each other. How long would it take before the shine went out of her eyes at first sight of him? Being together long term might dull some of the pain of what he did to her before, but it wouldn't ever ease his guilt.

He climbed into the seat beside her and held up a take-out bag. She eagerly reached for it. "Nothing to report," she said. "Celia hasn't budged and there haven't been any visitors."

"The widow lives a pretty quiet life considering we suspect her of conspiracy, forgery, and maybe theft."

"There's a fund raiser tonight that she'll attend. When Axel was alive, she made sure everyone knew to the penny how much he was donating. It would be noticed if she didn't make an appearance."

"I'll pick you up at eight," Rayder suggested. "Nick can watch her house while we're there. Maybe Jack will return while she's out."

"Shouldn't Nick be at the Ryan's? He's expecting to go."

"No, Celia shouldn't know he's returned. We'll keep her in the dark, it's more confusing. When she makes her move, I want us prepared."

"All right, but we'll go to the Ryan's separately. Celia shouldn't know you and I have had anymore contact than what she saw in the gallery."

He agreed. But would have preferred to arrive with Ellie on his arm. If only for one night, he'd like to pretend she was his.

ELEANOR PUT HER HAND on the door handle to open it, intending to return to the gallery and continue her day as if nothing was amiss. As soon as she'd decided to keep her normal routine, she'd had nothing but disruptions.

"I have to get back to work," she said unnecessarily, watching his eyes watching hers. The moment stretched as she continued to sit with her hand on the door handle. "I swore I wouldn't ask you, but I have to know."

His lips quirked up into a lopsided grin. "You want to know why."

"It's crazy to care after all this time, but. . ." her voice caught and she stopped, mortified that she was showing him, bare-faced, how much it had hurt to waken and find him gone on that long-ago afternoon.

He reached for her hand and she tugged it back. He held on insistently, placing her palm inside his coat, over his heart. His body heat quickly warmed her hand, arm and on up into her own chest.

"I loved you, Ellie. But you scared the hell out of me. There was no way on God's earth your protective, high-toned family would ever have accepted me. I was in law because my family needed a lawyer they could control. I came from a family of grifters. Generations of con artists. You and I couldn't have fought both my family and yours. Not then." The sadness in his eyes was genuine, forcing her to remember his words as she'd dozed in his arms. He'd tried to explain but she'd been too drowsily content to listen.

"Thank you," she said quietly and opened. He released her hand and she climbed out, determined to return to the gallery and act as if this was any normal day.

The rest of the afternoon went rather dully, considering the frenetic pace she'd been living with the past forty-eight hours. A gentleman she'd seen several times before, finally purchased a small bronze cast by a new artist she'd found in Pennsylvania. The work was intricately done and yet looked amazingly simple. The clean lines of the Madonna and child gave way to incredible detail on closer inspection.

Happy with the sale, Eleanor completed the transaction. "Shall I have one of the staff prepare it for shipment to you?" Eleanor asked her customer.

"Yes, thanks. Would it be possible to have the delivery man dress up like a clown?"

"Excuse me?"

"It's a gift for my wife's fiftieth birthday and I want her to know I still see the girl I fell in love with. She used to be MayBelle the Clown on the Wild Willy Show."

"Wild Willy was my favorite," she replied, delighted. "School day mornings at six, right?"

He smiled, obviously pleased she remembered the popular children's entertainer.

She explained the request to Anne, who immediately got into the spirit of the surprise and took the man to her desk so they could make the correct arrangements.

Eleanor left them to it and went back to the gallery to decide how to rearrange the pieces now that she had a blank space to fill. She'd very nearly lost her patience with the portly man a couple of times because she was so edgy.

Learning he was married to one of her favorite childhood memories made her feel guilty. She sighed and tried to remember the last good night's sleep she'd had.

She heard the telephone ring and hurried to answer. She rolled her eyes in dread when she heard her father's voice. Coming so soon after Rayder's amazingly accurate description of her family, she was in no mood to be solicitous. "Yes, Dad, what is it now?"

"Is Nick around Eleanor? I wanted to speak to him about Jacqueline Ryan's fund raiser. He should be aware—"

"Dad," she cut him off. "Nick's not going tonight, so you can tell me."

"Oh? Well, then, I suppose you've seen the small Dali they have in their library?"

She curled her fingers into her palm and squeezed. "Yes, I have. What about it?" Her voice held an edge that said her patience had worn very thin. Maybe it was time she told her father who was running the show here.

"What's wrong, Eleanor? You sound—"

"Frustrated?" Again, she interjected stopping him mid-sentence. "I am, Dad." She counted to three then plunged on. "I'm tired of your daily phone calls. Are you unhappy with the way I run the gallery?"

"No, but it's Nick's baby, we all know that. He appreciates all that you do, honey. Has he been hard on you? If he has, I'll speak to him about it."

The silent scream she felt inside manifested itself in a white-knuckled grip on the telephone. She fought for calm. Rayder had been right. At eighteen she wouldn't have had the strength to break away from her family's interference. But she was strong enough now.

The gallery had become her defining element. Her dream *was* her life and she couldn't sacrifice it, not for anything.

"You've got it wrong, Dad. Either that or you've been blind for the past year. I run the gallery and I'd like to know if you're unhappy with the way I'm operating."

"What do you mean, you're running the gallery? Where's Nick? What's going on up there, young lady?"

She took a deep breath. Then another.

There was no way on earth she'd tell him the whole truth, so she started with the easy stuff.

"Nick's lost interest in the business and I've covered for him for over a year." She let that sink in for a moment before going on. "I've had it with all the pretense. I suggest you and Nick have a long talk."

"I see." Her father's voice sounded doubtful. Under normal circumstances, Eleanor would hurry to recant, to soften the blow, to please, but no more. She didn't possess the stamina necessary to deal with her father's emotional demands on top of everything else. She glared at his portrait.

And, in a personal gesture of total defiance, she decided if Rayder ever made another move on her, she'd take him up on it. Knowing who her family was may have frightened him off before, but, by God, if she had one last chance to be with him, no strings attached, she'd grab it.

"Do you really see?" she demanded of her father. "Running the gallery's been my lifelong dream and you've always insisted it be Nick's too. But the truth is, the business is too staid for Nick. He's not satisfied, and I suspect he'll leave soon. I don't know what direction he'll take, or where his real interest lies, but you must decide whether or not you trust me with Macklin's. Think about it and call me back tomorrow." She settled the receiver onto its hook and sighed.

If her father decided to come back and run things again, she'd worry about it then.

She rolled her shoulders, getting the kinks out of her neck. A huge weight of guilt had been removed and she felt lighter than she had in a long time. Nick might be unhappy when she told him what she'd done, but it was time he confronted his lack of decision. When she went back out to the gallery, she found Anne alone.

The tall brunette turned to her. Her gaze was apprehensive. "There's weird stuff happening and Jack's at the center of it, isn't he?"

Eleanor couldn't deny it. "Yes, but we have no proof. Not yet. The gallery's in danger, Anne, that's all I can tell you."

"Can I help?"

"No. I don't want to entangle you in my mess. If the police are called in, I'd like you free to say with a clear conscience that you didn't know anything. Believe me, you'll be more help that way."

"I guess I should be grateful Jack was such a jerk last year. At least I'm not involved with whatever he's up to." Her smile widened. "Hey, the jerk actually did me a favor."

Eleanor laughed. "I guess he did at that."

Anne looked at her watch. "It's time to close. Shouldn't you be getting ready for this fundraiser? My mother's called twice to try and convince me to go. She's bound and determined to marry me off before I become an embarrassment. The way she gossips is worse for me than her having a single twenty-nine-year-old daughter."

"Have you ever told her to butt out of your life?"

Anne groaned. "Only every week." Then she took a closer look at Eleanor's face. "Are you okay?"

"Yes," she said, covering for her obviously distracted air. "But I'm flustered. I just told my father that I'm running the gallery and Nick's losing interest. It was weird, and difficult, but I do feel better. I hate lying and subterfuge."

Anne nodded. "Don't worry about your dad. He'll come around. Besides, your mom will be on your side right away."

Eleanor smiled. "I hope so, I could use a good ally about now." She thought of Rayder and grinned. "I need your advice about what to wear tonight. I haven't had time to shop." She mentally sorted through her clothes closet, discarding several outfits she'd worn in the past three months. Another problem with near-bankruptcy was that refreshing her wardrobe had taken a back seat to more practical considerations.

"Black's good. Why don't you wear that little dress with the yellow roses up the side?"

"Oh, no, I couldn't." When Anne said little, what she really meant was skimpy. Eleanor couldn't remember why she'd even bought the daring piece. "I only go to these things to promote interest in the gallery." That particular dress was far too short and sassy to stir up anything other than sexual interest. "I don't need the wrong kind of attention."

Anne looked at her slyly. "Still, it would do my heart good to know you were giving Celia a run for her money, honey," she drawled the last word in a distinctly feminine dare that piqued Eleanor's pride. She'd never been one to outshine her clients in a social setting, preferring to be relatively unobtrusive. But still, there was something tempting about Anne's suggestion.

CHAPTER TWELVE

ANY TIME RAYDER HAD imagined a scene from Ellie's life during these past ten years, it had been similar to this one: a mansion, the scent of old money, and a fundraiser full of people willing to open their hearts and wallets. The beautiful woman he remembered would have been here, smiling, charming, and perfectly comfortable.

The champagne sparkle and crystal chandeliers were outshone only by the jewelry worn. The glitter of the social elite extended into the conversation and subdued laughter surrounded him. Many people, including his younger self, were seduced by the sheen of wealth and power but the Macklins took it in stride. This was their milieu and Rayder had worried he'd never belong.

Eleanor would be as comfortable here as an actor in rehearsal. Sometimes, that was how he felt at these gatherings, as if everyone were simply playing a role, and no one noticed he'd forgotten his lines.

He didn't fit in here. He knew that, and yet, he'd made his living from people like these. His whole clan had. For generations, the Coles had been reivers, con men, and grifters. But the Brantons, on his mother's side, had been hardworking, decent people who never seemed to catch a break. Until lately.

Things had changed for some of his cousins and they deserved their slices of the pie. Just today he'd learned that Ashlee Branton, a single mom, had won a lottery and had gone to Tyce's place to sort out what her next move should be. Rayder approved, because young, pretty, single mothers were seen as prey by unscrupulous men. If Rayder wasn't tied up here, he'd head to Tyce's to talk to Ashlee himself. He had to trust that Tyce and his wife Lisa, would offer good advice and protection.

And when he'd walked away from the Cole family business ten years ago, all of them except Shamus, the uncle who'd raised him, had turned their backs on him when he'd decided to go legit. But the Brantons had embraced him.

The people around him reshuffled and he saw a chance to break through into the center of the large foyer. An elegant staircase rose along one side of the wall in a gentle curve and he made for it, determined to stand above the throng so he could find Celia more easily when she returned from the kitchen. He had no idea why she'd invade the Ryan's kitchen. She wasn't hosting and it wasn't her house.

He had been here for fifteen minutes and still hadn't seen Ellie.

He took the stairs up to the landing to overlook the room.

Not ten minutes later, Ellie arrived wearing a skin hugging black dress with some kind of yellow flower dancing up the line of her hip and waist. The material wrapped around her sarong style, separating her breasts and baring her shoulders. Rayder's mouth went dry.

He felt the pull to touch her and took two steps down. He halted when she bumped into some guy at the bottom of the stairs. They kissed each other and hugged like long lost friends. The guy leaned in too close and spoke into her ear.

She laughed and smiled, perfectly at ease with his hands on her elbows. Too at ease, he thought. He had no claim on Ellie, not anymore, and while he accepted his reaction was far from civilized, he could no more stop it than stop the tides. He moved farther down the stairs toward them, focused on Ellie, the man's hands, and getting them off her.

Ellie accepted a glass of champagne from a passing waiter and patted the guy's arm. She moved toward the staircase and Rayder stopped to wait for her to see him.

She made her way up three risers and turned to look over the crowd. Apparently, Ellie wanted a clear view of the crowd.

The guy she'd left at the bottom of the stairs was not moving on. No, he gawked at the hem of her tight swath of a dress and looked red in the face. Likely lack of oxygen, he thought. He'd suffered the same at first sight of Ellie tonight.

Rayder made his move.

From directly behind Ellie, he heard her say, "Are you all right?"

The guy nodded and took her hand, rising to stand beside her. "Whew, you took me by surprise there, Eleanor. I hadn't realized–what I mean is–you've got gorgeous legs and I never noticed them before." His glance swept down her body once more. His neck flushed.

"I've never worn a dress like this to a function of this type. Anne talked me into it. To be honest, there's a man I want to impress."

Another one?

"Hey, the dress is a knockout and so are you." He took a deep draft of his champagne.

Rayder stood behind her, on the step above and he pressed his palm to her bare shoulder. Her perfume rose to him, and her skin felt like rose petals.

"Introduce me to your fan, Ellie." He coaxed her to lean back against him as if she belonged there. She'd make him pay for this impertinence later, but he didn't care. For now, it had this guy on alert and that's all Rayder wanted.

She turned to glare up at him. "Rayder Cole, meet my old school pal, Dennis Traynor."

"It must have been in elementary school that you last tried to peek up a woman's dress."

Traynor coughed. "That's right, and coincidentally, it happened to be the very same girl's dress. Eleanor and I have known each other since we were what, five?" He addressed the last to her and Rayder let his outrage simmer down to a boil.

"Who the hell are you?" Traynor demanded, glaring back up at him.

Quickly, Eleanor shrugged off Rayder's hand and patted Traynor's arm. "He's an old friend from university. And he's quite a kidder." She turned to glare at Rayder. "Aren't you?"

Rayder blinked. "Yes, I am."

She winked at Dennis. "Now tell me who's been bothering you about your divorce and I'll tear them to shreds." Her easy manner helped Rayder relax. Obviously, this Traynor was not the man she'd wanted to impress with the dress she wore.

He'd find out more about the mystery man later.

Traynor chuckled. "Actually, it's Mrs. Hetherington. I seem to have caught her eye. Something about her daughter?"

Eleanor grinned. "She's Anne's mother. You remember my assistant?" Anne had begged off coming tonight because of her mother's persistent meddling and matchmaking. "She's a lovely person, Dennis."

"Oh no, not you too. I thought I could count on you to leave me in peace."

She raised her hands in surrender. "All I mean is Anne is a great catch. The rest is up to you."

With that, Dennis smiled and rolled his eyes. "Sure," he said. He glanced at Rayder, and smirked before he headed back down the stairs and disappeared into the crowd.

They'd been children together and this Traynor was every bit as comfortable in this crowd as Ellie was. Rayder didn't relish the sting of her next words. Ellie could be sharp-tongued, and he felt off-kilter by his rush of adrenaline to be cool when she laid into him.

But then again, there were times a good rush of adrenaline came in handy. Besides, the best defense was a good offense.

He gently squeezed her shoulder, letting his fingers linger a moment too long. "Time's moving on and we have to talk," he whispered next to her ear.

"Are you crazy?" she said in a harsh whisper. "You scared me half to death. What was with the Neanderthal man routine? Do you want to ruin everything?"

"I apologize. And if I bump into Dennis the school pal, I'll apologize to him, too."

"Where have you been?" she asked. "I haven't even caught sight of Celia yet. Have you?"

"She's in the kitchen last I heard."

"Probably checking to see if Jacqueline's skimping on any ingredients in the hors d'oeuvres."

ELEANOR AND RAYDER moved downstairs together. She was surprised at Rayder's possessive attitude. Nothing similar had happened at university. On a base level, one she was shocked to learn she had, she felt pleased to arouse a male display of territorial behavior.

"I'd expected to see you on Celia's arm, not loitering behind me," she said impulsively, "ready to pounce on anyone who spoke to me." Suddenly his grip at her elbow shot sparks of electricity along her arm and down her spine. He marched with her until they were out of the crush of people, in a quiet nook under the staircase.

"That's enough," he ground out, looming over her. "I thought you'd have more sense than to wear an outfit like this." His hands skimmed her ribs and moved down the curve of her waist to her hips. "It's hardly enough to cover you. How can I be expected to concentrate on Celia when you and this dress are center stage?" He tucked his fingertips down the front of her wrap-around bodice between her breasts. The erotic shock of feeling his skin brush hers so unexpectedly rushed her defenses. He tugged up on the material hard enough to make her breasts rise and fall. His eyes narrowed at the fluid movement.

"Oh, get a grip, it's not that bad," she said with a dismissive air she didn't feel. She immediately tugged the hemline back down to its barely decent former length. She studied him. Rayder, loomed darkly, standing squarely in her path.

She refused to give an inch or cower. Instead, she raised her face to his and glared right back at him. He smiled deeply, his eyes lightening. The sudden change sent shockwaves of awareness to a web of places inside her.

She forgot to be upset about his male display with Dennis. She forgot Rayder had been too aggressive, too growly, too much predator to tolerate.

It was there, in his eyes, in his stance, in the way he shielded her from view. He'd crossed a line he'd drawn for himself. She had wanted to impress him with this dress, and she had. A shiver of fear ran through her. Not fear of him. He was a gentle, caring man. It was fear for herself. Fear that if she wasn't careful, she might hand over her heart again.

The way she had before.

She shouldn't have listened to the feminine part of herself that had prompted her to display her body for him. But there was no turning back. The raider was poised for attack and she, wearing this silly little dress, was wide open for it.

Ridiculous, an inner, stronger voice told her. *You were no more than a girl then.* Full grown women can enjoy men without the kind of strings a girl expects.

"Stop it," she insisted. "We're not here to let you display your Neanderthal side, remember?" She made to move around him, but he gripped her elbow and held her still.

He opened his lips to speak, but a shrill laugh came from behind him. Celia.

Immediately, he set his face into an expression of cool amusement and turned away from Eleanor.

"Celia," he said easily, drawing the older woman toward him. "Come see who I've found hiding under the stairs."

"Rayder, there you are!" Suddenly Celia's voice rose above the crowd. "Why are you tucked into a corner where no one would ever find you?" Her eye make-up emphasized the cat-like tilt to her eyes and her lips were outlined to their fullest proportions. Drama personified.

Eleanor took one more fortifying sip of champagne before Celia descended on her, wondering at Rayder's chameleon-like ability to shift from dangerous to affable.

"Hello," she said uneasily, hoping Celia wouldn't demand information on her miniature.

Celia's gaze sharpened as she took in the clingy short lines of Eleanor's dress.

Eleanor stood quietly for the inspection. She'd kept her curls as tame as she could. Her make-up enhanced rather than dramatized, but nothing could change the brevity of the little black number she wore.

Celia's cold smile never reached her eyes. A warning shiver skittered along Eleanor's spine.

"Eleanor." Her name was said with all the warmth of a glacial cave.

A passing waiter stopped and offered them more champagne.

Celia declined with a wave of her hand. "Anything less than the best gives me a headache," she said to Rayder with a mean smile.

He inclined his head. "Say no more. I'll find you a mineral water, instead."

Her brittle eyes shifted to Eleanor. "I still haven't heard from your brother. I expected a call about my miniature before this," Celia said tightly.

"He's in Japan, Celia, investigating another matter."

"Really? Now, what could interest Nick Macklin in Japan?" The words and tone were cool, but the widow's gaze assessed her.

"I'm not sure," Eleanor admitted. "He doesn't keep me informed as often as he should."

"Yes." Celia nodded. "We saw that the other morning, didn't we? Poor Eleanor, it must be dreadful not to be trusted with important company business."

Stung, Eleanor wanted to retort that the business was hers, but of course she couldn't. However, Celia's glance flicked over her again and Eleanor saw a tightening around the older woman's lips. For the first time since taking Anne's advice, she was happy she'd worn this dress. Even Rayder's appreciation couldn't match the thrill of seeing Celia's unmasked dislike.

She wanted to ask Celia about Jack Burke and wracked her brain for the right way to turn the screws on her. Before Eleanor could frame the words, Celia noticed another woman she knew and waved in her direction. Without a word, she stalked off, leaving Eleanor with the amazing conclusion that Celia was more frightened of her than Eleanor had been of Celia.

Eleanor watched as Rayder tried to make his way back through the crowd and was snagged in passing by Celia. He gave her the mineral water he'd fetched and stood quietly while Celia wore him on her arm like a trinket. It was disgusting the way he smiled and nodded and allowed Celia's friends to size him up like a stallion at stud.

Eleanor smoothed her dress, tightened her stomach muscles and prepared to put an end to the ridiculous display of feminine possession, when Celia suddenly veered off in another direction, dragging Rayder along behind her.

Keeping her distance, Eleanor followed.

The chase was on.

Rayder, looking smooth and sexy, was doing what he was supposed to do, Eleanor told herself. She noticed that whenever Celia ran her fingers along his forearm he shifted away. At least he was keeping her at a distance, while still near enough to observe her closely.

Her prey stopped to chat with an elderly couple Eleanor recognized as former clients. Three years ago, the Robinsons had been among the first people to snub the Macklin Gallery by taking their business to a Montreal gallery instead. She sidled away, keeping her face turned from them. She wanted to prevent an awkward moment should the Robinsons see they were being watched.

Eleanor kept tabs on Celia's movement through the crowd until she spent considerable time with Anne's mother. Mrs. Hetherington, while a gossip, often knew far more about people's business affairs than the romantic affairs most gossips preferred.

Eleanor moved closer, standing behind and to the right of Rayder out of either woman's view. With any luck Anne's mother would steer the conversation toward business.

"How did you meet Celia, Mr. Cole?" Anne's mother asked pleasantly.

"He was introduced to my husband several years ago in Paris," Celia answered for him. Rayder placed his empty wine flute on a passing waiter's tray and caught sight of Eleanor in his peripheral vision.

Eleanor knew he'd seen her when his naughty fingers danced across her upper thigh, sending a jolt of electricity through her so explicit it nearly rocked her on her heels. She took a sharp intake of breath. She wanted to stand out of range, but another person moved too close behind her.

Forced to accept her own body's sinfully exquisite response to Rayder's touch, she vowed to find a way to avenge herself. Perhaps grinding her three-inch heel into his instep. The thought brought a small smile to her lips. Or maybe...

Celia's voice chimed louder, putting an end to Rayder's assault on Eleanor's senses. "It wasn't long before I found myself telling him how little I understand about the art world. I'm relying heavily on his advice." She clung to Rayder's side, and Eleanor saw her mash her ample breasts against his upper arm. The low, intimate chuckle that rose from Celia's throat made Eleanor grind her teeth. The image of

Rayder touching this woman, maybe even kissing her, shot a bullet of ice through Eleanor's heart. She didn't want to listen to another word.

The crowd around her shifted again and Eleanor was hemmed in, forced to hear even more of Celia's suggestive remarks.

Mrs. Hetherington, of course, was all ears. "It must be difficult being alone after a long, happy marriage," she said, in a sympathetic tone.

Celia had been twenty-nine when she'd married Axel. He'd been sixty-four and in tearing grief over the loss of his first wife.

"Yes, ten years was quite an investment." Celia's tone was shockingly cool.

There was a short moment of silence from Anne's mother before she said, "Speaking of investments, Celia. I've been hearing rumors that you've had copies made of all your jewelry. Are the originals for sale? I love your emerald pendant."

Celia Brand had one of the most spectacular jewelry collections in the city. Axel had been a generous, indulgent husband. Eleanor leaned closer, anxious to hear Celia's answer.

"Of course not, I've had the copies made for insurance purposes. One can never be too careful and now that I'm alone I need to protect myself even more." Celia's voice took on a wavering quality that Eleanor knew would prevent further questions. She felt Rayder shift slightly closer to Celia.

"I'll see to it that Celia's not being taken advantage of." Rayder said smoothly. "I've several contacts in Europe who shared Axel's fascination with miniatures." The tone in Rayder's voice assured both women that his only concern was seeing to Celia's best interests. "I'll see that she gets what she deserves," he said clearly.

Eleanor suppressed a chuckle at his audaciously ironic remark.

"There won't be any need to sell your jewelry, Celia," he assured her further. "The sale of your miniatures will see to that."

Celia made some comment Eleanor couldn't hear and suddenly Rayder moved away, out of earshot. People rearranged themselves again and Eleanor made certain she stood with Mrs. Hetherington. Happy with the overheard conversation, she now had an opportunity to pump Anne's mother for more information.

CHAPTER THIRTEEN

AN HOUR LATER, ELEANOR'S head felt full of startling revelations about Celia Brand's personal and business affairs, and she'd already written a check for the Burn Unit. Add the fact that she was sick of Rayder paying dutiful attention to Celia and all she wanted was to go home. She faded into the crowd behind Rayder and headed for the cloakroom.

Rayder caught up to her by the door into the library. "I need to talk to you. Now."

She barely nodded, aware that others may be watching. She didn't want any speculation about their relationship getting back to Celia. "In there. You go first."

She watched him knock three times. Getting no response, he opened the door cautiously. Then he slipped inside.

She joined him a few moments later. "Obviously, you've been caught in a darkened library yourself," she drawled, referring to his practiced knock. She didn't want to think of what he'd been up to at the time. She didn't want him to see that she cared.

He slanted her a look that raised her temperature. "Of course, I have, haven't you?"

"I wait until I get home." She spoke firmly to dispel the image of Rayder making love to a woman within earshot of a public party. The woman's image looked disturbingly like Celia's.

"That's too bad. Passion should be unstoppable." He leaned negligently against the closed door and studied her as she flicked on the lights, flooding the room with inhibition.

She strode to the French doors leading to the terrace. His reflection in the square panes of frosted glass looked choppy and unclear, but was undeniably, breathtakingly Rayder.

Rayder Cole in a tuxedo was every woman's fantasy come to life.

He came up close behind her. His hand reached up to her neck and sensation took over as he stroked her there. She wanted to tell him he had no right to touch her this way, but he'd only laugh. The scene with Dennis had pushed them both beyond denial of what was between them. "Where's Celia? Will she notice you gone?" she said, fully intending to move away. Soon.

"She won't miss me. She's following Mrs. Ryan around explaining how much to expect in donations." The stroking continued. "You heard that woman ask about Celia's jewelry?"

She arched her neck, stretching the stress-taut muscles he massaged. "That woman is Anne's mother, Mrs. Hetherington. She told me she's heard rumors Celia has already sold most of her jewelry, although Celia denies it. Celia's life has turned into a sham."

"Could Axel have left her broke?" He kept up the steady, hypnotic contact with the back of her neck.

Eleanor gave up the notion of moving away. It seemed a foolish idea when his touch gently soothed.

"It looks as if he was in financial trouble before he died," she explained. "Perhaps that's what brought on the heart attack. Rumor also has it that Celia's facing a tax audit." Her breathing changed as she responded to his strokes. She was dangerously close to moaning.

"That explains the why of this forgery deal, but we still don't know the how of it. Tax problems can make people desperate. Jack and Celia will make a mistake soon, and when they do, we'll be there." He moved his hands to encircle her neck, a band of warmth radiating heat in all directions, over and under her skin. His palms spread across her shoulder blades, inching the material of her dress down by millimeters.

"The police won't be interested unless we can give them proof of a crime," she said, rolling her head in time with his rhythmic movements. Celia or Jack had to break soon.

"This whole thing is shadow boxing. The only crime with proof is my returning the fake to the Calais museum and claiming the reward. The curator could accuse me of being in league with the forger." He drew tight circles on her neck with his thumbs, sending arousing messages skittering along her nerve-endings.

She turned and faced him. "Surely not. You've got proof you bought the fake in Japan. The only thing you're guilty of is being taken in a con." She smiled, enjoying the fleeting embarrassment she read in his gaze. "And isn't that ironic?" She continued to smile as she said it, hoping to take the sting out of the words.

"Returning the reward money should support my innocence. If all else fails, I can do that."

His hands slid down her waist to settle on her hips. He pulled her close.

"Except...he drawled. He nuzzled her neck, took a quick nip at her ear, apparently forgot what he'd been about to say.

"Yes?" She prodded. "Except?" But she didn't want to know. Didn't want to be pulled from the sensuous haze that had befallen her. She closed her eyes.

"Except Jack Burke has disappeared with a client's miniature in his possession. That's theft."

"That's right." She opened her eyes. "Nick handed the miniature to Jack. You and I corroborate that it wasn't in the vault the next morning and that Jack had left in the middle of the night. Celia would deny her involvement with Jack and be forced to act the part of innocent victim." The more Eleanor thought, the more she liked the idea of having that woman in a trap.

The light in Rayder's flame blue gaze dimmed. "No, that's wrong." He shook his head. As soon as the theft hits the media, I'd be implicated by the museum." He looked at her with a strange, sad light in his eyes and she realized what he must be thinking.

That Eleanor could have her revenge. That she wouldn't care what happened to Rayder.

"So, we're back to where we were, waiting to find proof that Jack and Celia are working together." Seeing Jack leave the house in his car couldn't be corroborated. Eleanor had been alone and had good motive to lie considering all she had at stake.

"It would help to examine the one I mistakenly returned, but there's no way the curator would allow it."

"What about Shamus?"

"No way, she mistrusts him more than me. After all, he's the ex-con. Some people put a lot of stock in a clean criminal record." His wry grin made her smile.

His eyes lit warmly in response. He closed the short distance between them, tall and broad, blocking out some of the light.

She felt cornered suddenly, by the man and the situation.

"There's nothing to do until morning," he said in a croon that reached into her vitals. "Nick can watch Celia tonight. I suspect she'll lay low." He brushed his knuckles across Eleanor's hot cheek and into her upswept hair.

"Why don't you ever let this down?" He tugged at her slim silver barrette and half her hair cascaded to her shoulder. "That's better." He reached for the matching barrette and the rest tumbled down. "I'm glad you didn't cut it."

Chills swept through her at a memory of Rayder tugging her hair to his face and worshiping it, letting it trail seductively across his lips. She opened her eyes and shivered with anticipation at his beguiling smile. Past images blended with the present. She felt exposed. Vulnerable. She had to stop him. Eleanor stayed his hand before he could gather her hair by the fistful.

"Why don't you back off and let me move away from this door?" She needed him to think the draft at her back had caused her shivers and pebbled nipples. She'd thought she wanted this, but now she wasn't so sure.

"I like you at a disadvantage," he explained in a husky whisper that did more to heat her than she'd have imagined possible. "It evens the odds."

"Odds? This isn't a game." If it was a game, she'd lose. She slipped inexorably into him, his scent, his feel, his sexual pull.

"Poor Ellie," he murmured in a warm brandy drawl, "you were always an open book."

"What do you mean?" Her thought clouded.

"You want me, no matter what's behind us. Even despite what's ahead of us. You want me to do this–" Rayder tugged her closer, "–and this–" he brushed one tight nipple lightly with the back of his hand. She flushed hot but wouldn't budge, choosing to pretend she felt nothing. He brushed his knuckles against her pebbled bead again, longer and slower this time, pushing for a response.

ELLIE'S SHARP INTAKE of breath hit Rayder like a blow to the gut. His lower body tightened. She stood with head held high, apparently in denial that his touch affected her. Proud Eleanor.

Warm indulgence rose in him at the sight of her, headstrong and determined. He tested the weight of one breast in his hand, running his thumb back and forth across the nipple.

She blinked, finally. She shifted her stance and his blood raced. Her body was telling him he'd neglected the other breast for long enough. Fascinated by the denial in her eyes and the invitation her body sent, he caressed the neglected breast delicately. Ellie blinked again, slower this time. Her breath shuddered out and his gut contracted with need. Her breast quivered in his hand. Ellie was shaking.

He reached for the top of her dress, determined to see what he'd been fondling. Slowly, he lowered the bodice. She shook in delicious, tiny tremors that rolled through her.

Her eyes drifted shut for a long moment, closing off from his view the war between denial and arousal she still fought.

Another tremor took her as he swept the material down and released her breasts completely. White and smooth and perfect, her breasts rose and fell with each breath she took. She was fuller than she'd been before, more luscious. He cupped each breast, rubbing her tight nipples with his thumbs. A small sound caught in her throat at the first contact of his hands on her bare flesh.

She was close to complete surrender. The bastard in him wanted her, here, against the cold glass door. His hands slid down to her hips and he pulled at the material, bunching it up. His mind took him much further along the road. He was already driving into her, hearing her urge him on, clasping her to him, enveloped in the wet heat she kept for him. Only for him.

Her expression alternated between fear and longing, desire and denial and the gentleman he wanted to be won out. He smoothed down her bunched-up skirt and took several deep breaths to regain control.

"Rayder?" she whispered in yearning, her eyes wide and luminous and staring into his. Quietly, as the sound of their heightened breathing surrounded them, a look of profound sadness entered her eyes. She covered herself before he could touch her again.

"I'll follow you to your place. Ellie, please don't turn me away." He grasped her hand and pulled it to his chest, placing her palm where she could feel his heart beating like a jack hammer beneath the tuxedo jacket.

He wanted her to understand how she affected him. "If we don't take this chance, we may never have another."

She nodded and a ghost of a smile lit her eyes. "They won't let us share a prison cell."

CHAPTER FOURTEEN

RAYDER MADE HIS EXCUSES to Celia and the hostess, Mrs. Ryan, and left the party fifteen minutes after Ellie.

It took twenty minutes for a thirty-minute drive to Ellie's building. Part of him couldn't believe she'd let him in. The other part was already there, drowning in her. The doorman smiled when he walked into the lobby.

"Your name, sir?" he asked.

"Rayder Cole."

"Yes, Mr. Cole, Ms. Macklin left word. You're expected." He couldn't credit the look of admiration in the man's eyes, but he didn't think much of it. His mind belonged to Ellie.

It wasn't like him to put pleasure before business. He knew better than to let a woman get under his skin while on a job.

The week the curator had given him was nearly up. Unfortunately, she was new at her post and thought the world had fallen in when the fake had been discovered. She'd been made to look the fool and she wasn't about to let Rayder and Shamus go unpunished.

And here he was, putting all that on the back burner while his libido jumped to attention. And for what? A woman who wouldn't want him in the morning. He had no illusions, what was true ten years ago was still true today. Rayder Cole wasn't good enough for Eleanor Macklin. He knew it at eighteen and he knew it now. Like sucking on a bad tooth, he couldn't get enough of the pain.

The elevator stopped at Ellie's floor and he got off. Plush carpet. Expensive lighting and doors. But sterile. Not the kind of place he'd have pictured her. He'd always imagined her in a big, old house with a veranda. Kind of airy and homey. There should be kids screeching in the background and rock and roll playing in the kitchen.

She'd wear her hair loose and free and have a small gallery in the front room filled with local artists' work. She'd smile a smile that said how glad she was he was home, and he'd steal a kiss, maybe nuzzle her ear, cop a feel.

He stood in front of her door for a long moment, lost in the dream. She yanked it open before he could knock. There was a noise as a neighbor's door opened behind him. Ellie grabbed his wrist and pulled him toward her. At the same time a woman came out into the hall behind him.

Ellie yanked until he stepped into her apartment.

"Embarrassed to have a man arrive at this late hour?"

"Of course not," she denied, looking flushed and distracted. And so damned beautiful.

"Or is it me you're ashamed of?" When she looked flummoxed for an answer he said, "Skip it." He looked around the apartment. Elegant. The furniture looked formal and stiff, except for one chair by the window. Big, with soft, sloppy cushions and arms broad enough to hold a dinner plate. Light from a reading lamp gave its deep green leather a rich glow. This was where Eleanor spent her time curled up comfortably reading or eating. He strode farther into the room to see the dining area.

"I just spoke to Nick. He watched Celia's house until I asked him to wait outside the Ryan's house for her." She followed Rayder into the room. "No one approached the house while Jack watched. Unless Celia goes to meet Jack after the party, she'll be alone tonight. Nick will call if Celia goes any place other than straight home."

"Does Nick need me to relieve him?"

She shook her head. "He had a nap and said he's fine for the night."

Anticipation rolled around the room and landed in his chest. "We're not needed for anything important?"

"No." The corners of her lips canted into a shy smile. She was nervous, and even more unsettling, so was he. What if he botched this, whatever it was?

To cover his nervousness Rayder studied the dining room, taking in the rattan and glass furniture. The cushions and wallpaper were silver and sky blue. Too feminine for his taste, but it sure looked like Ellie's.

A flash of her bedroom in the boardinghouse hit him square in the heart. He'd never seen so many ruffles, nor smelled anything so devastatingly female. He'd wanted to touch every shiny, silky surface, bury his nose in the lace-covered pillows, and drink in the sight of her as Ellie had settled across her bed and beckoned him. His head had roared with the rush of blood and overstimulated hormones. He'd fought the battle for all of ten seconds, he realized now; not bad for an eighteen-year-old who had no brain but the one in his jeans.

He tried to remember what she'd asked him, but he couldn't. He turned and looked at her. She appeared at a loss as to what to do with him.

"Tell me how life's been for the last ten years," he asked.

"Are you serious?" She glanced around the room as if expecting an exit to appear.

"Sure. Aside from the end, we were friends. There are lots of things I've wondered about you since."

She let go of her elbows and slid her hands down her thighs, left half bare by the ridiculously short dress. Her shoulders glowed smooth and inviting as she walked stiffly to the wing chair opposite him and sat down. "I've wondered about you, too," she admitted in a faint voice.

He sorted through all the questions he'd stored over the years, picking the one that had tormented him most. "You never married. Did you ever get close?" *Was there ever a man who loved you better, who taught you the things I've since learned?*

"No, I got busy with the gallery," she explained. "Nick and I had tons to learn." She smiled as if the strain and hard work of those years meant nothing.

"But you're happy now? With the gallery, I mean. It was always your dream." She looked pleased that he'd remembered.

"Yes, it was. Always. But it's like the old saying, be careful what you wish for, it may come true." She sighed pensively. "The gallery's become everything, eclipsing all other aspects of my life."

"I see. Can't Nick take some of the load?"

"No."

"Any other problems?" he coaxed.

"You mean aside from this mess we're in?" She smiled. "My father retired after Nick and I got comfortable, but he refuses to see Nick's interest has waned. My brother's impulsive, eager to be elsewhere. I've covered for him for the past year."

"I suspected you were the driving force."

"We were doing well until the investigation three years ago. You remember? You used it to blackmail me the other morning and forced me into that ridiculous charade at the gallery." Eleanor's voice took on a bitter edge he couldn't blame her for.

"I remember. I'm sorry I coerced you, but I didn't have any other way to get into your gallery without you giving me away. I thought it best to keep our first meeting in a decade private."

She nodded. "I guess I should thank you for the head's up, after all. Under the circumstances, we would have been in a bad state right now if I'd spilled the beans about our past in front of Celia. And you were right, I would have screamed it from the rooftops."

"Tell me what happened three years ago." He knew, of course because he'd had a hand in it, but he wanted her to talk to ease the tension.

She stood by the balcony door, looking out at the lights of the city below them. "A fraud investigation. As suspicion rose, we were considered guilty until proven innocent. Somehow, the investigation took another turn and Interpol shifted their focus to a man in France. We were never given the opportunity to clear our names." She flexed her fingers on her thigh. "It was frustrating. And such a long, slow road back for the gallery."

Rayder had never considered that aspect before. Of course, Ellie would want to clear her name, it was all-important to her. A tarnished reputation could kill a gallery and her career in one fell swoop. He frowned.

"We never got our day in court," she went on. "Even our most valued clients drifted away, afraid of being tainted by the scandal. A lot of them were there tonight. Some of them still turn away from me as if I stink up the room."

"Oh?" he said.

She was looking at him now, searching his expression. He deadpanned.

He had a bellyful of dread. The axe would fall any second. He had no choice but to confess. No more lies, not with Ellie. He lowered his head. He couldn't watch her when he said what he had to say. "It was me. I'm the one who turned Interpol onto the forger in France."

She gasped and he lifted his gaze. The horrified expression on her face said it all, but he couldn't leave without explaining. From the street below the distant wail of a siren whined.

"I saw pictures of both the copy and the masterpiece," he blurted, "in a French paper. In his own way, the forger had a distinct style. I recognized it. It was a simple phone call to Interpol," he shrugged to dislodge his guilt, but it didn't help. "I'm sorry, Ellie, I never meant to do you harm. I wanted to help."

"I suppose you think I should feel grateful?" she said sweetly. "If we'd gone to court, we'd have proved we had nothing to do with that forgery. Our clients wouldn't have left us, and Nick and I wouldn't have been *this close*," she pinched her thumb and index finger together, "to bankruptcy for three years."

"Damn it." He groaned. "I knew I should stay out of it. I knew you'd never understand." He sounded angry, but he couldn't ease up. He *was* angry. At her, for not accepting his apology and at himself for confessing. Why was every emotion he had surrounding this woman so damn difficult? If this was remorse, he'd had his fill.

"WHAT DID YOU EXPECT would happen when you nosed into my business?" Eleanor demanded. "Did you believe you were helping me? And why would you want to?" His stricken face gave her the answer in the sudden, cold stillness.

Penance.

She closed her eyes and held in a moan. *What a mess.* Rayder had wanted to make the scandal of three years ago better by helping her. But he'd made things worse by quietly stepping in. By keeping to the shadows, Rayder had made it impossible for the Macklins to overcome the whispers of dishonesty. A ruined reputation had resulted in near bankruptcy. "Oh, Rayder."

She made her way to her favorite armchair and sat heavily. She felt sick with heavy, confused emotions. Anger at the injustice, relief at learning the truth, even a weird gratitude for his confession, swirled within her.

Rayder loosened his bow tie with one savage twist and took a seat across from her. "Well, now you know. I thought I was helping, Ellie. I swear I did."

"It doesn't matter now." She sagged against the back of her chair. "This whole new thing could blow up in our faces and the old scandal will be revived when the new one hits the streets." They sat quietly for a few moments, each lost in thought. She needed time to sort her feelings and the only way to let them settle was to keep talking.

"What about you?" she asked softly, picking at a piece of fluff on the arm of the chair. "I seem to recall that you wanted a home, a wife, even two or three children." She didn't look at him. She was too busy wondering if that, too, had been a lie to string her along on the con job.

He looked startled by the question, which was a sort-of answer. He'd lied to her about wanting what she wanted. Of course, he had.

"On my last afternoon with you," he murmured. "I was filled with your love and the impossible seemed possible. I wanted that life Ellie. In those moments, I wanted it more than anything."

He shook himself as if the memories were painful. His eyes cleared and he looked directly into her eyes.

"I travel too much to have a family," he said tersely. "I don't even have a mailing address aside from Uncle Shamus's, in London."

He was rootless, totally uncommitted. He shifted, apparently unhappy with the conversation. Maybe she'd made him uncomfortable by dredging up his lies.

She took pity on him and shifted the focus to his uncle, a man she'd thought was fun and quirky. "I've been wondering if dear old Shamus still smokes those big cigars."

"Yeah, he does when he can get away with it," he said through a grin, his eyes warming. Rayder like this disarmed her and she felt her anger dissipate.

"The stroke he had." A thread of concern wove into her voice. "Was it serious?"

"No, it was a warning. He's got his blood pressure down with diet and exercise. He browbeats his doctor into allowing the odd day at the races."

Before long, Eleanor found herself smiling and laughing as they reminisced about other college friends and fun they'd had. The conversations they'd shared throughout the long day had only hinted at the enjoyment they could have in each other's company. Rayder was right. Before he'd broken her heart, he'd been the best friend she'd ever had.

It had been a long time since she'd felt connected to a man. Nothing would happen tonight that hadn't happened between consenting adults for an age.

"Coffee?" she offered.

"How about food? The hors d'oeuvres were hard to come by."

RAYDER FOLLOWED ELLIE to her compact, tidy kitchen. No ruffles or lace here. No memories to ambush him.

She opened the refrigerator and peered inside offering him a great view of her shapely legs and even shapelier behind. She straightened as if she'd suddenly realized the picture she presented.

"Not much here but eggs, cheese, lettuce and one sorry-looking tomato," she said breathlessly. "I still haven't had time to replenish my stocks since my trip." She stood up and looked at him, her eyes mischievous. "We could order in," she suggested.

"We could," he agreed, grinning. "Still love the old stuff?"

"Of course."

"Great." Anticipation hummed through him like a live wire. He retreated to the living room to get his cell. "What's the number?"

After she told him, he ordered from memory, with Ellie smiling and nodding as he listed their old favorites. She leaned close to him, her breasts snuggling against his upper arm, her breath a whisper against his neck.

"And sweet and sour pork," she said, snagging his glance with hers. She leaned closer and he slipped an arm around her as he finished talking. He smoothed his hand from her shoulder to her waist, memorizing each dip and curve along the way.

When he hung up, he found himself with an armful of adorable, seductive woman. Tempted to let his hands roam to points south, he kept them on her waist instead. She leaned into him and smiled.

"That was quite a show you put on for Dennis's sake." She laughed lightly. "All gruff and ready to–"

He cut her off by slanting a kiss across her mouth. She tasted of the sweetness of Ellie, the lush want of a woman as she parted her lips and arched up against him. The folds of her dress moved and stretched under his palms. He held the soft curve of her buttocks in both palms and squeezed, pulling her closer to his hips, aligning her with him. He pulled his lips from hers. "It was no show. Seeing that guy ogle you nearly sent me over the edge."

She pulled his head down to hers again, her only reply an open, urgent kiss. He should ease back, he told himself, set her away from him, but her kiss felt like absolution and he wanted it again and again. He kneaded her behind and tugged her closer, watching for any sign of doubt. He dipped his head toward her, then turned when the angle didn't seem right, and turned again, before settling his lips to hers.

THIS KISS FROM RAYDER was different than any Eleanor had had from him or anyone else before. It was passionate, but hesitant, fierce, but leashed; his lips burned and scorched, soothed and coaxed, drained her of all but her passion.

Her hands slipped from his hair to his shoulders. She touched his neck, felt his pulse beat in time to her own and knew sweet torture as she pulled back. Eleanor ached with wanting him, but she wasn't sure if it was an echo of the loving they'd shared long ago, or a new passion that grew between them.

The confusion of her senses was disquieting. "Rayder, stop." She removed his hands from her behind and held them between their bodies.

He touched her forehead with his and looked into her eyes. "Right, the food's on the way."

When she could, Eleanor stepped around him to head to the kitchen, hoping her legs would carry her. "I'll put the coffee on now. The China Palace has the fastest delivery service I've ever used," she said, relieved to focus on a different kind of hunger.

After the food arrived, they settled on the floor with their backs to the sofa and the food on the coffee table. Cartons and bags and paper wrap steamed with the succulent smells of their midnight snack.

"I've been thinking..."she let her voice trail off.

"Uh oh, sounds serious." He picked up a snow pea and popped it into his mouth.

"Serious enough that I want to talk about it before we go any further tonight."

"Okay."

CHAPTER FIFTEEN

"YES?" RAYDER FOCUSED his full attention on Ellie, afraid of what she'd say. He wanted tonight with her more than anything, but he'd walk if that was the end result of this conversation.

Her eyes gleamed as she studied him and took a deep breath. "I'm ready to accept that the last afternoon was partly my fault. No boy that age could have resisted what I offered and how I offered it." She looked at a box of rice, avoiding his gaze. "I'd thought about making love with you for weeks and when you didn't press the issue, I did. Teenage girls have hormones too," she said through a deep sigh.

She was a grown woman now, no longer that teen who would've died of embarrassment to admit to sexual desire.

Oh, thank God she wasn't kicking him to the curb. "You'll never know the six kinds of hell I went through as I watched you waggle your gorgeous ass up the stairs." His voice went tight and as she turned toward him; the hem of her dress rose.

"I wanted to bolt out the front door," he continued. "But you looked at me over your shoulder and told me you really, really wanted me. I aged ten years following you." His hands wandered down to her hips and held her loosely. Her scent, feminine and exciting, rose between them.

"Then when I saw your bedroom and realized what we were actually going to do, where I would touch you and with what, I almost lost it." His voice deepened to a rough rumble he couldn't clear.

"I remember." Ellie snuggled closer. "You looked as scared as I felt," she went on. "Until I saw you in my room, I hadn't considered the actual act, either. The responsibility, our relationship, the pattern of our lives was about to change.

"Instead of hiding behind the excuse of being carried away, I realized that I'd be in control of whatever happened next. You never forced me, nor manipulated me, nor coerced me in any way. I was wrong to remember differently."

Ellie's confession punched the wind out of him and sent his blood into a familiar raging pulse. She traced his arms with a light touch and ended up at his shoulders. The tips of her breasts tantalized his chest, but he still made no move to haul her closer.

"Ellie." He said her name with a reverence that shook him. He cupped her face with hands that trembled, smoothed her eyebrows with his thumbs, caressed her cheekbones. "I never meant for things to go that far. I never meant to love you. I never meant to take the gift that belonged to the man you'd love after I was gone."

"I understand that now," she said, and kissed him gently. "I buried my memories of your hesitation, the doubt I saw on your face, the battle I watched you wage."

He nodded automatically, caught in the mesmerizing reality of being here, with Ellie, and having her welcome his presence. She'd let her hair down. Completely. It curled and wisped about her face and the years between then and now drifted away. The pull of her body, her scent, his pounding pulse was more than he could bear.

"The hardest part was losing your friendship," she said quietly. "I had no one to go to on campus. They were all strangers to me. They had all buddied up by then. There was no one I could share with, so I left."

"The same night," he said, trying not to sound husky. He cleared his throat and started again. "You were gone by the time I got back."

"You came back?" Ellie's stricken, disbelieving voice shamed Rayder into looking away. She'd never even considered, he realized, that he might be sorry and return for her.

"Your landlady said I missed you by an hour." An hour, and his life had changed. An hour and every question he'd ever asked had been answered. An hour and every doubt had been confirmed. He was no good and never would be. And he'd hurt the only thing of importance in his life.

"An hour?" The despair in her eyes shifted and she jerked. And then, even with all the pain and the time wasted, she smiled. "I was on the freeway by then, hellbent on getting home. I moved in with my rebellious younger brother, got him on the straight and narrow and put my nose to the gallery grindstone." She tilted her chin up and met his gaze squarely, daring him to find fault with the way she'd handled the situation.

All this time, he'd told himself her family would have replaced the money he'd stolen. After all, they were loaded. Daddy should have rushed to his daughter's rescue. Rayder had convinced himself they'd have indulged her with an expensive gift to wipe away any dirty memory of those weeks. But, Rayder had misjudged his Ellie. Even at eighteen, she'd refused to be a victim. Instead, she'd been strong, independent, and resourceful and prouder than he'd imagined.

"Why didn't you tell your family, or at least your brother about me? I assumed they were there for you." He needed to know, needed to suck on that bad tooth one more time.

"I couldn't tell them I'd been taken in by a con man," she said dismissively, as if the thought of telling her family hadn't entered her head. "Look, all my life, they told me I was too trusting, too giving, too open. Even the boardinghouse had to pass muster. They interviewed landladies," she said, with exasperation.

The same qualities her parents had worried about had made Ellie the perfect mark for him. Trusting, giving, open. Rayder had looked for those things, had exploited them, had ruined them. For what? To take his place in a family who survived by exploiting those very same values.

She smiled at him, licking her index finger clean of plum sauce. Her tongue wrapped and curled around the tip. Her lips made a slight popping sound as she gleaned the last of the sauce from her skin. Her eyes danced with sensuous delight in the flavor.

"Where'd you learn to do that?" He hadn't meant to say the words out loud. She stopped in mid-lick and looked at him. Looked right at him and kept on smoothing her tongue along her knuckle.

Control shifted from his mind to another, much lower, part of his body. And, what's more, Ellie knew it, he decided, as he watched her start on the index finger of her other hand. A slow, steady pulse beat through him in time with each flick of her soft, pink tongue. He swallowed and followed every movement of her fingers and lips.

Ellie's feminine invitation sang to him. Lured him. Captured him. The shift in control was complete. His mind went on automatic and his hormones were in overdrive.

In one smooth motion, Rayder moved the table, took her hand away from her mouth and kissed her. Ellie kissed him back, using her tongue, teeth, lips and scent to drive him crazy. Invitation grew to demand, want grew to need.

Ellie was molten gold in Rayder's hands, moving, bending, molding to him. Her skin was soft and giving. Pliable. He eased her down to the floor between the sofa and coffee table. He gloried in her eagerness; his mind blown away by her seeking tongue.

She sighed into his mouth. "Rayder," she said between kisses, "I shouldn't want this."

He nodded and stilled against her, every nerve screaming to move. "But you do, Ellie, you do." Her eyes were filled with desire. Her hands slipped beneath his shirt and drew tantalizing circles across the flesh of his belly. She touched him and his nerves jumped, arrowed and dived south to sizzle into sharp pleasure.

"Yes, I do," she murmured next to his ear. "I want you even more than I did before." All they had was now, with no promise of a tomorrow. Making amends for the past was impossible. If making love to her added to the litany of charges against him, so be it.

She hesitated and her eyes clouded with thought as she stilled against him. "I'm scared," she whispered. "I want you, but I'm scared."

"Me, too." He smiled and took her hand, pulling it to his chest. He tugged it up to his mouth and kissed her knuckles. "If you don't stop touching me, it'll all be over, anyway." He groaned at the feel of her against him. "You always made me too horny too fast."

"I did?" Her surprised, pleased tone made him chuckle.

"I walked around campus with my books in front of my crotch." He grinned at the memory. "I didn't want to frighten anyone, least of all you."

She laughed with him. The sound slammed into his gut echoing somewhere around his heart. To slow things down, he propped himself on an elbow to watch her. She glanced up at him and then looked away.

"I guess it's foolish to be afraid," she said quietly, "but it's been a long time for me. Before, neither of us knew what we were doing so we were even, but this time is different."

He placed a fingertip on her lips. "This time, we'll both relax and enjoy," he said in a low tone.

She propped herself up in direct imitation of his position and looked at him squarely. She leaned closer and set her lips gently against his. "What are you waiting for?"

He shoved the coffee table out of the way. "Nothing," he said, reaching for her. A carton of food tipped over, spilling vegetables onto a plate. Neither of them cared.

FOR ELEANOR, THE MAGIC came back immediately. Where there'd been doubt, she found confidence, insecurity changed to contentment, feather light caresses created explosions of heat.

Rayder took her over. Completely.

He demanded and she gave. He coerced and she acquiesced. He squeezed the sensitive flesh at the curve of her hip, and she moaned encouragement.

"You're more woman than I ever dreamed," he said with a hint of wonder in his voice that sent thrills through her. "I dreamed about you. About your hair," he tangled his fingers in it. "About your lips." He nipped them between his own. "About your breasts." He encircled them, holding them up high so they jutted toward him. He pressed his chest against her hardened nipples, moving them back and forth across his flesh. Shooting sparks of awareness aimed for her heated, secret places.

She melted at his command. Every touch, every breath she felt against her neck, every nibble that burned and pulled and nipped, took her closer and closer to the hunger. She threw her head back in wild abandon, no longer keeping pace with him, no longer matching each of his caresses with one of her own. She was his, completely and totally to do with what he would.

Eleanor lost herself in him, not caring if she ever found herself again.

RAYDER KNEW THE EXACT moment Eleanor surrendered and his Ellie emerged. The ecstasy of triumph overcame him as he gazed down at her. Her eyes closed, her chest heaved, her hair splayed across the rug in all directions. Her neck flushed with sexual excitement. She'd be wet and soft by now. For him.

He had to fill himself with her; imprint every sigh, every touch, every look, every scent into his memory. He reached for her and held her tight against him, burying his nose in the sweet scent of her hair, inhaling her into his soul. She clutched him to her, and he clung, suddenly needing more than this one time.

Needing more than her body.

Needing more.

Needing.

His hands flexed on her hips, dragging them closer to his erection. He rubbed against her in his anguish to brand her. She moaned and he took it as a sign of discomfort. He had to ease off or he'd hurt her. When he pulled back, she lifted a leg to wrap around his thigh. She welcomed the heavy friction between her legs. Instead of hurting her, his rough handling had aroused her further.

Ellie wanted to be swept away, he realized, taken to places her rational self would never go.

She moaned and reached for his pants, fingers fumbling with the closure. The light brush of her fingertips against him were sweet torture. She cupped him fully, pressing her palm against him in measurement, sighing with delight at what she found.

"Oh, Rayder, you're everything I remember."

At her words, an exquisitely pulsing rush of blood roared through his loins. "Ellie, I have to see you."

She nodded; her eyes glazed. "Yes, please." She sat up and drew off her dress. He could see the darker skin of the areola, puckered and hard with the need to have his mouth. He brought her to lean over him and took each nipple into his mouth in turn, working his tongue. She moaned with each stroke, the sound taking him higher and higher, making him harder and harder.

Her flesh bloomed scarlet where he'd suckled and drawn on her deeply, pulling her into his mouth. He saw her eyes gleam as she watched him. Then she straddled him, cupping his erection with herself. She pressed down onto him and her eyes flared with delight when he growled his encouragement. She skittered backward and settled on his thighs. Before he could help, she was tugging off his pants.

In another moment he was free. Ellie drew in a sudden breath edged with a nervous sigh. "I had no idea," she said.

"You didn't look last time?" He couldn't keep the amusement from his voice.

She pursed her lips and shook her head. "I was too shy."

"I didn't hurt you before, so I won't this time."

"I lied." Her quiet voice flowed over him, and he stilled.

"What?"

"You, well," she hesitated, "you sort of stretched me. I remember a lot of pressure and a tear inside. Then it was over." She smiled a deeply mysterious and beguiling woman's smile.

He felt heat rise in his face. "The first time, I guess, it's like that," he explained inadequately. "Hell, Ellie, I exploded as soon as I felt you surround me. You were tight, like a soft, wet, hot pulsing glove." The image brought his erection back full strength.

"That's exactly how I feel now," she whispered hollowly.

"Ellie. For God's sake. I'm lying here at full attention. If you don't stop, I'll embarrass myself." He was ready to explode.

She slid both hands up his chest to his nipples and leaned close. Her hair felt like fairy dust as it flowed up and across his shoulders. She licked at his chest hair, making it damp and curl on his sweat-slicked flesh. Her breasts mashed softly against his ribs, the nipples hard as pebbles in the center of all that softness.

He laced his fingers into her hair and raised her face for his kiss. She let her tongue dance with his, stroking into his mouth, giving as good as she got.

"I'm sorry about the first time. I was young. It'll be better now. I'll be better," he promised.

"Rayder," she looked him in the eye. "The second time that afternoon was more than I'd ever dreamed."

He rolled with her until he covered her, the silky barrier of her panties an agonizing reminder of their unequal state of undress. He rolled her stockings down her legs, then suckled at her breasts again, loving the way she squirmed beneath him in silent demand. A demand for him to pay attention to what waited beneath the scrap of lace at the juncture of her thighs, already showing signs of the moisture beneath.

He set one exploratory finger to the task and felt burned by the heat he found. She softened and opened for him, inviting deeper exploration.

RAYDER'S MAGIC FLOWED over and around and inside her. Eleanor's breath caught when he touched her heat. She felt herself flower and open as his questing finger traced her.

She removed her panties and allowed him more room between her thighs. It had been too long since she'd felt this pull with a man. She opened her eyes and watched his face. Intent on pleasuring her, he didn't see her watching him.

Rayder's face was a study in intensity. Hard planes and angles with sweat shining on his forehead, hair damp from exertion and hard-won control, she memorized it all, needing to keep it for later. Her breath caught as the sensation he invoked spiraled higher and higher. There would never be another time like this.

If they didn't all go to jail, Rayder would leave soon, going off to other women, in other places, and she'd be left here, with a gallery to run. Suddenly desperation welled and she couldn't wait any longer. She bucked against the hand that cupped her, wanting to scorch him with her heat. He must remember her and this time. He might leave, but he'd never forget, her body screamed, echoing with the release that was yet to come.

"Ellie," he called to her. "I can't wait." He tugged at her hand in a mute request to encircle him. When she did, he moaned raggedly and moved against her urgently. He bit her neck with ardent arrogance. "Now, Ellie."

"Yes, Rayder, please," she urged, clasping his hips and bringing him close to her.

His fingers shook as he reached for his pants pocket and tore open their protection. As he slipped it on, Eleanor cupped him and squeezed lightly. He caught his breath, trying to hold onto his fractured control. The smile she gave him was pure devilment before he slipped into her waiting arms.

Rayder needed to brand her, to make her his, completely. He planned to enter her to the hilt on the first thrust, holding her until she moved against him, but her eyes widened in fear as he pressed against the folds he needed to part. He watched her, holding back all the tides of nature, shaking with his effort, until her eyes cleared, and she relaxed.

Ellie pulled him closer with an expression of such tenderness that he felt anointed. Blessed with the gift she offered, he entered her reverently and completely.

Slick and ready, Eleanor wanted Rayder never to forget this moment. She watched his face, awed by the intensity of concentration she read. Every millimeter was agonizing rapture as he filled her, every nerve ending alive with a billion messages of pleasure. His eyes closed as he stilled inside waiting for her inner muscles to adjust for him. She moved against him in a dance as old as woman, her excitement increasing with every undulation.

He kissed her then and growled against her neck. "You're mine. Mine!"

"Yes." she cried. It had been foolish to think she could claim him when all along the claim had been his to make.

They moved together in rapturous abandon, rough, hard, demanding release, no longer thinking or planning or deciding, caught in a cataclysmic desire to pleasure each other and themselves.

Eleanor's climax began deep and rose steadily until she swept up past the stars. She clamped her legs around Rayder's waist and rode it out, reaching for every sensation. When she relaxed again, he bucked into her fiercely and then stilled. He trembled with his release and she held him tightly.

"Rock me," he pleaded. His last spasm died away as he groaned her name again and again.

Rayder kissed her forehead, her nose, her chin and finally, her mouth. He blessed her with a kiss low on her belly as he left her and enfolded her in his arms. With a hand on her breast, he said, "Your heart's hammering."

"Mm. Feels good." She felt wonderful. Satiated. But one thought intruded. Rayder was falling asleep. Sleep meant waking and waking meant she might find him gone.

"Er, Rayder?" She nudged him. "Don't go to sleep, okay?"

Rayder heard her but couldn't rouse himself to speak. She'd been perfect. Hot, wild and not a recrimination to be seen. He tugged at what he figured was her arm, wanting to snuggle and hold her.

She tugged back, away from him. He opened one eye.

Eleanor glared down at him. "Wake up."

He didn't want to, so he closed his eye again. Maybe her glare was actually a loving, affectionate glance. He reached for her, but she slipped away just as he felt the weight of one smooth breast.

"Please, Rayder." She prodded him painfully.

"Okay, I'm awake." He raised himself onto his elbows and looked at her. He grinned. "Your hair's all over the place." He was about to say he loved it that way, but her frightened expression stopped him.

"Please get up." She stood and collected her clothes into a bundle in front of her. She used it to shield her body from him as she hurried, sideways, out of the room and into the hall. Once there, he heard her dash into her bedroom and slam the door.

"Hey!" he called. "Ellie, what's wrong?" He pulled on his pants and shirt quickly and began a ragged search for his socks. One was dangling in the beef fried rice container. He held it up. "Great," he muttered, "beef fried sock." He couldn't find the other.

He heard a sound behind him and turned to see her, dressed in jeans and a T-shirt, braiding her hair: a sure sign of trouble. He wondered if she realized her hair sent out signals. Touch me, touch me not.

She stopped and gave him a brisk smile. "Hi, sorry about the rush. Guess I wasn't as ready for reliving the past as I'd thought." Her gaze shifted away uneasily.

"This had nothing to do with the past. It happened because we might not have a future," he reminded her.

She finished the braid with a deft twist and flicked it over her shoulder in a gesture that dismissed him as well as her hair.

Obviously, touch me not. His fantasy of spending the night in her bed expired.

"If you keep looking at me like that, I'll think you blame me." He zipped his pants, the sound loud enough in the guilt-laden atmosphere to make her wince.

"I don't see where there's any blame to lay," she responded coolly. "We're adults. We had sex. End of story."

He dragged his tie around his neck and walked closer to her, disturbed by the doubt he saw in her eyes. She gave him a false smile as he drew her close.

"Maybe you had sex, but I was making love," he murmured.

She stood stiffly in his arms. "Even so, it's still end of story," she said briskly, looking from right to left but never up at him. "I guess I should say thank you, or, it was nice, or something."

"It was nice?" he demanded. "Nice? Honey, if that's your idea of nice, I'll stick around and find out what you think fireworks are all about."

"Don't tell me you'll stick around when we both know you won't." She pulled away. "Let's leave this as it is. A warm, lovely memory to replace the other ones that weren't so nice." He tugged her back, determined to clear the air. "Please," she placed her hands on his chest to hold him at bay. "I have enough confusion in my life."

"And you don't need more," he finished for her.

RAYDER CLOSED ELLIE'S door softly, but it could have been slammed with all the force of the Furies for the impact it made. No matter that he'd spent ten years of his life doing penance for that one unspeakably asinine stunt, no matter that he was at the top of his field, known internationally for his success, no matter that he was more in love with Ellie now than he'd dreamed possible, inside he was still that frustrated, egotistical doofus he'd been at eighteen.

Wearing the best tuxedo known to man, he was still standing outside Eleanor Macklin's apartment with his shoes in one hand, his sock in the other, his shirt undone and his cummerbund over his shoulder. He didn't know where he'd left his overcoat. But he was damned sure he wasn't knocking on her door to get it.

He stalked to the elevator. No way would he fall harder than he already had. No way would he waste more time with that woman. He should have known Ellie would tie him in knots. She only had to look at him to do that. He stabbed the elevator button twice.

The doors finally opened, and he got on, fuming all the way to the lobby floor. The doorman rose to attention when he stomped out of the elevator. The outside doors must have been open because there was one hellacious draft swirling around the cold, marble floor. Cursing with the shock, Rayder rose on his toes and hustled toward a chair in the sitting area.

"Hoo-ee, man, look at you. Kicked out?" The doorman smiled wide in amused sympathy. All six foot five of him.

Rayder was glad Ellie hadn't thought to call ahead and have this guy usher him out. He nodded and rested his head in his hands for a moment to get his bearings.

"I'm not sure what happened. One minute, I was doing fine, better than fine, and the next, I'm out the door." His legs still felt like butter, the afterglow of the loving slowly subsiding.

The doorman nodded in understanding. "Yeah, women can be like that. All sugar and spice and wantin' things nice but give them any excuse and..." He shook his head sadly, a lone diamond stud in his ear winking in the bright lights. "Still, you're the first I've *ever* seen Ms. Macklin invite upstairs, so you got further than any of the other guys she goes out with."

"Is that so?" He introduced himself as he put on his shoes. The only sock he had was the one that had come to rest in the food, so he went without.

"They call me Bruno," the doorman said, in a manner that indicated he was ready to pass some time. "I've got a thermos of coffee and an extra mug, if you want." He grinned. "Sometimes, people come down from upstairs late at night in no condition to drive, so I provide a wake-up service. If they refuse, I call 'em a cab."

Rayder grinned back and buttoned his shirt. "You're a good man, Bruno," he said, accepting the hospitality. After they filled their coffee mugs, he went on, "I guess you get a pretty good impression of people in the building."

"Yes, sir, I do." He settled back into the chair next to Rayder. "Ms. Macklin's a fine woman. Strong and knows her own mind. A couple of times I've had to help her out. You know, with guys that can't take no for an answer." The smile he gave left no doubt as to who won those altercations.

Rayder nodded. "I'm glad you're here for her."

"Yeah, I like Ms. Macklin. She's good people." The look that Bruno gave him then was measuring. "Must be something about you she likes, else you wouldn't'a been invited upstairs. Must be something she *really* likes about you if you got to take off your socks."

Rayder nodded, caught up in his own speculation about Ellie's reactions.

"Seems to me, if a fine woman like Ms. Macklin was willing to see a man's bare feet then there's got to be something there worth fighting for." He raised one eyebrow and considered Rayder. "Are you a fighter, Mr. Cole, or will you leave here whupped?"

"Oh, I'm going to leave all right." He smiled into the big man's eyes. "But I'm far from whupped." He tucked his shirt back into his pants.

AT THREE A.M. RAYDER pulled up behind Nick Macklin's car and parked. He flashed his headlights twice. Macklin turned in his seat, saw him and got out.

Rayder watched him saunter toward his car. Ellie's brother was a big man, who moved deliberately, cautiously. Rayder opened his window.

"You Rayder Cole?" Nick asked, giving him a penetrating look.

He nodded. "Anything happening?"

"Nope. Celia came straight home from the party and that's the last I've seen of her." He peered into the car, curious. Macklin yawned when he saw the empty back seat.

"No sign of Jack?"

"None. If he was here while you all were at the fundraiser, he kept himself in the dark. No lights came on, not even the exterior security lights." He yawned again, fiercely, this time.

Rayder nodded. "Makes sense. They're not careless. I just hope Burke's still in town."

"Yeah. If you're here to spell me off, I appreciate it. I'm exhausted."

"Go home, get some sleep. I've got a lot of thinking to do anyway."

At the cryptic comment, Macklin nodded. "It's too cold to hang around. Good luck," he said before hurrying back to his car.

Rayder couldn't blame him. Nick had a warm bed waiting for him. Rayder faced nothing but another sleepless night. He might as well spend it in his car.

Hunkering down into the heavy duffel coat he'd borrowed from Bruno, Rayder prepared to watch Celia's home. Thinking of Bruno made him consider his next move on Ellie. It should be unexpected. The doorman was right; Ellie wasn't the kind of woman who slept around. She was cautious with herself, her feelings, and her body. He supposed he had something to do with that, but he was sick and tired of wearing guilt like chain mail.

Oh, yeah, his next move needed to be something special. Something she'd never forget.

CHAPTER SIXTEEN

NEXT MORNING AT THE gallery, Eleanor enjoyed a morning mug of coffee with Anne.

"Dennis Traynor's nice," Anne said. "I met him last night. He told me he's an old friend of yours?"

"I've known Dennis forever. He's a good man. His divorce was difficult. He was surprised by his wife's decision to go to Europe to find herself as an artist. She's walking away from her whole life."

Anne nodded with a speculative look in her eye. "It's especially difficult when the reason for the breakup seems out of character," she mused.

"Do I detect a thread of interest in my old friend? I'll put in a good word for you with him."

"Hey, let's get off the topic, I'm not ready for another foray into a relationship," Anne shuddered dramatically, but grinned all the same. "Thanks for the good word, anyway. Now, what happened when you wore the dress? Did you get the reaction you wanted?"

She couldn't stop the heat from rising into her cheeks. She ducked her head to take a sip of coffee.

"Oh ho! It looks like something happened. Tell me who noticed. Was it Rayder Cole?" Anne lowered her face to get a better look at Eleanor's and Eleanor couldn't hide the grin any longer.

"He noticed," she admitted, "but I left him at the Ryan's at about ten." If Anne didn't ask if Rayder followed her home, Eleanor would be finished with her recap of yesterday's events with nary a lie being told.

The telephone rang and Anne, glowering defeat at Eleanor, went to answer it.

She should have regrets about having sex with Rayder. Good, healthy sex had a way of making the world seem brighter. She was glad, purely on a physiological level, of course, that she'd had such a cleansing release. She was a healthy woman in her prime and she needed sex. There was nothing wrong with wanting the touch of a man's hand. And there was everything right about that specific man's touch, a throaty voice in her head reminded her.

"But as for it happening again," she whispered in response, "forget it." The voice responded with a sly, "we'll see," as it had ever since Rayder had bemusedly walked out the door last night. She'd been surprised he'd gone as easily as he had, but a niggling part of her said it wasn't over yet.

He was an intuitive man, adept at reading signals and while he may have been initially confounded by her request that he leave, he'd soon figure out that it had been fear that had driven her to act the way she had.

The call Anne sent through to her office was from Nick. "How did it go last night? Catch any bad guys?" Eleanor asked.

"Nope. After Celia returned home, I stayed until three when Rayder showed up to relieve me."

"He did?" Rayder hadn't slept either. "Did you speak to him?"

"Not much, I was practically numb. My only thought was a hot shower and a good night's sleep."

"Of course." She wanted to ask if they'd discussed her but didn't want to give too much away. Nick could be persistent, and she didn't feel like sharing her feelings for Rayder with anyone; whatever they turned out to be, she thought ruefully.

"I should stay here," she explained. "I want my work schedule to be as close to normal as possible."

Nick agreed. "Dad called a few minutes ago, woke me up and chewed my ear off. What did you tell him about me?"

"The truth." This was not the time to hold back. "That you've been less than attentive to the gallery for some time. We need to let them know. I'm tired of Dad treating me like a child. And he needs to let you move on if you want to."

There was a long pause as her brother digested her opinion. He sighed. "You're right. It's not that I don't care El."

"I know," she broke in, "You can't get excited about it anymore."

"Yeah."

"What will you do?"

"I don't know."

"What does Dad think?"

"That I'm lazy and shouldn't have dumped it on you."

"Is he coming back to take over?" If he did, he'd have to be told about the forgery and all of this would have been for nothing. She tightened her grip on the telephone, her stomach clenching in dread.

"He's thinking things over. I said I'd call tomorrow."

"Good," she said briskly, to cover her fear. She refused to beg. If her father didn't know yet what the gallery meant to her, he never would.

Their conversation concluded; Eleanor put her mind on business. She spent the rest of the morning doing the unthinkable. She cancelled all the orders she'd placed during her buying trip to the southwest. It pained her to explain to these artists who had seen her gallery as a steppingstone to international recognition, that there was no way she could continue with her orders as written. A couple of artists were furious, but more of them were willing to work out a different arrangement.

Comforted that all was not lost, she was surprised to see that it was close to noon. She called Nick to ask him to relieve Rayder. "I imagine he's hungry," she said. "I'll take him to breakfast."

Eleanor told Anne she was leaving and drove as quickly as she could to the posh Rosedale neighborhood, trying to shut out the recurring images from last night. Rayder, leaning over to suckle her breast,

Rayder, sighing with the pleasure of her hands on his flesh, Rayder, confused and lovable as she escorted him to her door.

Seeing his car, she parked and approached it, keeping a sharp eye on Celia's house. Leaning close to the window, she tapped on the glass and peered in.

He looked tired, red-eyed and out of sorts. His beard had grown to a shadowed stubble. His eyes lit with recognition when he saw her, and she controlled a smile at the warmth in his eyes. He unlocked the passenger door for her.

"Hi," he said, letting his gaze travel the length of her before she settled in the seat next to him.

She handed him his sock. "Sorry, I forgot your coat at my place."

The growth of whiskers on his face was so black she could easily imagine him with a full, luxurious beard. Would it be bristly or soft? Would it scratch her delicate skin or feather it?

"I was just thinking about you," he said quietly.

"Good thoughts, I hope."

"You don't want to know what kind. Not right now, anyway."

She tried to ignore his sex-laden voice but found herself mesmerized by the level gaze that matched it. His fingers brushed at her hair on her shoulder. "What's this? No braid?"

"I wanted a change," she said primly, but she allowed his caress of her hair. "I didn't come here to be seduced."

"Oh? That's too bad. I haven't made out in the back seat of a car in years." The lascivious expression on his face was so deliberately corny, she laughed out loud.

He yawned and stretched, rubbing his face hard enough to redden his cheeks. "I'm afraid that even if you did want to do the back-seat rumba, I'd be asleep before we got started."

"Nick's on the way to relieve you. I'll drive you to your place and make you some breakfast," she offered, sure he'd be too tired to drive himself.

The look he passed her made the backs of her knees sweat. She wondered if he was truly as tired as he let on.

"I've only got an hour," she said, reminding herself as much as him that time was too short for dallying.

Rayder's studio apartment was over a garage with lane access. It was only two blocks from the Brand mansion, but the area was full of converted apartments whereas Celia's street was a preserve of single-family homes. Eleanor had to block the garage door in order to park.

She experienced an odd blend of nervousness and anticipation as she followed him up the outside stairs to his door. She had the curious sensation that she was under Rayder's intense scrutiny, which was ridiculous seeing that he wasn't even looking at her.

Unlocking his apartment door, he stepped inside and turned to her, his blue-ice gaze burning with desire. She had no time to react beyond the realization. He kissed her full on the mouth before she caught a breath, warming her from the inside out. When she responded, he opened her coat buttons quickly, holding her around the waist in a deliberately intimate embrace.

She was in a whirlpool with no will to fight his seductive pull. His hands ran the length of her back, her waist and down to her hips. He kissed and nibbled at her lips and each corner of her mouth. Rayder dipped his tongue into the soft, wet place between her lip and her bottom teeth. She moaned and slipped her hands into his raven-black hair and held on.

Rayder coaxed Ellie into his apartment, keeping her in his arms, warm and tight. After several teasing kisses and desire-heightened caresses, he shut his door, locking them inside where they had privacy. She flushed warm with deep longing.

"Miss me?" he asked on a husky note.

"I might if you give me time to," she quipped. She craned her neck to see around his broad shoulders. Window seats were a feature of three dormer windows; the floors were dark-stained pine, burnished to a rich glow. A heavy, beamed ceiling completed the impression of an old English loft. The walls were a rich cream color; the windows framed in black. A small open kitchen was tucked into a corner at the far end and a floor to ceiling bookcase divided a section of the room into a sleeping area.

"Like it?" he asked with a grin as he stepped aside. "It's not big, but it's a lot better than staying in a hotel. I pretend this is home."

"I guess you've spent a lot of time in hotels." She walked into the living area.

"I try not to think about it." He took her coat and hung it up on a coat rack by the door. "Sorry there isn't room for a closet or a proper hanger."

"Anne will need me back at the gallery, and I'm expecting Nick to call," she said quickly, to dispel any hopeful plans he might have that she while away the day in bed.

"Hey. I get it." He put his hands up palms out. "I'm too bushed for anything more than breakfast and a nap," he swore.

"I'll make some food," she said, not bothering to point out the charged sexual energy she'd just experienced in his arms.

"There's not much here in the way of breakfast food," he said.

"Out," she said when he followed her to the kitchen. "Take a shower, shave, and do whatever else you have to, but stay out of my way. I work alone."

She set to work and found he was right about the selection of food. Breakfast would have to be ham on a roll with lettuce and mustard, mayonnaise, a large dill pickle and a bottle of ginger ale in an ice bucket. She decided against coffee, thinking he needed sleep more than caffeine.

The food was ready by the time Rayder emerged from the bathroom, his hair damp and his face freshly shaved. He grinned when he saw the laden plates she'd set out on the bar that separated the kitchen and living area. He pulled out a stool for her to sit on and she settled onto it with a flourish. "Thank you, kind sir."

He presented the ginger ale as if it were the finest champagne. She inspected the label. "Canada's best."

"Of course," he teased. "I taught you about pastrami and you introduced me to ginger ale. On the rocks, right?"

He filled their glasses and settled onto his own stool beside her. He lifted his sandwich with two hands and moaned with delighted intent when he bit into it. "I was starved," he admitted.

She watched his strong fingers pop an errant piece of meat into his mouth and felt a thrill go through her.

"I've been wondering if the forgery now is connected to the case three years ago," she mused aloud. His incredibly erotic capture of a smudge of mustard from the corner of his mouth caught her attention. She cleared her throat. "When you made that call to Interpol to deflect suspicion away from Nick and me, where did the trail lead?"

"To a forger in France. No one special. He wasn't even good enough to camouflage his own style."

"There was no connection to Celia?"

He frowned in thought. "I don't know. Once the investigation shifted away from you, I lost interest. I'm not sure where it went from there."

"What if Axel had something to do with it?" If Celia's husband had been involved in dirty deals, then maybe she'd continued the family sideline by using Axel's contacts.

He stopped chewing and looked steadily at her. She watched him as the gears of his tired brain began to grind. "It's possible. Axel was less-than-honest when it suited him. And if a network had been set up during his lifetime, Celia might be shrewd enough to revive it after his death. And she's certainly desperate enough to look at any avenue to maintain her lifestyle."

"How can we find out more?"

"Shamus."

"He has contacts at Interpol? People who tell him confidential things?"

"Always."

"You two are scary."

The scent of the sandwich called to her and she hefted it to her mouth for the first succulent bite. "Mm," she moaned. "Heabenny." She tried to speak around a mouthful. She swallowed. "I mean, heavenly."

Eleanor, too, was starved. The upheaval she'd felt since Rayder's arrival had dented her appetite, but now, with her equilibrium coming to rights, she attended to it.

"By the way, what did you do with my money?"

He grinned and made her breathless again. "Nothing."

Right. She let the subject drop and moved onto the matter at hand. "Did Shamus check to see if Celia or Axel laundered drug money, or got involved in human trafficking, or any other nasty things?"

"He says not," Rayder assured her around a mouthful of pickle. "And yes, he checked."

She shouldn't be this shocked, but she was. "I was joking."

"I wasn't." He gave her a steady look. "When you're dealing with extreme wealth, there's no telling where it came from."

She pondered that until the food disappeared, the ginger ale bottle was emptied. They talked and laughed over stories she told of life as a gallery owner. He spoke of some of the finest pieces of art in the world being stolen, never to be found. She was fascinated by the daring of art thieves.

"Once, I found paintings stashed in an alley. The thieves stuffed them into the office trash and the cleaners were dumping them, unaware. Once I figured it out, I hung around at night, pulled everything out of the dumpster and received a decent reward."

"What happened to the thieves?"

"I assume they went on to steal other things."

"But—"

"But what, Ellie? Why didn't I turn them in?" He raised an eyebrow at her. "Some of the most prestigious museums in the world have basements full of stolen booty. One of the finest museums in New York has several pieces they refuse to return to rightful owners. The courts are loath to prosecute the receivers of these stolen goods, yet the thieves themselves get hefty prison sentences. It may be wrong for me not to turn these guys in, but isn't it morally reprehensible to reward the men who create the market? Not everything is black and white. And justice isn't always served in the courts."

"Before this forgery threatened my gallery, I'd have disagreed with you."

"But now?"

She thought a moment. "I want to get out of this mess. I want my life back."

"And you'll forego some of your principles to get it." He said it with an understanding smile, but it hurt.

"Putting it that way seems harsh."

"No. It's human." His smile lit his eyes with a warmth she was coming to love.

But Eleanor had no answer. She was aware, of course, of the inequities in the legal system, especially when powerful men and high-profile institutions were involved. All she could do was shake her head in wonder. The conversation shifted to quirky artists and even stranger collectors. They'd each had dealings with their fair share of them.

Rayder asked about several pieces of pottery he'd seen in the gallery. Eleanor spent the rest of the time explaining how much she enjoyed working with living artists. It was much less stuffy than trying to sell the works of long-dead ones to people she didn't much like.

"So that's why Nick's been missing from the auctions in London and New York lately. You've been taking the gallery in a different direction."

"Not through choice. It's been a purely defensive decision, but I've enjoyed it." She didn't feel like explaining Nick's recent lack of interest in gallery business.

She excused herself to freshen up for the afternoon at work. When she returned to the living area, Rayder was sitting on the sofa.

She sat beside him, allowing him to take her hand in his. He squeezed her fingers and pulled them to his mouth. He planted a big, noisy, wet kiss on each knuckle, pretending to devour her hand in the process. She giggled, but arousal rose deep inside.

His eyes betrayed his yearning as he looked up into her face. "Don't go. Spend the rest of the day making love with me."

"I can't," she said doubtfully, hating to have to deny them both. "I shouldn't," she tried again, more firmly, but his tongue had started to play havoc with the tender flesh at the apex of two of her fingers. He licked her there with long, wet strokes, setting up images better left alone.

"Then at least let me kiss you before you leave," he said in a honey-sex growl that caused the aroused warmth inside her to spread wider and deeper.

"Oh," was all she could manage as he slipped one of her fingers full into his mouth and sucked hard.

He put his palm to her chin, fingers splayed up to her lips. He smiled a deep, knowing smile and slipped one long finger into her mouth. She opened for him and licked along his fingertip to his knuckle, knowing she had to stop this, knowing she was powerless for as long as he touched her.

He sucked more strongly on her finger and she moaned as he pulled her to the edge of the sofa. "I want to kiss you," he said again, setting her shoulders against the broad sofa cushions. Quickly, he knelt between her knees and reached up inside her skirt. Tugging forcefully, he took off her panties and hose.

"What are you doing?" she rasped on a panting breath. He'd completely disarmed her, filling her with wondrous heat and even more desire.

"Preparing to kiss you." He smiled slowly, a sex-stirring, slow-boiling kind of smile that oozed a promise of wild, abandoned fulfilment. She could hardly wait to see what he'd do next.

He started to unbutton her silk blouse. When he had the blouse gaping enough to unsnap her bra, he did, letting her breasts free to his seeking mouth. He kissed her royally, passionately, fervently, suckling at each hardened nipple in turn. Back and forth, back and forth, he went, nipping and sucking and making her drown in her own desire.

She reached for his belt buckle, but he slipped away from her hands. He bent his head to the soft flesh on the inside of her knee and bit her hard enough to make her flex. Then he did it to the other side.

"Did I hurt you?" he asked with concern.

She rolled her head from side to side. "No, I just can't believe what you're doing."

He smiled like the raider he was and trailed kisses closer and closer to her center.

Eleanor looked at him. Poised between her thighs, Rayder's face took on a triumphant gleam. He dipped his head and lapped at her once. He grinned like a pirate finding treasure.

She squeezed her eyes shut. The delicate, exquisite pressure of his tongue again made her lose her mind. He scraped his palm across the teased, sensitive bud of her nipple and she lost all control. Bucking against his seeking mouth and nibbling lips, she shattered into a climax she didn't know was possible.

Her skirt was shoved up to her waist, her blouse was agape, exposing her wet, flushed breasts and her legs were sprawled open. Rayder stood between her knees and looked down at her. His hair was mussed, and his eyes were wild with triumph, but other than that, nothing was out of place. His shirt was still tucked neatly into his trousers, bulging though they were, and every button that should have been buttoned, was.

Eleanor slid her palms along his hips and tugged at him. He didn't budge. "What's wrong?"

"I wanted to kiss you, and I did."

"That's all?" There was something not right here. How could he give her so much and take nothing for himself? The evidence of his desire was blatantly swollen in front of her.

He tugged her skirt down to her knees and handed back her panties. She snatched her blouse closed as she felt her face flame into embarrassed heat. "Why?"

He knelt beside her and smiled wickedly into her eyes. "We don't have time for more." With that, he helped button her blouse with fingers that trembled.

CHAPTER SEVENTEEN

WHEN ELLIE LEFT HIS place to return to the gallery, Rayder took a cold shower. He placed his palms against the wall and stretched back, letting the icy water sluice across his shoulders and down his body, doing little to cool his arousal. He'd planned on doing something over-the-top and unexpected and he had.

And he was suffering for it now. He laughed, letting the water fill his mouth.

He was six kinds of fool. He'd taken a real chance on the sofa. Ellie wasn't as experienced as most women her age. The surprise in her eyes had told him this had been another first for her.

Another first. The thought was enough to turn the icy spray to steam.

He soaped and rinsed quickly, wondering if she'd ever showered with a man. Wondering what else Ellie had yet to learn. The ideas and images he let bounce around his desire-fogged mind finally set themselves into an ordered pattern and Rayder contented himself with counting down the list, realizing he was a long way from "whupped."

He decided to thank Bruno for more than the loan of his coat. His challenge had changed Rayder's approach.

After his shower, he called Shamus. "Check into the forgery investigation from three years ago. We want to know if there was a connection to Axel Brand. If there was a network set up, find out how organized it was, and if it could have been re-activated after Axel's death."

"We?" The single word question hung in the air like a balloon, dancing with promise. Shamus chuckled quietly.

"Yes, we," Rayder retorted dryly. "Call me back with whatever you find out before four p.m. We need to figure out Celia's next move in advance."

He set his alarm clock for three hours sleep and crashed into a deep slumber as soon as he felt the soft cushion of the pillow at his head. He even dreamed he was sleeping.

BACK AT THE GALLERY, Eleanor told herself it was fair to leave Rayder in that unfortunate state of arousal, but she couldn't force herself to believe it. Even as mind-shattering as her experience had been, until she felt his weight on her and his strength inside her, something was missing.

As, she realized, he'd planned all along. This was the only way for Rayder to ensure she'd return to him for more. Rayder, the consummate con man, was trading on her innate sense of fair play.

She saw right into his scheming heart and was beginning to understand his convoluted way of thinking. Should she be scared that she could see his trail of breadcrumbs that led back to him? Probably. She wasn't sure what that said about her mind, but it was fun, too, she admitted begrudgingly.

Rayder called shortly after four p.m. "Hi," he said. His voice sent humming, thrumming messages through the line. She picked up a breadcrumb with a light sigh.

"Hi yourself."

"Any word from our intrepid investigator?"

She checked her notes. At some point she hoped to turn this mess over to the police and she'd kept track of everything.

"Celia had a dental appointment at one, then she stopped at a bakery on the way home. Nothing suspicious and no movement since. She's pretty cool for someone who's supposed to be desperate."

"I've got Shamus checking into a connection between the forgery three years ago and this one. There must be a link. Axel was wily enough to avoid being caught, but his widow may not be."

She sighed in frustration. "I feel as if we're sitting at a carnival game waiting for the row of ducks to shoot and the operator's gone home."

"Fraud investigations aren't nearly as exciting as they're shown on television, Ellie. During this waiting period try to fill your mind with other things." His voice dropped to an intimate croon that sent arrows of desire down her body. "So?" He stretched the word into a question. "Will you come back later?"

"You know I will," she said, letting the smile on her lips enter her voice. "You are getting more and more transparent every day," she teased in a sultry come-and-get-me tone.

He laughed deeply, making her temperature rise. "I'll expect you at six."

"Fine, now let me get back to work."

"Ellie?" he called her back to the receiver.

"Yes?"

"Bring a toothbrush and a change of clothes for work tomorrow. We're pulling an all-nighter." His voice sounded strange, as if he wasn't getting enough oxygen. Neither was she.

The heat of a flush rose from her toenails to her ears and she reveled in it. "All right," she said softly, stretching to flex her legs under the desk.

ELEANOR WAS IN THE showroom an hour later, rearranging the pottery pieces Rayder had admired. This Christmas shopping season was shaping up into a success, after all.

"You made good choices with these pieces, Eleanor," Anne said.

"Thank you. The artists are being well received." If her father returned from retirement, she'd take what she'd learned and create an entirely new enterprise, one devoted to living art and artists. The surprising thought immobilized her.

The Macklin Gallery was everything to her. She'd spent her life trying to live up to the expectations of the past Macklins.

Could she move on some day? Have a gallery of her own?

"That one needs a balance piece, Eleanor. Larger, I think, and about one foot to the right." Anne's sudden comment pulled Eleanor out of her reverie.

"This one?" Eleanor pointed to a bowl painted in light, translucent blasts of color. It was an interesting contrast and she loved it.

"Yes," she agreed. "I'll set it up for you. I hear your cell."

"Great. Thanks, I left it to charge on my desk." She dashed to her office. Snatching up her phone she exhaled a long breath. "Nick."

"Jack just pulled into Celia's driveway and drove around the back of the house. She's closing the heavy drapes in the living room so I can't see inside anymore."

The telephone on Anne's desk rang and she heard Anne answer.

"I wish we could hear what Celia and Jack were talking about." Eleanor said to Nick. "If they leave, follow them and call me as soon as you can."

The intercom buzzed. "Hold on, Nick, Anne's buzzing through. It must be important."

"Sorry, Eleanor, but it's Celia Brand on the line. Will you take the call?" Anne asked.

"I'll take it," Eleanor agreed, a spear of excitement shooting into her voice. She returned to Nick. "Celia's on the other line. Hold on while I talk to her." Her heart rate sped up.

Eleanor took a deep breath spiked with adrenaline. Was this the misstep they were hoping for from the widow? Eleanor answered the call. "Celia." she said breezily. "What can I do for you?"

"Is Nick back yet?" Celia's tone was brisk and businesslike. Had she seen Nick watching her home? If she had, what game was she playing?

"Nick should be home in a few days," Eleanor replied slowly, to stall for time to think. But it was no good, thoughts and images ricocheted back and forth.

"This is ridiculous," Celia said testily.

Eleanor could only agree, but she said nothing as her mind slowly cleared. During the pause she recalled one of her father's negotiating tactics. He'd taught her that the first one who speaks, loses. So, she waited.

Celia sighed, clearly put out. "I want my entire collection returned to me before noon tomorrow."

"You do realize that the Lady Emma has still not been returned to us? The repairs–"

"Yes, I know," Celia snapped.

Bingo. Eleanor held her breath. *There it was.* Celia's slip of the tongue spoke volumes. Celia had admitted that she knew the Emma Hamilton miniature hadn't been returned to the gallery yet. Eleanor couldn't see how to make the widow admit to knowing where the miniature was. Still, this was good news.

"That is," Celia amended, "I'd hoped you'd have it back by now."

Too late to retract. We've got you.

"The work hasn't even begun, I'm sorry to say." Eleanor cleared her throat to hide her elation.

Celia had blundered badly. Rayder had been right about Celia and Jack. Obviously, they'd decided to make a move. If only Eleanor could figure out what it was. Were they leaving the city together? Or was this a one-time partnership? *Copy the miniature, sell it as the real thing, and keep the original to sell again later.* Maybe. Maybe the pair wanted to do the same with the whole Brand collection?

"I'm extremely disappointed," Celia said harshly. "Ray Cole is the only nibble I've had on that collection and I don't want him to lose interest."

"I'm sure Mr. Cole be willing to wait a while longer," she suggested. "If you'd like, I'll talk to him myself. Surely, I can persuade him that waiting a few days will be worth his while." Nick was so much better at this type of cajoling than she was. "Especially if I tell him other people would be interested in a collection of such importance."

"I still want the rest of the collection by noon tomorrow." Celia's voice came through the line like a whip. "And don't think people won't hear of this botch of yours. People have long memories. Three years ago seems like yesterday."

Eleanor jerked in response to the implicit threat.

"Of course, Celia," she said quietly, to let the widow think she'd been cowed into submission. "I'll take care of it." They said goodbye amicably enough, but Eleanor put the receiver down with too much force.

She picked up her cell phone and told Nick what Celia had said. "Call her and let her know you're home. Sweet talk her and see if you can get her to let anything else slip. Anything at all."

"I'll wait for this evening. It will look suspicious if I call right now."

She agreed. "You can pretend you just got in and are unaware of everything that's happened. You'll get an earful of complaints about me but try to get a clue what her next move will be. Whatever it is, it'll happen tomorrow after she comes for the rest of the collection."

She called Rayder as soon as she could, unwilling to wait until she saw him at six. When he answered her call, her mind flashed to those shattering moments at his place earlier. But she had to turn away from those memories and fill him in. Business was business.

"Nick's calling Celia later and pretending he just returned. When she and I spoke, Celia let it slip that she knew the miniature hadn't been returned to us. Then she tried to retract."

"This is coming to a close faster than I hoped," Rayder responded. "Shamus called with information on the European connection. I'll fill you in when you get here."

On the short drive to Rayder's apartment, Eleanor came to terms with the idea that this merry-go-round would soon end. She would get her wish and return to her usual, busy life. Solitary and work-focused, her life would be what she'd become accustomed to. The life she enjoyed.

Nick would admit he needed more fulfilling work, and in time, her parents would accept her brother's decision. All these changes seemed poised to shift into high gear and take on a life of their own. Her confidence soared that she, Nick, and Rayder would come out of this unscathed. Celia and Jack would be the ones burned by their own greed.

Rayder—she felt a sharp stab of anguish at the thought of saying goodbye—would return to the life he clearly loved. International travel, exotic women vying for his attention, the excitement of tracking down stolen booty and outwitting art thieves, could never hold a candle to a dull life with her. It might be selfish, but she wanted to fill her remaining time with him with glorious memories.

She'd wasted too many years hating him. For all the years to come, she'd prefer to dwell on good times when her mind turned to Rayder Cole.

She parked and he opened his door as she climbed the stairs to his apartment. He must have been watching for her. As she neared him, she saw that his bloodshot eyes had cleared, but he still looked overtired. He was in jeans and his shirt hung open. His feet were bare.

"You'll catch cold like that," she admonished, rising to the landing to stand in front of him.

"Then you'll have to warm me," he said, pulling her into the apartment and into a bear hug. He kicked the door closed. Flushing with pent up sexual energy, she wallowed in his hug, enjoying the length of his body against hers. "Too many clothes," he muttered, and helped her out of her coat.

When she dropped her purse on the floor, he frowned. "You didn't bring a bag for the morning."

"It's in the car. I forgot it." The lie sat awkwardly on her tongue, but the truth was, she didn't want to fall asleep in his arms. Spending the night with Rayder would only be courting hurt and more disillusionment.

He didn't seem to notice her lie because he grinned and draped his warm palms on her hips. He tugged her tight to his pelvis and she fell, fully, willingly, into Rayder's appeal.

"You took forever to get here," he murmured next to her ear, nibbling and kissing her along her hairline. His arousal pressed against her and he growled into her hair. "I'm sorry, Ellie, I need you now. Right now."

"I couldn't have said it better myself," she whispered on a groan.

HOURS' WORTH OF REPRESSED arousal welled through Rayder as he half pushed, half carried Ellie to the sofa. He delighted at the flush in her cheeks when she looked at where they'd spent their last moments together earlier today. He remembered in full, vivid detail how she'd responded to him. She'd been so damn beautiful; flushed, sated, wrung out from the climax he'd given her. Seeing her splayed open, melting from the inside had played through his mind since she'd left. Desire and need destroyed whatever control he had.

"Oh, my," she said on a sigh when she realized his intent. Her eyes widened and her lips, soft and full, parted for his kiss. Heaven would taste like this.

He sat on the sofa and pulled her down onto his lap. Desire rose like heated mercury as Rayder stroked and kissed her, his Ellie. The banked fire of his need burst into flame as she allowed the kisses to become more volatile. They sank down into the cushions, aware only of each other and the inferno between them.

CHAPTER EIGHTEEN

RAYDER REACHED UNDER Ellie's skirt and tugged her hose and panties off. In a ragged effort to control his need, he held her away from him. "I can't wait," he warned her in a guttural voice. "I've wanted you all day." Every day since he'd first seen her in that parking garage.

She undid the fly of his jeans, her knuckles brushing against his low belly. He gasped at her heated touch. Her fingers were featherlight and quick. He must've been out of his mind to let her leave today without completing.

"You don't have to wait an extra minute," she promised. His erection was so full she had difficulty freeing him, each brush at the denim a painfully sweet ecstasy. With a growl, he shucked his jeans to his knees, and she settled over him, cradling his shaft against her. She held still, letting the sensations they shared multiply tenfold. Her wet heat dragged against his hard flesh.

He protected them quickly, with hands that trembled. He gritted his teeth against the rush.

While he worked, her fingertips brushed his temples, the side of his face, and then tipped into his mouth. She lapped at his tongue and settled onto his mouth for a deep, erotic kiss. She willingly gave whatever he sought, whatever he wanted, as he groaned against her and held her with arms that shook.

He needed and she gave.

Rayder bucked hard against her in silent tribute to the loving that would come. Ellie cradled him and urged him on with unsteady hands. She moved with him, pleaded with him, reached for him, and rose up so he could press into her. She slid down all the way, drawing a hoarse cry from his throat.

Rayder bucked into her deeply, heard her sharp intake of breath at the ferocity of his thrust. Carried beyond endurance, he spilled into her, suddenly and completely, pulsing with release. "I'm sorry, sorry, sorry," he crooned as she cradled his head between her breasts.

"That'll teach you that loving should be reciprocal," she said tartly. "Denying yourself this morning was foolish." Ellie softened her teasing words with a nibble on his earlobe. "My turn will come."

"You can bet on it." His voice sounded dark as smoke, but that was how he felt.

ELEANOR FRAMED RAYDER'S face with gentle hands and fell totally, irrevocably in love. "I'll keep coming back until you leave," she promised him. She bit her lip. He'd leave and she'd miss him. And love him. And always, always, remember him.

He searched her gaze, his own a study in affectionate tenderness. "Can we go to bed now?" he asked, trying to gather her in his arms and sit up at the same time. "This sofa's fun but the bed's a whole lot bigger. And we've got some serious love to make."

"Yes, yes we do," she agreed urgently. "But do we have time? With Celia and Jack moving things along..."

"She said noon tomorrow. We've got all night. Besides, I won't get my fill of you even with all these hours to fill."

She smiled. "I feel the same way. Like we're kids again."

"But Nick will need to be relieved. Call him to find out when he'll need a break. Between now and then, we stay here."

She nodded and got her phone out of her purse. "How goes it?" she asked when he answered on the first ring.

"I rented a car for this. I don't want her seeing the same vehicle two nights in a row."

Rayder hitched up his pants and straightened the rest of his clothing while Eleanor flushed hot, remembering the feel of his bare flesh against her. She forgot to speak.

"There's nothing going on, it's quiet as a tomb." Nick broke through to her. "I doubt they're going anywhere tonight."

"Do you need me to spell you?"

"You could bring me a burger later."

"Okay, I'll be there in a couple of hours," she responded hastily. "I'll take a turn there while you have a break."

"Sounds good. Wait. It looks like they've got a food delivery coming in. Yeah, I guess they're not going anywhere."

"At least not for dinner," she said. "See you later." She hung up. "We've got a couple of hours."

"Great. You take the evening shift, then when Nick returns, I'll be waiting here for you."

Waiting for her. That sounded nice, however unlikely a shared future with him would be.

They undressed and snuggled under the covers, legs and arms intertwined. Their faces inches apart they studied each other until Eleanor giggled and Rayder grinned. The urgency between them had been unyielding earlier. In the aftermath, their release made things easy between them and she found it amusing.

Rayder crossed his eyes and stuck out his tongue. He might be the most sophisticated man she knew, but he had a goofy kid living inside him, too.

"Stop," she said between breathless giggles. "Sex is serious business," she intoned with mock severity, raising an eyebrow.

"Yes, it is," he agreed solemnly. "Ellie, I need to tell you—there's so much—"

She cut him off with two fingers at his lips. "No, Rayder, please—not yet—not now. This will take some getting used to, for both of us. And we have no idea what's going to become of us. Let's neither of us say anything we'll regret, happy or sad. Deal?"

"Deal," he said, disappointment darkening his eyes.

"Now, what's this European connection Shamus told you about," she asked, determined to talk about something less threatening than their romantic future. "Interpol suspects the forger they charged three years ago knows a good deal more than he's saying, but he's refusing to implicate any others in the scheme. So far, they've concluded that the copies were made of *stolen* masterpieces."

"The reason being?"

"Owning stolen art, these people and institutions are perfect crime victims. Criminals themselves, who could they complain to?"

"The simplicity is flawless." Despite her abhorrence of the crime, she had to admire the ingenuity. "You said 'copies', there were more than one?"

He nodded. "And more than one forger, apparently. It's an intricately woven network of forgers, each a specialist in his field."

Eleanor was shocked. "A network? This is much bigger than I thought." The implications were astounding.

"With Axel knowing so many semi-honest collectors, he'd have known who would make the best victims." Rayder's voice was soft as he sank into thought.

"Yes," Eleanor mused. "Even worse, they'd need an inside man in Interpol to have the investigation stall for this long," she suggested. That idea worried her. He tugged her closer. "How will we ever get clear of this?" she whispered.

Rayder looked lost in thought as she waited. His brows furrowed and he frowned more deeply.

"What is it?" she asked, growing alarmed.

He looked at her, understanding dawning. "Not what, who? Who is it in Interpol? Who is the inside man? Ellie, can you recall who was in charge of the investigation three years ago?"

"I can't remember, we talked to a slew of detectives, including some local men. I don't know who was really in charge."

"Shaughnessy. I'd bet my life on it."

A swell of excitement came over her when she heard the name. "That's it. I did speak to a man named Shaughnessy. He was arrogant and tried to bully me, said he'd be waiting for me to slip up."

"He's the reason the forger won't talk. How could he tell what he knew when one of the conspirators is the guy questioning him?"

"You believe Shaughnessy is involved in this now?"

"Why not? This whole set up probably started with Axel, but Celia still has a collection that's worth millions. Why would a forgery ring fall apart just because one of them died?"

"You're saying even the police are in on it."

"Just Shaughnessy. He's a bastard and if he knows I'm anywhere around he'll do his best to bury me."

"Let me guess, he was unhappy when you shifted the investigation to his own forger when he could have sent me and my brother to jail. You interfered."

"I wondered why he went from vague dislike to hating me. Things suddenly turned personal after I blew up his phony investigation. He's pulled some sleazy stunts over the years. Helped himself to some nice pieces when he thought no one would know, but I never indicated I was aware. Like I said, I don't catch criminals. My only interest is in retrieving what's lost."

"With a little luck, you can start catching bad guys now."

He rolled his eyes. "I suppose you want me to go completely legit and turn vigilante." He sighed theatrically. "Over stolen art?"

"Could you hide the fact that it's you? Would you be satisfied with that?"

He groaned. "Ellie, my work's a fine line between catching crooks and getting back stolen property, no questions asked."

She looked at him steadily.

He sighed. "I'll think about it," he promised. "If I'm going to turn in bad guys, the first one I'd like to send to jail is Shaughnessy." He nodded. "Yeah, I'd like that. I've always seen Interpol as simply doing the job, with nothing personal at stake. But this is different. Shaughnessy wanted to send you to jail three years ago and I ruined his plans."

"He must have been furious. How can we fight against a professional like him? He has even more contacts and support than you do."

Rayder considered her comments. After a moment he spoke. "By putting the focus on Celia. She's not Axel. She doesn't have his skill, experience or wiles. She's scared and desperate." Rayder lifted Ellie's chin to see into her face. "Celia will make a mistake and when she does," he snapped his fingers, "we'll be there."

"But first, check in with your uncle. Maybe he can find out more about what Shaughnessy is up to. Do you know where he is?"

"Shamus can find out in minutes." He called his uncle.

While he talked with Shamus, Eleanor fretted. Depending on someone else grated. She was used to being in charge and coping with whatever came up in her gallery. In her life. But now, she was dependent on an old man in London and a former con man to get her life back on track.

When Rayder hung up, she realized they would have to wait. Again. "But doesn't waiting this way leave too much to fate? Can't we *do* something?"

"I've told Celia I have people interested in buying other pieces," he said after a thoughtful pause. "I could up the stakes for her."

"You want to con her?" The idea held delicious merit. Despite having been conned herself, conning Celia wasn't the same. Celia was in the thick of a conspiracy to defraud museums and honest collectors while Eleanor had been a naïve college freshman.

"We don't have to make any move. We can go on waiting." He studied her, holding her gaze, his blue eyes calm and measuring. "Or you could trust me."

"What's your idea? Because I'm sure it's more than another white lie." She pulled herself up to a full sitting position with her shoulders against the headboard.

"Greed," he explained, "is the essential ingredient in any scam. Without a greedy mark most con jobs are doomed to fail."

She snorted. "I wasn't greedy," she pointed out.

"Not for money, no. But there was something you wanted very badly, and I gave it to you."

Eleanor pursed her lips. *Love. Respect.* Those were things Rayder had given her ten years ago. He'd given her what she wanted more than anything else, so she allowed him to take her money.

"Celia's avarice is clear, and it's the only thing we have to bank on."

"So," she said, wanting to understand the psychology better, "even you would not have been conned into buying the phony miniature if a part of you hadn't been greedy for the reward money."

"Right. I got sloppy, choosing to see what I wanted to see because it was expedient to my business. And then when I found out you and your brother were involved," Rayder said, "I wondered if this was a twisted plot to exact revenge."

Surprised, she frowned at him. "What? I had no idea where you were or what you were doing now." She'd assumed he'd fallen into the abyss of crime, never to be seen again. Or he was in prison for fraud.

He shrugged. "I decided you'd like to see me suffer."

"You assumed I set you and Shamus up?" Dismay rose into the slow burn of affront. She shifted away from him in the bed. "How dare you think I'd want such a vicious revenge."

He made a guilty face.

"Maybe drizzled in honey and tied down over an ant hill," she allowed, warming to the subject, "maybe telling your girlfriends you had a contagious disease. Or seeing you with your pants down in a restaurant while the other patrons laughed and pointed, but, never, never, would I try to ruin you."

"Do you want to see me with my pants down?" He grinned lasciviously and waggled his eyebrows at her. "And would you laugh and point?"

Eleanor struggled against a smile and lost. "Under the circumstances," she lifted the blankets and admired the view, "I wouldn't laugh and point." He reached for her and tugged her beneath him. His powerful, steady heartbeat soothed her as she raised her face to his.

"That's better," he murmured as he dipped his head for a kiss.

A long time later, after a loving that left them breathless and sated, Eleanor and Rayder shared a cramped shower in the apartment's small bathroom. Amazed by all the wonderful things two people could do in a shower, she hardly noticed when the hot water ran out.

Towel drying her hair, she wandered out into the main living area and found Rayder already chopping vegetables for a stir-fry at the tiny kitchen counter. "I can do this in any kind of pan, in any kind of kitchen, with any kind of oil. Living the way I do, cooking has to be flexible especially when I don't have much opportunity." He passed her a knife and she started to chop broccoli.

"This will be wonderful. I'm starved," she said over a rumbling stomach. "Is there enough to take to Nick?"

"Sure." He glanced at the clock. "But you said he asked for a burger." He checked his phone. "You'll have to leave soon; the two hours are almost up."

"I've got work to do while I'm watching Celia's house. My laptop's in my car."

He nodded and frowned. "Bring in your laptop and your overnight bag when you come back. You are staying the night?"

She hesitated, not wanting to spoil the warm fuzzies between them. "Don't push me, Rayder. I can't promise I'll stay overnight." No more than he could promise to stay with her when this was over, and his life was calling.

He opened his mouth to speak but closed it again with a sad smile. "Okay. *If* you return, I'll be grateful. But no pressure."

Thankfully, he let the subject drop and they enjoyed a quiet meal together.

An hour after she took over from her brother, she looked up from her laptop to see a woman walk past Celia's house with a dog on a leash. She closed the lid to hide the light and lowered herself into the seat keeping her eyes at window level.

The little dog sniffed and watered a pillar that stood at the front of the driveway. The woman looked across the road and straight at Eleanor's car. Two long seconds later the dog pulled ahead, and the woman resumed her stroll.

Eleanor eased out a breath but kept her head down and her laptop off. Her phone rang, making her nerves jangle. The display read 'Private Caller', so she assumed it was Rayder.

"Hello."

"Is this little Ellie Macklin?" A gruff male voice asked.

"Shamus?" Surprised and delighted at hearing the old man's voice, she asked how he was.

"Fine, girl. Just fine. I see you're making yourself useful." At his words, she glanced around the quiet street, wondering if he could actually see her.

"I'm watching Celia's house right now. Although, we doubt she's doing anything tonight."

"I know. I said I see you're making yourself useful."

She processed his comment. "The woman walking the dog?"

"An old friend."

She shivered in reaction. "Rayder told me you have a lot of contacts."

"My nephew called earlier wanting some information. I'm calling you with it."

"Right," she said with a nod. "Have you learned where Shaughnessy is?"

Shamus chuckled. "I was wondering how much my nephew told you. Obviously, he's told you everything."

She laughed at the obvious lie. "I suppose he has." Rayder would never tell her everything.

"Shaughnessy is in Kyoto, sniffing at your brother's trail. Shaughnessy's a bloodhound. And this time he's out to get you."

SOMETIME AFTER THREE a.m., Rayder felt Eleanor shift away from him in the bed. It dipped and moved as she got up. He opened one eye and watched her. She stood by the dresser, her hand on the pile of clothes she'd left there. Her hair caught the faint luminescence from the moon filtering in through a crack in the curtain. Her back, long and straight, flared into well-shaped hips. His response was raw and immediate. If she left now, he may never have another opportunity to let her know.

"Ellie, come back to bed," he said, his voice a rough-hewn plea.

She turned her head and looked over her shoulder at him. She smiled shyly, her eyes sad pools. "I thought I wanted to go home."

"Why? It's cold and I've spent too many nights without you." He lifted the blanket in invitation. She'd come back to him upset and frightened after talking with Shamus.

"It's silly, but deep down I have this fear that if I go to sleep, I'll wake up and you'll be gone," she said in a broken whisper. She walked closer and perched on the end of the bed.

He'd left her sleeping that afternoon so long ago. He recalled watching her, soft and warm, snuggled under the sheets. Trusting, sweet, Ellie who'd just given him five thousand dollars and her virginity.

She searched his gaze, no longer trusting, but still sweet as honey. "You said earlier that greed is an essential part of a con game. What was I greedy for?"

Her steady directness disconcerted him. *Love.* She'd wanted love. The tragedy was that he'd been too young to appreciate that he had it to give her. He'd loved her then, but he'd also wanted to prove himself to his family. He'd let his family win but had ended up losing them anyway when conning Ellie had changed him.

"Come back to bed," he coaxed. "Otherwise, you'll never know if I'll still be here in the morning. Come back to bed, Ellie, and let me love your fear away."

She shivered in the cool night air.

He scooted to the end of the bed and gathered her in his arms. She clung to him. "Don't worry about Shaughnessy, I won't let him near you or Nick."

"It's not him I'm afraid of. I'm afraid of myself, mostly, and you, a little."

"You're afraid because you don't want me to hurt you again," he guessed. "I can't believe you've given me the power to hurt you."

She sniffed and nodded into his shoulder. "I can hardly believe it, either."

"I won't leave you, Ellie. Not tomorrow, not the next day. Not ever." He guided her up the bed and cocooned with her in the warmth.

"When this mess is cleared up, one way or the other, we'll work out a solution. We'll be together," he promised.

"How? You're based in Europe and I can't move the gallery." She rested her head over his heart and tucked her leg between his.

"I can change my base to here, maybe help out at the gallery." He tilted her chin up so he could see her expression. Her beautiful face held a blend of caution and tenderness. He decided to tease the caution away. "That is, if you'll let me take some early flights before you wake up."

She grinned and tweaked his nipple between her thumb and forefinger.

"Ouch. You wound me, woman." He growled and tossed her onto her back. "For that you must suffer."

"How?" She laughed, low and seductively, causing an immediate leap in his heart rate.

He settled his lips on her nipple and suckled hard. "Like this." He entered her in one bold thrust. "And like this."

IN THE AFTERMATH, ELEANOR wasn't surprised to find Rayder in bed beside her early the next morning. They decided to go to her place immediately so she could change for work. "And to think I could have had my clothes with me," she muttered as she hurriedly dressed in yesterday's outfit.

The drive to her building went by quickly. Traffic was lighter at this time of the morning.

"I'll pick up breakfast while you're getting ready for work," Rayder offered as they stepped into the elevator from the parking garage. He held up a long wool coat. "I'll return Bruno's coat to him before he goes off shift."

She made a mental note to get Rayder's coat out of her hall closet so he wouldn't forget it again. "I found one of your socks," she said around a chuckle. He gave her a sly wink, and a kiss on the cheek, then exited the elevator.

Twenty minutes later, her doorbell rang, and Eleanor looked through the security viewer and saw Rayder holding up a white bag bearing the logo of a popular bakery.

She opened the door. Mouth-watering smells emanated from the bakery bag. "What did you bring me?" She waved him in.

"Fresh bagels." He grinned and kissed her cheek. "Mm, you smell like flowers and Ellie," he said into her ear. Then he headed past her into the kitchen.

"Help yourself to coffee while I finish my hair," she said, hurrying to the bathroom for the hair clasp she'd left there. She got his coat out of the hall closet on her way by and draped it over a kitchen chair.

Rayder cut an intriguing figure as he opened and closed her cupboards. His hair, sweeping the bottom of his collar, shone blue-black against the dull sheen of his black silk shirt. "Butter?" he asked when she came up behind him.

"Soft is on the table, cold is in the fridge. You'll find cream cheese on the second shelf." She settled into a chair with a cup of coffee and watched him. Tall and lean, he made the kitchen seem too small. He still carried a faint scent of the outdoors with him. Eleanor propped her chin on her fist and watched his strong, capable hands cut the bagels and slather them with butter and cream cheese. "This is nice," she said softly.

"What is?" He looked up from what he was doing, pinning her with his direct blue gaze, but he knew what she meant. The glitter of enjoyment in his eyes told her so.

"Having you here, like this," she told him anyway. The details of their future were uncertain but their commitment to each other was everything she could ask for. Although he hadn't said the words that would bind him to her, she knew he loved her.

The doorbell rang again. Sorry they'd have even a short interruption; she muttered a curse. She went to the door and saw her brother through the security viewer.

"Nick." She opened the door. "What are you doing here? Where's Celia?"

"Getting some kind of weird thing done to her hair. She's got these tinfoil thingies stuck in it and she looks like something out of an alien movie. I called and asked how long a procedure like that would take. I've got lots of time for breakfast. She's not going anywhere looking like that."

Eleanor laughed.

Rayder frowned. "Why didn't I think of that when she had me chasing all over town with her? I sat in a coffee shop across the street while she got ready for the Ryan's fundraiser."

At Rayder's words, Nick's warm brown gaze went past her toward the kitchen, landed on Rayder and cooled to a chill.

She turned, tracking her brother's gaze and frowned. Rayder leaned negligently against the kitchen doorway, looking as if he'd spent the night. A stubble of beard shadowed his cheeks and his eyes glinted with humor. He knew how this looked to Nick and he didn't care.

Rayder inclined his head slightly but said nothing. Nick stared, sizing Rayder up, weighing and judging, taking in the cut of his suit, the quality of his silk shirt. He shifted his gaze to Eleanor, encompassing her from the top of her head to her feet.

"Rayder brought breakfast over." She felt the heat of a flush to her hairline. "This morning," she finished lamely.

"Great. I'm starved," Nick said blandly. He pushed past Rayder and went into the kitchen. His lips quirked into a grin when he saw Rayder's coat hanging over the back of a chair.

"Great." he said again, more easily. He poured himself a cup of coffee. Then he grabbed Eleanor's bagel and took a good-sized bite out of it. "Thanks, El," he said with a grin.

Eleanor hadn't realized Nick would be eye to eye with Rayder. They were the same height. And she'd forgotten how wide her brother's shoulders were. That's where the similarity ended.

Nick's eyes were warm brown and no match for Rayder's icy blue. Nick's usually friendly face encouraged trust and friendship.

Unless her brother was crossed. She'd never seen a man imitate a cyclone better than Nick. Slow to anger, he boiled rage like a cauldron when he had reason. She hoped Rayder never gave him reason.

"Rayder Cole." Nick broke the silence. "I've heard a lot about you." His eyes remained hard. Not a good sign.

She glanced at Rayder. He put on his most disdainful expression and sat in one of her kitchen chairs. "Sat" wasn't quite the word, she thought, "sprawled" or "lounged" would be better. That wasn't a good sign, either.

He waved for her to sit down in the only other chair in the room. Rayder was saying in his own insolent way that he had every right to lounge in her chairs, drink her coffee, bring her breakfast, and know what was in her cupboards.

She tidied his coat before sitting across from him at her round breakfast table.

"And what have you heard?" Rayder asked Nick with an edge in his voice most people would take for a warning.

Nick smirked. "You're the best," he replied.

Rayder's eyes flashed surprise.

Nick grinned at Eleanor, obviously scoring one for himself. She sighed dramatically. She'd never understood the male need to keep score.

"You've tracked down stuff that's been a cold trail for years," her brother said. "Even back as far as loot from World War Two." Nick swirled the coffee in his cup. He looked at Rayder quizzically. "No one's sure how you do it."

Rayder glanced at Eleanor and winked. "It's a gift," he said. "A sixth sense."

Eleanor laughed out loud. "Baloney. It's his uncle, Shamus Cole. He's a wily old con man who knows everything and everyone and if he doesn't, he knows someone who does. He pulls in favors, does research and knows names." She'd learned that herself a few hours ago.

Rayder shrugged. "Anyone with connections could do what Shamus and I do."

"Shamus Cole," Nick said with a nod. "Spent time in jail about ten years ago. Had a stroke and got released on early parole." He glanced at Eleanor. "Since he'd never been violent, they figured a sick old man wasn't much of a threat to society," he explained, surprising her with how much private information he'd gathered.

Rayder scowled but looked impressed. "My uncle has never been dangerous. He crossed the wrong man. A well-connected contractor using substandard material in a seniors complex got taken for a nice sum." Rayder shrugged. "The seniors got the therapeutic whirlpool they'd been promised. Shamus got jail."

Nick grinned ironically. "The con man with a heart of gold."

Rayder's lip curled in a grimace and his glance caught Eleanor's. "Something like that." He looked back to her brother. "I've got a plan to turn this waiting game of Celia's to our advantage."

Nick grinned and the tension dissipated like fog in the early morning sun. "Fire away," he said and reached for another bagel.

CHAPTER NINETEEN

STANDING IN NICK'S office, Rayder watched Ellie stare at a portrait of an old man in a pinstriped suit, wearing spats. One of the great-grandfathers, he guessed. Sour-looking old cuss.

Shamus had considered Nick a minor nuisance. At best, an eager amateur. His uncle had underestimated the younger brother. Nick was quick and wary with a well-hidden street edge that made Rayder wonder if he'd inherited his traits from these old men.

He turned his mind back to business, which consisted of talking to Celia on the phone. She was still at the hair salon. Raucous female laughter added to the sound of running water in the background.

Rayder needed to soothe Celia. "My client is prepared to make you an offer on the collection providing you include the Lady Emma," he said. "He's adamant about having the entire collection."

"Of course, I'll include it," Celia snapped.

"Oh?" His heart rate quickened at her admission. "You got it back from the Macklin Gallery?"

"Yes. It looks wonderful."

"So, the collection's intact?"

"I said it was," her impatience put an edge on the words.

"Fine, then I expect to have the details of the offer emailed to me shortly. I'll firm up by two p.m."

"Surely you can move faster than that. You've already been here for days." Celia's petulant voice scraped his spine.

"There is the time difference to consider," Rayder said smoothly, unmoved by her impatience. "The banks in France are ready to close for the day. We'll have this cleared up tomorrow at the latest." If she and

Jack had plans to flee, this new, unexpected promise of further wealth should keep them in the city.

"Oh, very well," she snarled. "Don't be late."

When Rayder hung up, both Nick and Ellie slapped their palms to his in a high five. They all smiled and exchanged looks, pleased with the plan.

Then Nick called Celia using his cell phone on speaker so Ellie and Rayder could hear. "Celia? Nick Macklin here. My sister tells me you've been looking for me."

"Where the hell have you been? I want my Lady Emma back. I have a buyer for the entire collection and he's due to meet me at two."

Nick gave Rayder and Eleanor a thumbs up. "Then I suppose I'd best find Jack and get that piece back for you. I wouldn't want you to lose out on a sale. But didn't my sister tell you we expect to make a killing with that collection at Sotheby's?"

"I can't wait until then. I need the money now."

"You said the buying agent's meeting you at two."

She hesitated. After a moment, she said, "Yes."

"I'll be there as soon as I collect the Lady Emma from Jack Burke."

"Fine," Celia snapped. She disconnected the call.

Nick laughed. "She's done it. If I testify that Jack had the miniature and I had no idea where he'd taken it, and Rayder buys the entire collection, we've got her. She's the one who will be caught. We'll all be in the clear."

"You'd best get back to that hair salon, Nick," Rayder said. "And make note of everywhere she goes for the rest of the morning."

"I will."

"I promised myself I'd keep the regular work of the gallery moving ahead," Eleanor said as she headed for the connecting door to her office. "I'll get things done while I'm waiting."

Rayder watched Ellie leave Nick's office and hoped to get a few moments alone with her before he left. But Nick looked coolly at him and indicated he should take a seat. Nick settled behind his desk, looking stern.

"Before I go," Nick said, "what's going on with you and my sister?" Nick stared at him, taking his measure. Macklin was likely coming to conclusions Rayder wouldn't like. Dressed in casual slacks and a brown leather jacket, Macklin slouched in his chair. He looked like an insouciant big cat, more interested in idle contemplation than fact.

Rayder wasn't fooled. "What has she told you?"

Nick's brown eyes narrowed. "Nothing. That's just it. Eleanor doesn't let men bring her breakfast, even if it is the day of and not because of the night before." Nick watched him closely and the skin on the back of Rayder's neck itched. While Nick's body hadn't shifted one iota, his demeanor changed. He was now a big cat on alert. Dangerous, watchful. Lethal.

"I love her." The words were simple and yet complicated, filled with more history than Nick would ever know. "I always have."

Nick frowned deeply. "You knew her before?" He sounded doubtful, but interest and concern filled his gaze. At Rayder's nod, Nick tilted his head. "At university," he guessed. It was a statement rather than a question.

Confession time. "I messed up in a big way. I left her. But I loved her more than I realized. I was young. Stupid with a capital S."

Nick nodded. "I always wondered what brought her home, but she never said. I gave up pushing. Yeah, well, what do you plan to do about it now?"

"Marry her."

The grin that split Nick's face was contagious and Rayder beamed back at him. It felt damn good to say it out loud.

"All right." Nick jumped up from his seat, confirming Rayder's suspicions. Macklin was a man of fast rebound and even faster reflexes. He clapped Rayder on the back and shook his hand.

"Maybe Ellie should go along to keep you under control," Rayder said. But he felt his chest expand and relax. He'd been tense without realizing it. "You look about to burst. This is serious business, Macklin. If you tip our hand, there's no telling what will happen."

"Don't worry about me, I'll be fine." But his grin looked mischievous and Rayder wondered how Ellie managed a brother with this much rabid enthusiasm. But from what she'd said, he'd been losing interest in the family business. He wondered how she managed that, too.

"Play it cool," he instructed, "as if the only thing you know is that Celia's been chomping at the bit for your return. Remember, she doesn't know we're in touch with each other. She doesn't know about Ellie and me, either."

Macklin nodded thoughtfully.

Rayder continued when he saw Macklin's focused expression. "Celia believes I'm a buying agent representing an unknown collector in Europe. You're the gallery owner storing her collection. *Simple.* Get her to sign a release for the missing piece, stating that she'll take delivery when it's returned from cleaning."

Nick nodded. "Anne's printing one up now."

"Good, then we're set."

Nick ducked his head into his sister's office to tell her he was leaving. Rayder followed and after Nick left, he leaned in, planning to offer a simple word of encouragement but he caught a look of stark terror in her eyes.

"Oh, Rayder, what if something goes wrong?"

He shrugged. "We'll come up with something else. We've already uncovered enough to put the spotlight on Celia and Jack."

She leaned back in her chair, looking lost and forlorn. "I'll still lose the gallery." Her hair splayed along the headrest of the chair, reminding him of the way he'd caught it in his hands when they'd made love the evening before.

"No, you won't. I promise you." He kicked the office door closed behind him and drew her to her feet. He held her and felt his world shift as he realized how deeply he needed her. "I want to make up for all the years of pain I caused you."

He wanted to share what he'd told Nick about loving her, but until this problem was behind them, he didn't have the right to speak about a future with her.

"I understand you thought that was what you were doing three years ago and that helps a lot." She sighed. "And now I have to work, or I'll lose what's left of my mind."

"I'll help with anything. Tell me what to do." He figured he could get a jump on how the gallery ran for future reference.

NICK RETURNED A COUPLE of hours later from his meeting with Celia. He breezed into the gallery with his arms held wide, looking every inch the carnival barker. Eleanor sighed at his carefree expression. "How goes the battle?" he asked blithely. "Nerves stretched to the breaking point?"

Eleanor huffed and led both Rayder and Nick into her office. "You could say that. How did it go?"

"First of all, she ran more errands, like she had all the time in the world. When she finally headed home, I waited about fifteen minutes before calling her to say I had the collection and I'd be right over."

"And?" Rayder asked as a nerve jumped in his jaw. It was the only indicator of his impatience. He'd been a big help shifting displays. He'd done the work that had been set aside when Nick left for Japan. It had been nice watching his muscles bunch and work with the heavier pieces. She and Anne had shared some smiles over that.

"And I was great," her brother replied to Rayder's brusque question. "Fantastic! I had her eating out of the palm of my hand," he announced with no shadow of modesty to interrupt the flow of words.

"You're a natural," Eleanor drawled. "Now get to the point."

Rayder's sharp glance made her wonder what she'd said to spark the look. "Keep talking, Nick," he said, "I want to hear it all." He sat on a chair in Eleanor's office, intent on her brother.

"I walked in with the collection and she practically grabbed it out of my hands. Then she checked every item against an inventory list she had and signed for the delivery."

"Did she balk at noting the missing piece?"

"Yeah, she did, but I handled it. She said she was curious why we'd be so careful now when we'd been lax in keeping the piece secured before. I told her Jack Burke was in possession of the miniature and that he was a slow, meticulous man. I acted as if everything was going smoothly with the frame repairs. What could she do, call me a liar?"

Eleanor shrugged. Nick fairly hummed with adrenaline. He was so hyped she could feel it from five feet away. She and Rayder exchanged glances and waited for Nick to continue.

"She gave a good performance. I said what you told me to say, Rayder: that we were protecting her investment and by noting the missing piece, she could prove we hadn't returned the Lady Emma yet. She didn't seem to like it much, but she signed. There were a couple of sweaty moments, though."

"Excellent. You did well, Nick." Rayder nodded, as if he knew exactly what it felt like to live through those sweaty moments. "By signing that the piece was not returned and then selling it to me at two p.m. today, Celia will be admitting her connection to Jack. We'll have her right where we want her."

"You sound as if you enjoyed yourself today, Nick," Eleanor said, conceding that she'd have loved to have been a participant in the thrust and parry of the game.

"Celia thought she was going to win, and all the time, I *knew* she was going down. That's quite a rush." He held his palms out. "I loved it."

He and Ellie had talked about Nick's lack of interest in the gallery and his enthusiasm for handling his side of their hunt for the truth.

"Nick, if you're serious, I could set you up with some interviews." Rayder looked levelly at Ellie. "I think you've got the edge necessary for this kind of work. You'd have to tone down the megawatt enthusiasm a bit. That kind of thing tends to spook your average art thief," he commented dryly. "Cool, calm and collected. But you know your way around the art world."

Nick mused a moment, then he looked at Eleanor. "What would Dad say if I wanted to leave?"

"I've already talked to him about the situation here at the gallery. I've explained how much I've been doing and that I believe you're unhappy. He won't be as surprised as you think."

Nick nodded. "Thanks for laying the groundwork. There's no time like the present. Even if I decide not to take Rayder up on his offer of a reference, I don't want to stay on here. It isn't a good fit for me. Not anymore."

Ellie checked the time. "If you're calling Dad, make it now. They'll be getting in from a golf game. I swear he calls me every day while Mom makes him a snack."

Nick smiled. "As scared as I was when I found out about the Lady Emma in Kyoto, I still loved the adrenaline kick. I've been on a high ever since I took off a few nights ago."

Rayder nodded. "There's nothing like closing in on the trail of a missing piece. Someone knows something somewhere and it's all up to you to find out who it is, what they know, and where the piece is. Usually, you're running on a hunch."

Ellie shook her head and grinned. "Oh, please. Save me from you two adrenaline junkies."

Nick left them, preferring to talk with their father in private. When he returned, he looked much more subdued than he had when he'd left.

"WELL?" ELEANOR ASKED. "What did Dad say?"

"He asked if I'd found something else to do. When I told him my decision, he said I was crazy to give up the gallery, but I think he understood. Did you know he tried painting for a few years?" Nick asked Eleanor.

"I had no idea." The whole thing seemed unreal.

"Seems Grandpa cut off his allowance and his inspiration died," he said with a grin.

"What about me, Nick? Is he coming back to take over?" She held her breath, not daring to hope their father would trust her with the gallery.

"You talk to him about that yourself, El. He's on hold."

Rayder stood immediately and followed Nick from the office. She took a moment to collect her thoughts and picked up the line where her father waited.

"Hi, Dad. You spoke with Nick?"

"Eleanor. I had no idea Nick was leaning on you so much. If you'd told me, I'd have come to help."

"I don't think so, Dad. You'd have come back and taken over. I," she grappled with the right words, "needed time to prove I could do it on my own. Time you wouldn't have given me."

There was a long pause.

"Dad? Are you there?"

"Yes, honey, I'm here. I'm just surprised you know me so well. And that you'd think I don't trust you. I know you love the gallery, that you would give up everything for it. Maybe too much, Eleanor. I don't want you losing out on life for the business, honey. Don't do what I did, what my father and grandfather did. No business is worth that."

All she heard was that her dreams were within reach. The Macklin Gallery would be hers to run with no interference.

RAYDER RANG CELIA'S doorbell at two o'clock sharp. Security lights blazed across the front of the house, illuminating every nook and cranny. It was odd for mid-afternoon, but it was cloudy, so he shrugged away his disquiet. The lights must have been installed for the new security camera he noticed.

Nick hadn't reported the camera installation and it hadn't been there the last time Rayder watched the place. It could have been installed today while Celia was at the salon. Maybe Nick hadn't noticed or thought it had always been there.

No matter. What difference could it make? Celia's actions would bring about her downfall, not the comings and goings of her visitors. He dismissed the camera. After all, they were so close to success, one small error wouldn't cost them the game now. Just the same, he wished he'd known about it, he would have been careful to keep turned away from the lens. As it was, she had a full shot of his face.

He rang again.

Finally, Celia answered the door. "Ray. Won't you come in?" She stepped back as he entered. "Would you like a drink?"

"No thanks, it's early for me."

She led him into the living room where he saw the now familiar carrying case that contained Axel's miniature collection. It sat on the coffee table. All the drawers were closed.

"Ah, the collection. Lovely," he said. "And you have the Lady Emma? It was returned from repair?" he asked.

She smiled a smile that could freeze a lake. "Yes. Here it is." She pulled open the drawer that had been empty on that first day in the gallery offices.

He gazed on the tiny rendering of the face of Lady Emma Hamilton. Smaller than palm-sized, the miniature's ornate frame barely left room for the actual likeness. An elegantly dressed woman with a wide, clear forehead and rather small eyes looked back up at them. She had thin, upturned lips that hinted at a smile. All in all, the portrait was ordinary, showing no dash of genius in the execution, but rather, a workmanlike effort to create an exact likeness that only hinted at the real woman's vitality.

Judging by this original, the forgery he'd returned to the museum was excellent. The thought assuaged his ego a trifle. At least he'd been duped by one of the best.

"She looks like any one of a thousand women whose portraits hang in halls and drafty castles," Celia observed. "Hardly interesting enough to create a curse or a legend."

Rayder agreed. All of this plotting for a too-ordinary likeness of an extraordinary woman, he thought. He wanted to examine it more closely, but Celia closed her fingers over Emma's face.

He grinned. "Did you know Lord Nelson actually bequeathed her and their daughter, Horatia, to the people of Great Britain?" he said.

"Were the citizens impressed?" she asked.

Rayder snorted. "Not particularly. Emma and her daughter were ignored when news of his death reached England."

"Then she died a pauper, so beginning a legend about widows dying penniless. And to change that particular part of the legend, it's time you made your offer." She sighed dramatically. "Although I must admit, I've been having second thoughts about selling."

CHAPTER TWENTY

RAYDER WASN'T SURPRISED by Celia's rudimentary bargaining ploy. Pretending sudden disinterest in an offer was standard practice. "You do recall your promise to give my client first refusal," he reminded her.

"Well, I do, of course, but ..." she trailed off expectantly.

He announced the amount of the phony offer, calculated to arouse her interest to fever-pitch.

All he got from her was a slight lift at the corner of her mouth.

If necessary, he could up the stakes to include a Picasso as well. He needed her well and truly hooked.

Celia declined the initial offer with a shake of her head and an eye roll. He wasn't surprised by that ploy either, after all, negotiations had just begun.

"I'm authorized to go one hundred thousand higher, but that's my buyer's highest bid."

She shrugged. "There's always putting it up for auction. Nick Macklin mentioned the spring auction this morning. If your buyer is so interested, it makes me wonder how much better I can do there."

"My buyer specializes in miniatures and he mentioned Axel beating him to a few over the years. He's been disappointed on a number of occasions and tells me this is a last-ditch effort. If he doesn't get the collection for his price, he'll give up altogether."

She raised an eyebrow. "Ray, tut tut, true collectors don't ever give up. They can be very patient and focused."

He nodded and considered opening discussion on the Picasso; but decided to hold out a few more minutes. He shifted the conversation to small talk about the Ryan's fundraiser and some of the people he'd met.

She went along with him, until he saw the impatience he'd been watching for.

"I thought we had an understanding, Celia. You said it yourself, I want to buy, you want to sell, a match made in heaven."

Cool and deliberate, she smiled. "I'm sorry Ray, the pearly gates are closed."

What the hell was she up to? He asked question after question, trying to get the mood to shift back to congenial, but she deflected consistently. As she continued to decline, he realized there would be no deal.

What's more, she had never intended to make one.

Like an amateur, Rayder had been played like a mark.

He had no choice but to retreat.

"Your attempt to squeeze my buyer will fail Celia. I'd be remiss in my duties if I didn't tell you he'll be very disappointed. And he has an unforgiving nature. Word will get out that you don't play by the rules and you'll have a far harder time selling anything in the future."

She shrugged. "I'll manage, I'm sure. A smart woman always does."

He headed to the door and stormed to his car, furious for falling so easily into her trap. He'd been blinded by his feelings for Ellie. But that was no excuse. He should have seen what was coming, should have realized Celia was more conniving than he'd anticipated.

Then a truly disgusting realization hit. He *still* couldn't figure out what the widow Brand was up to.

He decided to sit it out and wait. He moved his car along the street pretending to leave, then returned to watch the house. He called the gallery and told Ellie what had happened.

"Call my uncle and ask him to find out how close Shaughnessy is. Tell him to have Jimmy Matsukawa send Shaughnessy on a wild good chase."

"Too late. Our friend from Interpol is already on the way here. Shamus called a few minutes ago."

"Damn. I'll stay here, keep an eye on the house and think."

"Do you want me to come over?"

It was on the tip of his tongue to ask why, but he already knew. She still didn't trust him, not completely. This screw up would cost him. He had promised her nothing would go wrong. "No, don't leave the gallery. Behave like it's a normal day."

"What should I do if Shaughnessy shows up here?"

"Tell him that a far as you know, Jack Burke has the miniature and he's working on it. Let Shaughnessy find out for himself that Jack's in hiding."

"That's good. I can show him that Celia signed for her collection minus the Lady Emma."

"Exactly," he said. "And Ellie, try to stay calm. Nothing's gone bad, yet. We could still get through this."

He heard a sharp sigh. "I'm okay," she said softly.

They said goodbye and Rayder was sorry he'd bitten his tongue. He should have told her how he felt. She should know he loved her.

Ellie didn't want to hear the words right now. He'd said them too often on that afternoon ten years ago, just before he'd walked out. If he spoke of loving her, she might wonder if history was about to be repeated. Ellie had enough to worry about.

The afternoon soon moved into early evening as he sorted through any number of con games Celia could be playing.

The front door opened, and Celia emerged, dressed in party finery. She carried a small evening bag. She locked the door to the house and climbed quickly into her car and drove off, leaving her house dark and empty looking.

He considered following her but decided the collection should be his focus. Instead, he called Nick. "Celia's left dressed for a party. Find out where she's going."

"No problem. There's a political fundraiser tonight at a hotel downtown. I'll start there."

Once he spoke with Nick, Rayder decided to stay until something interesting happened. It didn't take long.

A dark sedan crept out from beside the house, lights off until it passed Rayder in the street. He'd bet anything it was Jack Burke driving. From the looks of things, Jack had helped himself to a lot more than one small carton of miniatures. The back seat was filled to the brim with stuff covered by a blanket. Paintings, most likely.

Rayder started his car and pulled a U-turn to follow his quarry.

Once on Bloor Street, Rayder followed Burke at a cautious distance. In the dark, it was more difficult to keep the car in view and the traffic was congested. Jack proceeded east, away from downtown.

Jack stayed in his lane and took no sudden turns. Apparently, he was unaware of being tailed.

Eager to see where Jack was headed, Rayder grew bolder and got closer. Eventually, Jack turned into the parking lot of an old rundown motel unit on Kingston Road, miles from Celia's house. It would be the last place anyone would look for a fortune in artwork.

Parking his car behind several others in a pub parking lot across the four-lane road, Rayder used binoculars to watch as Jack Burke unloaded several paintings from the back seat of his car. When the car was empty, Jack opened the trunk and several other pieces followed the rest into the unsavory motel.

He had to see what was happening. He crossed the road, dodging eighteen-wheelers, SUVs and mini vans.

He crouched under the motel room window and risked a peek into the room. The curtain didn't reach the bottom of the window and he saw enough to know Jack was alone. He was talking on a cell phone. His arms waved excitedly.

Rayder cupped a hand over the ear farthest from the window so he could block out some of the traffic noise. Snatches of conversation came to him. Jack was planning to pack and ship the goods. Then he'd go to the airport at–he couldn't hear the time. He heard something about a claim. Insurance, most likely.

Damn. He'd walked right into an insurance scam and he was the patsy. Now he knew why the security camera had been installed. Celia had wanted his face to be the last one at the front door. She and her partner stole her own paintings and Rayder would get blamed. Then, Jack could forge the originals whenever the insurance settlement ran out.

Furious, he checked the lock on the door. It was original and the wood on the door frame was old, probably rotted.

One shove and he was in. Jack had no time to hang up, so his conspirator would probably hear the commotion. Rayder found the thought peculiarly satisfying.

"Hey!" Burke yelled. He tried getting up off the bed but Rayder was on him like a nightmare.

Jack was bigger than Rayder expected and he found himself thrown back against the wall between the window and door. A foot to the left and he'd have been through the glass. He bounced back with an upper cut to Burke's chin that connected with a solid *thunk.*

Burke growled and went for his eyes, trying to gouge them. Hearing a sound at the door, Rayder shifted to see a young man staring into the room. He had a phone in his hand recording the fight.

"Call 911!"

"Already did," the newcomer replied excitedly. "This is wild." The young man swung the phone to record the artwork leaning against the walls and on top of the bed.

Rayder cornered Burke by the shoddy dresser, away from the artwork. Burke grabbed the television with both hands and hoisted it over his head. Rayder dodged to the right just as the set crashed to the floor where he'd been standing. Burke meant business.

The wail of sirens alerted the two men they had no more time for games. Rayder moved in, determined to get the upper hand.

Next thing he knew, he tasted the salt of his own blood on his tongue and a man's arm was around his neck in a choke hold. Realizing immediately that he had to appear calm and rational, he ceased struggling.

Burke was in much the same circumstance.

"Holy cow, Martin, look over there," the younger of the two officers said, pointing to the goods stacked in the corner. Empty packing cartons were testimony to the next step in the plot.

"He stole it!" Burke's voice exploded into the scene and the arm on Rayder's neck tightened.

Rayder, determined to appear non-threatening, said nothing, and waited for the officer to release him. When he did, he calmly denied being the thief and accused Burke of the crime. By this time, the younger officer had taken a closer look at the paintings.

Outside, the young man stood with another officer and watched the video on his phone.

"I think we gotta live one, here, Martin. This stuff looks valuable, even the ones that don't look like anything."

"If you have an officer who specializes in fine art crime, I suggest you call him," Rayder advised. "Those 'ones that don't look like anything' are Picassos stolen five years ago from a London museum."

"Yeah, and how do you know that?" the officer named Martin said.

"Because he's the one who stole them," Jack answered with a sneer. "This is your lucky day, boys," he said expansively, "you've caught yourselves an international art thief. You check with Interpol if you don't believe me."

Shaughnessy was behind this frame.

Standing in the parking lot beside the police cruiser, Rayder watched the street traffic flash by. The young officers had called for back up to protect the goods and deliver both Rayder and Burke separately to their police station for questioning.

In the few minutes they waited for assistance, Rayder said little and kept Ellie's name out of the whole sorry mess. He planned to call Shamus to pull in a couple of favors. One of them would be a call to Interpol.

Shaughnessy wasn't liked at Interpol. His superiors wanted to send him to prison. Interpol also knew Rayder, up until now, wouldn't testify against Shaughnessy and without Rayder, they could do little to police the policeman.

Until now. If breaking his silence about Shaughnessy's thievery would save Ellie's gallery, Rayder would spill everything he could prove. And he could prove plenty.

He smiled and shrugged away the tension. It was nice to have an ace in the hole.

Idly, he became aware of intense scrutiny from the officer called Martin. Paying closer attention, he heard his name and description over the police radio. He didn't want to ask what the code words meant; he had a pretty good idea. It sounded to him like theft. Big-time theft.

Officer Martin tilted his head and looked curiously at him. "Sounds like your buddy was right. Seems some society lady called in an art theft tonight. You've got big trouble, fella."

"Yeah," Burke agreed. "And so, does that uncle of yours. He's going to rot in prison." Rayder threw himself across the short distance, wanting to smash his forehead against Burke's laughing mouth. His arms, already aching from the handcuffs, screamed with pain at the lurch when one of the officers wrenched him to a stop.

"Settle down, Mr. Cole," he was instructed. It was clear now that Shaughnessy was in league with Burke and Celia. Why else would Burke threaten Shamus?

He looked forward to his interview with Daniel Shaughnessy. He'd love seeing the smug bastard's face when he started talking about all he knew.

He still needed to be careful about mentioning the Macklin Gallery. If this forgery ring found out his feelings for Ellie they'd go after her, too.

He only hoped that when she came down to the station, she'd keep her cool and not expose their relationship in any way. He should have warned her about that. He should have called her when he saw Jack leave Celia's house. There were a lot of things he should have done.

ELEANOR CONTINUED TO wait at the office for a call from Rayder. The lights were out in the gallery and she sat with her feet up on the desk and her chair tilted back. Her hands were folded over her stomach. Her fluttering, nervous stomach. She'd been chewing antacid tablets for an hour.

Until a few minutes ago, Nick was waiting with her. Nick couldn't find out where Celia had gone tonight so they'd done nothing but sit and wait, with the tension rising around them as she visualized silent men walking through the gallery and taking pieces out as the business died around her.

In desperation, she'd sent her brother over to Celia's house to get a report from Rayder. If he wasn't going to call, the least he could do was let Nick know what he decided to do.

The phone finally rang, and she jumped to answer, afraid it wouldn't be Rayder, more afraid it was Shaughnessy.

It was Nick. "Ellie? I'm in front of Celia's place and I can't see Rayder or his car."

"Maybe he decided to follow Celia after all," she suggested.

"Ah, no, I don't think so," he said with a note of caution Eleanor found alarming. "There's a whole swarm of reporters and photographers and TV news types here. It looks like something big."

Eleanor touched the power switch on her television remote control and found an on-the-hour news update from a local station. "Go over and ask what happened. Call me back."

But she didn't have to wait for Nick. As soon as she hung up, she saw a distraught Celia Brand on her television screen, her coal black hair aglow in the camera lights.

"Mrs. Brand," the reporter from a local station asked, "what time did the robbery occur?"

Celia sobbed into a linen hanky. "Between six and seven p.m., when I was at a charity function at Sick Children's Hospital. They took *everything*. All my dear husband's art." She sobbed harder, turning Eleanor's stomach. "They took all the pieces he spent *years* collecting."

The reporter asked, "Do you know who did this?"

Celia rallied admirably. "I suspect it was a man who called himself a buying agent. He identified himself as Rayder Cole, but it was probably a phony name."

Sickened and appalled, Eleanor gasped. Was it true? She sank into her seat because she wasn't sure she could stand. Had Rayder tricked her and Celia at the same time? Had he painted Celia a villain to keep Eleanor from telling what she knew about him? Doubt and self-recrimination filled her.

The telephone rang and she made a grab for it, hoping on some deep level that it was Rayder, calling to reassure her.

It wasn't Rayder.

"Nick. I heard," she said dully. "It's on Channel Nine already."

"I can't believe how fast these crews got here, El, and there are more arriving all the time. It's a madhouse. The scuttlebutt is that they've got video of Rayder going into the house."

"Wait, it's back on." She fought for control, all the while picturing Rayder climbing in a broken window at the back of Celia's home. She held herself tight. She couldn't break down, not with Nick on the line.

"The reporter says Rayder's already in custody." The news update ended with the happy reminder to tune in again for the full story at eleven.

"I'll be over in a few minutes," Nick said. "We'll think of something." All Eleanor felt was pain. She'd been conned again.

CHAPTER TWENTY-ONE

RAYDER WAS SURPRISED by the media already at the police station. Vans that looked like miniature television studios were parked around the street. Cables and wires were strewn across the sidewalk.

"Mr. Cole," a microphone was shoved to within inches of his face. "Celia Brand claims you stole her husband's entire art collection. What's your reply to that charge?" a disembodied voice asked from his right. Officer Martin tugged at his upper arm to keep him moving and told the crowd to let them through.

"No comment," Rayder replied, trying to edge by the reporter. With Ellie's penchant for charging into the fray, he wondered how she'd weather the storm of interest she'd arouse when she arrived. He hoped none of these vultures recognized her. If they did, he'd never keep the gallery out of it.

Inside the station, the atmosphere was quieter but still charged with the scent of the hunt. Some officers, apparently unused to thieves of international caliber, openly stared at him. He ignored them, concentrating on the facts that would keep Ellie's gallery out of the investigation.

With Celia's insane plan to defraud her insurance company with a phony theft, there was no need for the forgery to be brought to light, he realized. All Ellie had to say was that he'd been interested in purchasing Celia's collection when they'd been introduced in the gallery. A simple statement from her and Ellie would be clear of any taint. He needed her to corroborate his story. Nothing more.

He controlled a smile, envisioning her bursting through the doors of the station screaming, "He's innocent!" Ellie to the rescue.

ELEANOR SAT IN HER favorite armchair and stared out across the city. Rooftops blended into the blackness of the night; lights winked off slowly as the people living in neighboring towers went to bed.

The media had milked the theft story without giving the public one iota of fact. Sickened by the innuendo and speculation that had run rampant on television newscasts, she'd turned everything off.

She needed the dark and the quiet in order to think. Tears tracked down her face, dropping off her chin. Her skin was sore from rubbing them away, so she left them to drip. It was easier. The raw skin on her cheeks would heal quickly, but her heart was another matter.

She continued to sit and stare out the window wondering why she couldn't accept that the future she'd planned with Rayder was over before it began. After a while, she rocked back and forth, taking small comfort where she could.

This was how her brother found her an hour later.

"El, what are you doing here? Why aren't you answering the phone?" Nick leaned over her and set his hands on her shoulders. "El. What's this about?" Concern and loss converged into a ball at his question.

How to tell him his sister had lost her future with a man she loved, *for the second time*. She didn't have to, not yet. She'd answer his other questions.

"I won't answer my phone because I'm afraid it's the media. I don't want to speak with anyone. Not even Rayder."

"Which brings me to my next question. What will you do about him?" Nick asked.

"Nothing," she sniffed and wiped at her nose with a torn, soggy tissue.

Nick passed her a fresh one.

"Thanks." She blew her nose.

"We've got to go to the police. We've got to get him out of there."

She raised her eyes to meet his. "No, we don't. Believe me, he'll talk his way out of this. He's one smooth talker, that Rayder. You don't have to worry about him."

"That's callous. He's on our side, remember?"

She sniffed and stood up to get another drink from the scotch decanter she had on a side table. She held the bottle up in offer. "Rayder will land on his feet, believe me." Shamus was likely already pulling strings.

"No, thanks, I don't want to show up at a police interview stinking like scotch."

She chuckled at that. "There won't be a police interview, because you're not going down there either." When he looked about to protest, she raised her hand to silence him. "You still don't get it, do you?"

"Get what?"

"We were conned, both of us." She fortified herself with a long deep sip of scotch. She didn't usually drink the hard stuff, but under the circumstances, what the hell, it wasn't every day a woman got fried for the second time.

"What do you mean, conned?"

"Rayder Cole is a stinking, lowdown con man. He made me think he'd changed, Nick. I swallowed his whole act. Again!" She shook her head. "God, I can't believe I did that." She smeared a hand down her face.

Her brother went still. "What do you mean again?"

"It was when I was away at university. Remember? I came home?"

"Rayder told me you two met then. He also told me he messed up badly. You mean to tell me *he's* the reason you came home? Because of a fight or a mistake he made?"

"Not exactly." She took another long sip, then poured herself more scotch. Warmth stole through her and she wondered if she could cross the room on steady feet. *Maybe best not to try.*

And then she told him. Spilled the whole, sorry story. Told him about her broken heart, the rumpled sheets, the race to Rayder's dorm room. Discovering he was gone with her money. Everything.

Nick's face went stark with anger. "El, I get why you didn't tell Mom and Dad, but you could have told me. It killed me knowing there was something seriously wrong and there was nothing I could do for you."

She shrugged. "It was a long time ago." This new deception was what mattered now. "There was nothing anyone could do. I had to pick up the pieces and move on. Which I did." She swayed a bit as she wandered back to her green leather armchair. The bottom of the chair rushed up to meet her as she sat. "Which I did very well," she corrected with a wave of her hand that held the glass of whiskey. "Until, of course, I let the bastard do it all again."

"No, I don't believe that. What do you think happened tonight?"

"His face was on Celia's security camera. That's what they said. They told you he was the last one in the house before it was robbed." There was something wrong with her image of Rayder as a thief stupid enough to have his face framed in a camera lens, but her heart was breaking so loudly it interfered with her reason.

"But Rayder wants to marry you."

She snorted. "Yeah, and he's setting you up with a job interview, too. He'll give us everything we've ever wanted." One more sip and the whiskey was gone, but no way could she get to her feet and go for more. The glass slipped out of her hand and landed with a dull thud on the floor.

"You're such a lightweight," Nick chided with a smile as he picked it up and put it on the side table. "Your pity party's over."

"Don't you get it? We're greedy, Nick. You want to move on and I'm still the girl I was. I'm greedy for someone to love me. He dangled everything we wanted in front of us so we wouldn't see the truth."

"Okay, that's enough," he said. "I'm putting you to bed now. You'll sleep it off, and in the morning, we're doing whatever we can to help Rayder."

"The only hope I have to salvage the gallery, is Rayder keeping his mouth shut about us. If he does that, at least I can keep my life the way it was. I can keep the gallery, Nick, if none of us speaks. I hope he's got enough decency to do that one little thing."

Suddenly, she felt an uprush as her brother lifted her into his arms. She settled against his shoulder. "Oh, Nicky, I love him."

"I know, El, I know."

"Promise me you won't tear his head off."

"He loves you El, I won't tear his head off for that."

She patted his cheek and smiled. "My little brother, still so naive. I hope love never hurts you, Nick."

RAYDER HAD BELIEVED Ellie would come charging to his rescue. But now, hours later, he knew different. She believed he was guilty. She must or Ellie would have been here.

He sat in a small room off the main hall, giving his statement, for the umpteenth time, in short, crisp sentences. His credentials had finally been confirmed with Interpol. Shaughnessy was down the hall being questioned and Celia had been brought in to make her own statement.

From what he heard; Jack was singing like a bird. Apparently, the idea of the insurance fraud had been Celia's. Only Rayder, Eleanor, and Nick knew that their own investigation had tipped the scale of Celia's desperation.

Shaughnessy's part in past art thefts was being exposed as more and more calls came from his superiors. Every call was for Rayder and he knew his information would put the disgraced cop away for a long time.

But that wasn't his problem, nor was it Ellie's.

No, Ellie had what she'd always wanted: her gallery, free from scandal, free from her father's control, even free from Nick's disinterest.

And now, she was free of Rayder, too. By not coming to support his story, she'd let him know loud and clear how she felt. The gallery must come first. Eleanor Macklin would not besmirch her reputation by being linked with Rayder Cole.

He'd done everything he could think of to gain Ellie's trust. And for what? At the first sign of trouble she bolted into a hole and hid. When he needed her, she was in the wind.

He couldn't blame her. What he did before was too big to forget.

She didn't trust him, so she couldn't love him. Love couldn't survive when there was no faith. He knew that now. He'd learned his lesson.

The officer slid his statement across the table to him and he signed it.

His police business finally concluded, he walked out, promising to be available for more questions if need be. A couple of weeks and the episode would be in his rear view. Eventually, the museum in Calais would have their Lady Emma restored to them. Even better than before, because now the story of its most recent curse victim, the widow Brand, would enhance the legend.

He stepped outside, surprised by a faint lightening in the sky, relieved to see the news crews had taken shelter in the vans. A rush of wind and sleet tore at him as he buttoned his coat. He turned up his collar and huddled into his shoulders as he headed for the nearest corner to hail a cab. It would be faster than calling one.

Then he saw a woman across the street, in the shadows by a streetlamp. *Ellie.*

He stopped and stared at her, drenched and shivering in the cold. He walked to where she waited. She moved into the light where he could see her better. Her skin was pale, the hair that had escaped the scarf around her head was whipped into nearly straight cords as it blew about her face. Her eyes, large and luminescent, peered up at him.

Not Ellie.

He shook his head in chagrin at the hope he'd felt bloom. Stupid to think she'd lurk out here, waiting for him.

The woman shrugged and moved on.

He hailed the first cab he saw and headed for Ellie's. She'd want to know what happened. He also wanted her to know, once and for all, he wasn't a thief. And then, he'd walk out.

Bruno looked surprised to see him. He was clearly curious but kept his questions to himself. "Mr. Cole. I'll ring Ms. Macklin and let her know you're here."

"Do that, Bruno. She'll want to be warned," he said as he walked to the elevator.

Ellie opened the door on the first knock. "Rayder, I planned to call later. It's barely dawn."

She'd been sleeping in her clothes. She looked rumpled and worried and worn out. But he froze his heart against the pain he saw in her eyes.

"Were you planning to leave a hearty message of support?"

"What do you mean?" She stepped back and followed him into the living room.

He didn't sit down.

"I mean, you didn't come to the station. You didn't give a damn what happened to me as long as your gallery was safe." He spun to face her. "Am I right?"

"No, that's not right. I was confused. The news reports said they had video of you going into the house." She folded her arms and stared defiantly at him.

"And you took that to mean I was breaking into the house. God, Ellie, is that what you believe? I'm a thief? I guess you think everything between us was another con?"

She bit her lip and said nothing. *Answer enough.*

"I've done everything I could think of to redeem myself to you. I can't go on thinking twice before I speak, double checking everything I've said, worrying whether you believe me or not. It's impossible for anyone to live that way. Hell, you can't even trust that I'll be there when you wake up from a nap!"

She blinked and still said nothing. But her fingers worried at her sleeves.

"So, I'll tell you what happened and then I'll leave."

Her eyes stricken with emotion he couldn't name, she nodded.

"The gallery's safe. I didn't mention you or Nick. You've got what's most important to you."

Her eyes lit up at that. "Do you think Celia will mention us?"

"She's not stupid. She doesn't need forgery added to the list of complaints. For now, she's being looked at for conspiracy to commit fraud."

"What will happen to her? To Jack?"

"Probably not much. She'll play on the sympathy of the court. Jack will play the dupe, although I doubt it'll help." He shrugged, not caring, and trying hard not to see her. Trying hard and failing. Even now, if she showed some real affection, he'd gather her close and fall for her all over again.

"And Shaughnessy?"

"His superiors are pleased with me right now. He's busy doing damage control, but it's too late. The forger he hung out to dry three years ago is spilling his guts. Shaughnessy's out of the picture." He'd be in prison for years. "Europe takes art theft seriously."

"Oh." She looked uncomfortable, disconcerted with him. He took that as a sign to get out while he still could.

"Don't sweat it," he said with an edge in his voice he recognized as bitterness. "I'm not much for long goodbyes."

A WEEK LATER, TRUE to his word, Rayder left a message at the office for Nick that an insurance investigator was willing to give him an interview. Nick called Rayder to get more details. It was past closing time and Anne had left for the day.

"When do you leave?" Eleanor asked her brother.

"After Christmas. I'm meeting with a Mr. Lindquist in London." Nick could hardly contain his excitement.

Eleanor knew her smile was stiff, but she kept it on her face anyway. She'd lost Rayder because of her lack of faith in him. She knew that now. Rayder was right. He couldn't love a woman who wouldn't accept him at face value. That wasn't what love was about.

"Great," she said to Nick, "We'll tell Mom and Dad about your interview when we see them at Christmas."

She put on her coat and boots. "Rayder didn't say anything else?"

"Nope. That's it," he responded, crushing her hope that Rayder may have asked about her.

"Oh, he said it looks as if Celia may be off the hook. Good lawyer, I guess."

Eleanor froze. "That's so wrong. How can that be?" A notion pestered at the back of her mind. If she thought too hard, like now, it escaped. But soon, it would show itself, and she would grasp on and remember.

"I don't know, El, I guess Rayder was right all along. If you're powerful enough, you can get away with anything."

"But still there should be evidence she planned to get away with this. That she planned ahead of time to be off somewhere with her paintings and the insurance money."

Nick shrugged.

Eleanor worried at the elusive thought all the way home.

Bruno helped her from her car to her apartment door with her Christmas packages. The doorman was particularly solicitous this close to the holiday.

She asked him to wait while she went to get the gift she had for him. "I hope you're a Blue Jays fan, Bruno," she said, handing him the gaily wrapped package.

The big man accepted the baseball-sized box with a smile, shaking it for a hint of what was inside. She laughed. "Go ahead, open it now."

"Thank you, Ms. Macklin, I will." His pleasure at the autographs scrawled across the ball reminded her of the joy of the season. "This is the 1993 Championship team. Thank you again, and Merry Christmas. And please say hello to your man, Mr. Cole." The curiosity in Bruno's expression was unmistakable.

She was suddenly and excruciatingly aware Rayder was not her man. "He's not my anything," she responded. She backed into her apartment, mumbled something passably cheerful and closed the door, jamming her knuckles into her mouth to hold back the sobs that rose from her throat.

This was wrong, so wrong. Rayder should be here, with her, not alone in that studio apartment waiting to testify against two crooks who probably wouldn't get half what they deserved.

And from what Nick had said it looked as if Celia would be free. What a travesty. She would lay odds Celia talked Jack into this whole scheme in the first place. Jack simply wasn't mastermind material. Not from what she knew of the man.

And now, Celia would get away with everything because Eleanor was too frightened of losing a business that didn't mean anything to her anymore anyway. She may have lost Rayder because of her stupid lack of trust in him, but she refused to lose her self-respect as well.

Eleanor hurried back to the gallery offices to collect the notes she'd kept throughout their whole investigation. There must be something in them the police could use.

She didn't know admissible evidence from her elbow, but she needed to be honest with the police, about her involvement, about her hesitancy to come to Rayder's rescue. Without all the facts in their hands, how could they hope to sort out the truth from the lies Celia Brand would utter?

She turned on the lights in Nick's office and went to the locked drawer in the desk. She opened it and pulled out the notebook. Yes, it was all there. Even the name of the neighbor who'd first told her Jack was gone away. Surely, Brian would corroborate her story.

Eleanor walked back to the door and put her hand on the light switch. Turning, she studied the portraits one last time. They were all there, like ducks in a row: her father, who'd finally accepted that she was a capable businesswoman, to her Great-Great-Grandfather who'd started the Macklin Gallery on nothing more than a dream and a wife's appreciation for good art.

She saluted the dusty old portraits of dusty old men, in a grand gesture of defiance. She no longer cared about the Macklin Gallery, not if she had to keep silent about what she knew. A curious weight seemed to lift from her as her decision to act took shape.

She should have done this the night it all went sour. When she still had a chance to save her relationship with Rayder. *Too little, too late.* He would see this as simply setting the record straight, not as an act of faith in him.

Maybe he'd be right to think that. Maybe he'd never believe she was abjectly sorry for not believing in him.

She reached for the light switch and a glimmer caught her eye. The display light over one of the portraits glinted on a frame and suddenly the elusive memory she'd searched for earlier, rushed back.

She called Nick.

"Hi," she said as soon as he answered. "When Celia went to the beauty salon and had those foils in her hair, what color hair did she have when she came out?"

"What? Why?"

"Because I want to know if she planned to disguise herself when she made her getaway with Jack. I think she was wearing a black wig on the night of the theft. No one gets black streaks in black hair, Nick. What color was she?"

"Damn," Nick's voice went soft as he pulled up his memory. "She went salt and pepper. Looked a helluva lot older, too."

"Thanks, it's not much, but it's something. Maybe the prosecutor needs one more piece of the puzzle." A media circus had surrounded the phony theft and Celia seemed to thrive on the attention, making a mockery of the justice system.

"El, this will ruin the gallery. You're willing to sacrifice everything?" Nick sounded astonished.

"I'm setting myself free of a ton of guilt," she replied with true conviction of purpose. "And that's worth anything."

Eleanor drove to the offices of the city's largest newspaper and asked to see the reporter covering the Brand case. The man was at a Christmas party with his wife, but after a brief conversation, agreed to meet with her as soon as she'd made a statement to the police. She called Police Headquarters and told them she was coming in.

THE NEXT TIME ELEANOR surfaced, it was a week later, time enough to be yesterday's news. She and Nick had spent Christmas in Florida with their parents while she'd pretended to be happy. Her father had kept his thoughts to himself for a change, but her mother watched her with sad eyes. It was hard to hide heartbreak from your mom.

She stepped off the elevator into her underground parking garage. The first blizzard of winter had roared in by way of Buffalo and she dreaded the drive to work. Her plans were to auction off the remaining gallery inventory. Later today, she'd look at a small house that had a perfect front showroom area with living quarters in the rear. With some luck, she'd have enough money left over from the auction for a down payment.

Nick supported her decision to rebuild her life and had suggested she clear the air with Rayder, but she couldn't face him. She knew how hard he'd worked at earning her trust. He'd never forgive her for thinking the worst. Hell, she couldn't forgive herself.

Her father was less understanding than Nick, but that was no surprise since she hadn't been able to tell him everything. Admitting that her love for a man had caused her to sacrifice the gallery was tantamount to telling her father he'd been right all along: that she wasn't cut out to be in business because she let her emotions rule her head.

Her father was wrong, but it would take a lifetime to explain it.

She rummaged in her purse for her car keys as she strolled to the car, in no hurry to begin the treacherous drive. The snowplows would be out in full force, but still she'd be glad when the day was over. Every moment spent in the gallery chilled her. It, and those painted, disapproving faces in the portraits no longer held sway on her decisions, but she'd be happier out of the place.

At twenty-eight, Eleanor Macklin had taken control of her life. She found her keys and quickened her pace toward her car.

It wasn't until she'd climbed into the Volvo that she saw him. A man, standing in the shadow drawn by the pillar across from her.

Rayder. Her heart caught in her throat. Tall, looming; just as he'd been the first time she'd seen him here. He stepped into the light and strode toward her, his face a mask of angles, shadows, and planes.

She climbed back out of the car and waited, her heart pounding in the stillness.

He stopped when he was close enough to touch her. "Why'd you do it, Ellie? You had it all, everything you wanted, and you threw it away."

She drank in the sight of him, his blackbird hair, shorter now, neater, the hollows under his high cheekbones, the pucker in his lip. She fought the temptation to touch it with one fingertip. She put her hand on top of the car to steady herself.

"Only the gallery." *And you.* "In the end the gallery turned out not to be all that important to me." She didn't want to stand here and dissect the decision she'd taken far too long to make.

"How so?"

"I lost my faith in myself, in my judgement, and I can't live my life that way. I had to do what was right."

"That's funny, I believed the only one you lost faith in was me."

The pain his comment went bone deep. "You have no idea how sorry I am about that. I should have believed in you. I should have trusted what I was feeling, what I knew you were feeling."

A nerve jumped in his cheek as he listened without speaking.

She went on, "I don't expect you to forgive me, Rayder, but I hope you at least understand how it looked to me. The reporters were sensationalizing everything. I was frightened and you looked angry when you arrived at the station. I hesitated and the longer I hesitated, the more the doubt grew. I was wrong not to go to you, and I'll spend my life regretting it."

He still didn't speak. This was it. What they had was gone. She blinked back tears. She had to say this next part, she had to get the words out before she broke down completely. "I understand you not forgiving me. I didn't forgive you for over ten years."

Horrified that she'd bared herself so completely, she went on in a desperate ramble to make sense. "I couldn't let Celia and Jack get away with it. All they faced was an attempted fraud charge. Nothing of the truth would ever come out. It's like you said, Rayder. No one important ever pays for their crimes in the art world. It sickened me." It struck her that he hadn't been paying much attention to the last part of her rant.

"But the gallery means more to you than anything else. Doesn't it?" He gripped her forearms and held her still when all she wanted to do was jump into her car and speed away.

She bent her head, refusing to look at him. "Not anymore. I was wrong to put the gallery ahead of you. I was wrong not to trust in you. I said I forgave you, but when push came to shove, I let you down. What kind of person does that make me? It's you who can't depend on me, Rayder."

"I tried everything I could to let you know how committed I was. When you didn't show up to help me, I thought you believed the worst. How could I not?"

"And you were right. I did believe the worst. And I'm ashamed, okay? Ashamed." She dashed a couple of errant tears from her cheeks. "I have no idea what I can do, how I can act, to make you believe how sorry I am."

"Is this a stalemate? Have we hurt each other enough now to be even?"

"I don't understand." Confused, she could only stare.

"I want to start again," He said quickly as if the words were too big for his mouth.

She raised her chin, still unsure. She sniffed. "What do you mean, start again?"

"How do you feel about the gallery now? About losing it?"

"The damn place is a mausoleum. Old and musty and dead." She was shocked by his reaction. He was grinning like a man who'd found gold.

"What will you do now?" he asked.

"I'm moving on. Whatever happens, I'll be building the life I choose, not following blindly along a path set out four generations ago. The Macklin Gallery's dead and I don't want to die with it."

He reached for her scarf and pulled it down, exposing her long, unruly curls. He filled his hands with her hair, and she ached for more of his touch, but she couldn't move, afraid that even now he'd reject her. "Is there room for a husband in this new life you're forging?"

"This doesn't make sense." He couldn't mean marriage. Not Rayder.

"Marry me, Ellie. I love you."

"How can you? I deserted you, left you to rot in a police station. You said it yourself. I was too afraid of losing the gallery to stand beside you when you needed me most." Her voice dissolved under her guilt.

"You had every reason to wonder. Hell, in the beginning I even suspected you and Nick." He stepped back, his voice firming with resolution. "We've spent too many years apart because of guilt. Let's not waste anymore." He tugged her face close, his hands entwined with her hair. "This is my final appeal, Ellie." His eyes blazed into her. "Do you want me or not?"

The intensity in his gaze frightened her. Then she saw a glimmer of warmth glowing deep in the recesses of his pupils. *Love.*

"Oh, Rayder, you pirate." She grabbed his shoulders, yanked him to her and kissed him for all she was worth. When she was done, he looked much less threatening and infinitely softer around the eyes. "Just try to get away from me this time. I'll hunt you down like a dog. I've got investigative experience now."

Rayder hauled her close and tight, so tight, and kissed the tip of her nose. "I remember. I had something to do with teaching you."

"Got any other lessons up your sleeve?" She pressed her hips to his in an unmistakable offer.

"Yes, but before we start, I need to hear it, Ellie."

"I love you."

"Again."

"I love you. And trust you."

"Heart and soul?"

At her nod, he nuzzled her neck. "That's my girl. And for the record, I love you, too."

Epilogue

RAYDER HELD ELLIE'S hand as the deck of the *Sandjack* swayed beneath their bare feet. His cousin Teri had just said her vows and she was kissing her groom, Jared MacKay, the captain of the boat. The *Sandjack* was a honeymoon charter boat that Teri had booked before her previous groom ditched her at the altar. Yes, his sweet, funny cousin had been hurt and humiliated in the worst way. The guy who hurt her was still on Rayder's list of things to take care of.

But today was a day for happy thoughts, and he set aside plans for the loser that Teri had narrowly escaped. As soon as she'd heard Rayder was marrying Ellie, she'd insisted on sharing her special day.

And, not to be outdone, his other Branton cousin Ashlee wanted to make it a triple ceremony day with her fiancé, Brick Harcout. When the Brantons partied, they included everyone. His heart warmed as he looked around the deck at his family.

Tyce and Lisa Branton stood beside Ellie, while Cousin Ashlee stood with her fiancé Brick beside Rayder. As he'd promised, Shamus was somewhere behind the group with Tyce's mom.

The Caribbean was the perfect setting for a wedding that brought the whole family together. The Branton side of Rayder's family had had some strange twists and turns in their romantic lives, but none were stranger than his own.

He pulled his Ellie in closer to his side and nuzzled her just above her ear. She raised her face to his. "I love you," she whispered. "Marry me."

"I'm planning on it," he said with a chuckle.

The bride and groom turned to face the family group and a wild cheer went up as they hugged all the guests.

Ten minutes later Rayder called the group to attention. "Our turn!"

He and Ellie stepped up to the front and their service began. The vows were simple but meant the world to him. The Cole family played fast and loose with people and especially their emotional connections, so hearing these words of commitment, loyalty, and love made his eyes sting. *Must be the breeze and salt air.*

He held his breath while he waited for Ellie to complete her vows. His chest swelled with pride as she looked up into his eyes with her own swimming in happy tears.

He had his Ellie at last. And he had everything he'd ever craved, love, commitment, and even renewed family connections. These Brantons, a simple family who all worked hard, loved well, and supported each other were everything a man could need.

Love, well-earned and deep as the sea beneath them all, bound them together.

THE END

I hope you loved Rayder's Appeal so much that you leave a review! If you do, thank you, thank you, thank you. If you choose your books based on reviews, I hope you'll pay it forward and share your thoughts on *Rayder's Appeal*[1] where you purchased it.

I'd love to see you on my mailing list. For a free introduction to another series, Last Chance Beach, in *Hangover Husband*, sign up for *Bonnie's Newsy Bits* on my website.[2]

---

1.   *https://books2read.com/Rayders-Appeal*

2.   https://landing.mailerlite.com/webforms/landing/t6w3o6

Other Romances* by Bonnie Edwards
Return to Welcome Series

Return to Welcome A Collection
Finding Mercy – Book 1
Loving Logan – Book 2
Craving Jake – Book 3 (Also in print)
Claiming Shandy – Book 4
Christmas to the Max (A Return to Welcome Novel)
Love at Christmas Collection
Not-So-Blue Christmas
Invitation to Christmas
One Crazy Christmas
Christmas to the Max (A Return to Welcome Novel)
Last Chance Beach
Hangover Husband **
Fake Me

Take Me (and My Kids)

Christmas Come to Dickens
The Tinsel Tango
The Rumball Rumba
The Winterland Waltz
Second Chance Dance
Stand-Alone Contemporary
Love in a Pawn Shop
Sweet Ride!

Long Time Coming (A Short Romance)
The Stone Heart (Paranormal Short)
Thigh High
Rayder's Appeal (Romantic Suspense)
The Brantons (Steamy)
Body Work Book 1
Slow Hand Book 2
Whole Lot O' Love Book 3
Boxset The Brantons
Rayder's Appeal Book 4
The Diamond Series (Steamy)
Twinkle, Twinkle, Little Thong
Diamond at Heart
Tales of Perdition (Erotic Paranormal)
Perdition House Part 1 An Erotic Saga
Perdition House Part 2 An Erotic Saga
Rock Solid- Tales of Perdition 3
Parlor Games- Tales of Perdition 4
A Breath Taken - Tales of Perdition 5
* CHECK EACH TITLE FOR Print
** FREE for subscribing to Bonnie's Newsy Bits

About the Author

AUTHOR BONNIE EDWARDS once received a note from an influential editor saying: "You write great sex scenes, but there are just so many of them." The author was ahead of her time. Eventually, the market for steamy books opened up and caught up to her. This is what you're reading now; her sexy, well-written, gloriously fun romance.

She has written novels, novellas and short stories for Carina Press, Harlequin, Kensington Books and Robinson (UK) although now she publishes her work herself.

Sometimes her stories have a paranormal twist, like ghosts. But they're always entertaining and guarantee a happy ending. Bring a fan...it's hot in here.

With 40+ titles to her credit, she has been translated into several languages and sold books worldwide. Learn about more exciting releases and get a **free** romance by subscribing to her newsletter, Bonnie's Newsy Bits[1].

Cheers and happy reading!

Bonnie Edwards

Learn more: https://www.bonnieedwards.com/

---

1.   https://landing.mailerlite.com/webforms/landing/t6w3o6

Don't miss out!

Visit the website below and you can sign up to receive emails whenever Bonnie Edwards publishes a new book. There's no charge and no obligation.

https://books2read.com/r/B-A-JXD-BADGB

BOOKS 2 READ

Connecting independent readers to independent writers.

Did you love *Rayder's Appeal The Brantons Book 4*? Then you should read *Craving Jake Return to Welcome Book 3* by Bonnie Edwards!

Returning to Welcome was easy...staying will be a challenge. Especially when someone is determined to drive her out.

Brianna Bowler has returned to Welcome to help run Bowler's Dog Rescue. She's also doing everything she can to set aside thoughts of her high school crush who appears to be with a perfectly perfect sprite of a woman. (Not that she minds how opposite she and the sprite are. Really, she doesn't.)

Paramedic Jake Morrow has a woman in his house, cooking, cleaning, clinging—and irritating the hell out of him. He'd felt sorry for her, injured, alone and broke, and offered to help. Big mistake

.

Jake set himself apart from everyone who used to know him. He can't take their pitying looks, their sympathy, or their avid interest in his tragic past.

What would really make his day? His ex-girlfriend finally moving out. But Theda won't take his word for it that things are over.

What's worse is Brianna Bowler's return. Their shared secret and attraction burns between them as Jake accepts that things aren't quite right with his ex. A break-in at the dog rescue, smashed windows, and a stolen laptop all add up to serious trouble for Jake and Brianna.

All Jake's protective instincts rise as the strange events take a deadly turn and Jake knows his loner life will never be good enough again.

Some women can't be set aside, not even for their own good...but others want revenge.

Also by Bonnie Edwards

Dance of Love
The Tinsel Tango A Dickens Holiday Novella
The Rumball Rumba: A Dickens Holiday Romance
The Winterland Waltz A Dickens Holiday Romance

Last Chance Beach
Make Me
Fake Me
Take Me (and My Kids)

Return to Welcome
Finding Mercy
Loving Logan
Craving Jake Return to Welcome Book 3
Claiming Shandy Return to Welcome Book 4
Christmas to the Max

Tales of Perdition

Perdition House Part 1 An Erotic Saga
Perdition House Part 2 An Erotic Saga
Rock Solid
Rock Solid
Parlor Games
A Breath Taken
The Tales of Perdition A Collection

The Brantons
Body Work
Slow Hand
Whole Lot O' Love
Rayder's Appeal The Brantons Book 4

The Diamond Series
Twinkle, Twinkle Little Thong
Diamond At Heart

Standalone
Long Time Coming
The Stone Heart
The Brantons A Collection
Thigh High

www.ingramcontent.com/pod-product-compliance
Lightning Source LLC
Chambersburg PA
CBHW050422260626
47156CB00003B/1122